THE LIFE SIPHON

The Life Siphon, Book One

Kathryn Sommerlot

A NineStar Press Publication

Published by NineStar Press
P.O. Box 91792,
Albuquerque, New Mexico, 87199 USA.
www.ninestarpress.com

The Life Siphon

Printed in the USA
First Edition
May, 2019

Print ISBN: 978-1-950412-77-8

Also available in eBook, ISBN: 978-1-950412-76-1

Warning: This book contains some acts of violence, one of which involves the death of a secondary character, as well as some xenophobic and ableist language.

To my husband Masaki—
my official partner in the zombie apocalypse

Part One

Runon

CURLED INTO A ball at the bottom of the stairs, the servant lay shaking like a leaf.

As hiding places went, it wasn't the best—a high traffic area, the connected hallway linked the guest rooms with the kitchens, and the boy hadn't scooted back far enough to be hidden in the shadows. I stopped by the doorway to stare at him, assuming he'd glance up and see me waiting, and he did nothing of the sort. He just sat with his arms wound tight around his knees, trembling like his bones were threatening to jump out of his skin.

It was only when I crept closer that the burn marks along the tender inside flesh of his arms became noticeable. The blistering skin summoned a sharp wave of irritation; Zakio had been *playing* again.

The servant didn't notice me until I was standing directly over him.

"What's your name?" I asked, more frustrated than anything else.

He leapt to his feet as if his heels were on fire, and the shaking he'd gotten under control erupted again. He looked like a willow tree caught in a summer storm the way his limbs were flailing to either side, and I had to take a step back to avoid being hit.

"I'm so sorry, Prince Yudai," he sputtered, "I wasn't being lazy, I was—"

"Hiding from Zakio," I interrupted. "I know."

Gods, he was young. His bottom lip jutted out as his eyes started to water, and I moved away because I didn't particularly want a servant crying all over me. He attempted to pull himself together in the breaths that followed, though he wasn't nearly quick enough in twisting his burned arm out of sight. Even though I'd already noticed the red welts, he gave me ample time to note them again before remembering it was evidence.

But he didn't lack common sense; I'd give him that. He knew showing off the bubbled skin would only result in worse treatment the next time around.

"Do you need something, Your Highness?" he asked.

Two fat tears rolled down his cheeks, smudged with kitchen grease. All I'd wanted was to get to return to my room and avoid my father's endless parade of nobles practically throwing themselves down to get the chance to kiss his boots, and instead, I found this. Zakio assumed himself above the rules of common decency, and my father had never put the mages on a short enough leash. This was the *worst*.

I sighed. "Where is he?"

"What?" The servant's eyes went so wide I could see my reflection suspended in them. "Who?"

"You know who," I said. "Zakio. Where is he?"

"Your Highness, I don't—"

"Either you tell me, or I set the whole castle on fire to smoke him out."

I'm not sure the boy really believed me, but his fingers were trembling against his thighs again, so maybe he did. I wondered what stories about me were circulating the servants' quarters in whispers that week; at the very least, I hoped they were more flattering than the last bunch.

Of course, if the visiting nobles and their daughters got wind of a few more inventive rumors, the lot of them might go running for the hills, but I'd never get that lucky. I doubted anything less than my death would stop my father from bargaining away the princess crown that would come twin to my own.

Honestly, he'd probably conduct a grotesque marriage auction around my corpse.

"He's...he's in the mages' quarters," the servant said, which meant he either believed my threat or simply wanted the conversation to be over.

"Lovely," I replied, and I meant it; blowing off steam was exactly what my black mood needed. "That's just where I would have thought to search first."

IT WOULD BE tempting to sing Zakio's name as I made my way to the mages' quarters, but better not to announce my presence without knowing if he'd be the only one there. The torch-lined hallway, filled with the slightly sweet scent always following the mountain rains, sat quiet enough to bounce my footsteps back at me. My father had the castle scrubbed every summer from rafter to cellar trying to chase the smell away, but I found it comforting, and in the back halls where the ceilings hung lower and the rooms shortened, it lingered more strongly.

My arms tingled as someone within the hallway used their abilities. So, the rooms weren't deserted. I stopped, paused just outside the first doorframe, and waited to see if anyone emerged. The magical aftershocks left a thin film at the corner of my mouth, and sweeping my tongue over it produced a burst of sweetness.

Muffled rustling sounded from the opposite side of the heavy wooden door, and despite two more echoes of magic against my ears, only one set of footsteps sounded inside. Good—maybe the day wouldn't be so horrible after all.

When I walked in, Zakio started so badly he dropped the flask he was holding, and it shattered on the stone floor. I'd be lying if I said it wasn't satisfying.

"What are you doing here," he asked through clenched teeth, "sneaking like a rat through the halls?"

"Your insults are so boring," I replied. "I mean, could you put some effort into making them more original?"

His mouth stretched, teeth glinting in the flickering candlelight. Zakio was lanky and towering, taller than me despite being a year younger. He'd cut an intimidating presence if I didn't already know what a sniveling weasel he was, hiding behind his High Mage mother's unjustly influential robes. She wasn't here, however, and he knew I had him cornered.

"Get out," he ordered. It lacked punch.

"Look, as royalty, I really think you should be using inventive, unique insults for me," I said. "I deserve at least that much."

"You've no idea what you deserve." Flecks of spit accompanied the syllables, and the stack of books next to him teetered close to collapse, swaying each time he stamped his boot against the floor. Most people would know better than to needle a strong mage.

I wasn't most people.

"It seems you've been toying with the servants again," I said. "You wouldn't have held him with *magic* when you were torturing him by any chance? Since, as you are well aware, using your abilities against another human without permission goes against the laws of your station."

Zakio deflated, but only a little. "You've no proof."

"The boy's got burn welts all up his arm."

"He works in the kitchens, that's a common injury."

I cocked my head at him because I knew it'd annoy him when I batted my eyelashes. He lost his temper so easily. "And who do you think my father will believe, me or you?"

"Surely, he knows better than to believe anything that comes out of your mouth," Zakio said with a growl. "Though I'm surprised there's any time for stories considering all the other things they whisper you put *in* your mouth."

"Oh, now *that* was almost good," I replied, smiling widely. "You saved your best ones for last, didn't you?"

Zakio's hand came down hard on the table, knocking several quills and an inkpot to the floor. He didn't seem to notice when the ink spread black around his boots. "Get out!"

"Stop hurting the servants, or I report you to my father."

"You're an arrogant bastard," he said.

"My mother was queen, but try again."

If I were anyone else, he'd have had me up against the wall with his magic, holding me in place as he summoned flames from the hearth to blacken my skin. As it stood, all I'd really done was deny him an outlet for his rage, which in hindsight might not have been my best idea. I made a note to make sure the servants stayed away from the mages' quarters until he'd calmed down enough to avoid doing anything monumentally stupid. As much as I'd like something to take Zakio down with, having blood on my hands didn't sit well.

It could get me out of the evening's banquet, but— well, it probably wouldn't.

"One day—" Zakio was breathing so hard his chest heaved beneath his dark robes. "One day, you'll get exactly what you deserve."

"If you've been listening to my father, that will probably come wearing a ball gown and dark rouge." I turned to leave, clasping my hands behind my back.

Then I paused and turned. "Oh, and Zakio?"

His eyebrows rose to his hairline as I pointed at a haphazard stack of parchment. Some of the characters on the top one were smudged, as if written in a hurry and hadn't fully dried before an errant sleeve dragged across them.

"Those papers look awfully important," I said.

His shouts of alarm as I sent the papers flying toward the crackling hearth were worth any punishment my father doled out later.

BY NIGHTFALL, THE banquet hall had filled with people and sound. Glasses clinked as servants distributed my father's finest vintage made from the sweet grapes that had survived the first frost settling down the mountainsides—a drink I'd never been particularly fond of. In the space not taken up by nobles, their eligible daughters, and their sizable entourages, sat long tables draped with fine red silk, as if the color itself could stir romance—or at least the illusion of romance slipped over promised favors and heirloom jewels. Walking through the crowd took considerable skill, but I'd long grown adept at snaking away from conversations I didn't wish to be part of. And the watered wine, though teeth-numbingly saccharine, offered a buzzing escape.

My father must have invited all of Runon. I wondered who was guarding the borders he steadfastly refused to reopen; perhaps, in the past, there'd have been foreign dignitaries present, and maybe they, too, would have brought potential matches for me. A princess from a neighboring kingdom would probably be just as bad as the daughter of one of my father's simpering minions, but at least it'd be different and offer me a chance to use my Common, which had fallen sorely out of practice. Chayd to the south, for example, might have been willing to mend our broken relationship through a political marriage. My father had closed those roads before any of the others, however, and Runon was effectively an island in the sea of our mountains.

The whole affair churned my stomach. If I focused my eyes too long at a single point, all the colors blurred together to make me dizzy. The wine helped, but not nearly enough, and the crown already weighed heavy enough on my head to drag me down through the castle cellars.

In my effort to avoid making eye contact with any of the invited nobles—lest they get the wrong idea and shove their daughter at me— I turned in a slow circle until I spotted Zakio on the far side of the hall. His mother stood next to him, plainly annoyed, as if *she* was the one being offered for trade like a prized warhorse. Zakio glared at me and normally it would have brightened my thoughts, but the walls were too close and the air too hot. I'd find no respite in angering him further tonight.

I'd made it to the bottom of my second glass of watered, too-sweet wine by the time my father strode to my side. The large crown around his head was ornately studded with gems rendering it impractical to use for anything but ceremonial events. I wondered, not for the first time, how much heavier it must be than my own. I'd never bothered to try it on, since I'd find out sooner or later and would rather not hasten the inevitable.

"I expect you to be on your best behavior tonight," he warned, like I was still a child ducking beneath the draped tables.

"If only I knew what that was," I replied.

He clearly wanted to answer but never got the chance, for my cousin appeared at his side in one of the garishly dyed cloaks he favored. A buffoon, the only good thing he'd ever done was siring a daughter, but, at two years old, she hadn't joined her father this evening. A pity—it would've been a nice diversion to chase her between guests' legs.

"Your Majesty," my cousin said, bowing low. "There's a fine crowd in attendance tonight."

"So many beautiful young women as hopefuls for the crown," my father added.

They both looked to me, expecting a response.

"Beautiful," I echoed. They might be, but I wouldn't know. If the defining emotion of the rest of my life was going to be misery, I hoped my future bride would at least have a good sense of humor. In truth, I didn't know why my father continued the charade, but maybe we all clung to the lies we desperately wished to believe. I knew I did.

That path was too melancholy to go down with so many others staring at me. I grabbed for another glass of wine, ignoring the ache already starting in my temples. At this rate, I'd be out cold before the dessert course and couldn't find it in myself to care.

My father reached for my glass and didn't make it. Instead, my reactive jerk away splashed wine over the goblet rim, hitting my sleeve. I didn't much care about that, either; I'd pull the fires free from the kitchen and make the flames dance with whatever wine remained, and they'd all be properly dazzled again.

These parties were so predictable.

"Ah, here comes Wahara now," my cousin said, as if my father and I were both blind to the approaching figures. He just wanted to be part of the inner circle. Despite all his bumbling, he was calculating when he needed to be. I wished I could push him out the east tower to avoid his tales when he'd had too much to drink.

Wahara brought with him his daughter—whom I'd met twice before, each time in a more expensive silk gown—and three others. One of them, a young man about my age, was pushed forward beside Wahara's deep-bowing daughter, which must make him the son and heir.

As both Wahara and his daughter lowered their heads to my father's crown, the son's eyes roved over me from head to toe and then back up. *Ah.* Tonight was shaping up to be far better than I'd dared hope for. He was certainly easy on the eyes, and locks of his black hair were falling over his forehead just enough to give him a sultry look, the kind his sister probably pined for. The look slid effortlessly across his features, and she pursed her lips beside him in a pale imitation.

"Wahara," I said, "it's genuinely good to see you again."

If he brightened because he assumed I was pleased to see his daughter alongside him, well, it wasn't *my* fault he'd mixed up the sentiment.

THE SON DIDN'T even make it an hour before he was hovering deliciously at the side of my vision, just beyond the nobles with their shrewd gazes and the princess-hopefuls with their layers of silk. The amount of silver in the room might have emptied an entire mine, and at least one of my father's advisors owned one deep within the mountains, so the excess made sense.

The party guests had made short work of my father's good wine stores, and the servants began pouring fermented *niyun*, a red fruit that soured considerably when the alcohol was released. The brew was a sign my father thought the party was going well enough to risk losing favor with the lesser-quality drink.

I'd had enough that my vision was spinning the chandeliers overhead, but with Wahara's heir loitering nearby, the blur wasn't a bad thing. Making inadvisable decisions came easier when I couldn't quite get my thoughts in order.

One of my father's advisors cornered me against the largest table, his bony fingers wrapped around his daughter's thin wrist. She looked like she'd rather be anywhere else, her small silver eyes darting around the room much like a frightened doe. I didn't blame her; being paraded around like fine merchant's ware got old before the first course was served. She couldn't be any older than fifteen. Even if I *were* interested, she was far too young to be desirable, and any attraction her father hoped to cultivate lingered in the realm of wishful forward thinking.

My eyes slipped over his shoulder to Wahara's son. He played coy at first—as if I couldn't tell he'd been finding excuses to remain in my line of sight—but finally met my gaze with defiance. The resulting rush turned my blood to fire. I finished my goblet without caring about the sour aftertaste of the *niyun* wine and set the glass on the table.

The castle had a thousand small nooks in which to hide, and I knew all of them. All it took was a vague excuse to extract myself from the noble's animated conversation, though as I was walking toward the double doors separating the banquet from the rest of the winding halls, I raised one eyebrow in the direction of Wahara's heir. Either he'd get the message and follow, or he wouldn't, and I'd escape the humiliation early. Both outcomes meant victory.

The halls were full of servants with trays full of shredded, smoked meat and new bottles of *niyun* wine, but none of them gave me more than a passing glance. They were clearly familiar with me sneaking out of royal parties before the ringing of the midnight bells, but my mother, before she'd died during my childhood, had always told me to forge my own path. It just so happened my preferred path led in the opposite direction of my father's wishes. I suspected, had she lived, my mother would have been proud.

I wished I knew for sure, though, and the sudden nostalgia and longing swept through my body with such force I stumbled back into the cool stone wall. I missed her, an ache in my heart only sometimes soothed with magic and drink and stolen kisses. Speaking of, however—

Wahara's son stood just outside the doors, staring at me with an expression hovering between desire and fear. It wasn't as endearing as he'd probably liked it to be, but I was in no position to be picky. I grabbed his wrist and led him through the twisting halls I knew by heart until we reached one of the small servants' closets.

I didn't know why anyone bothered locking things in the castle. The iron clasp, heavy and solid, took only a single ripple of magic to heat until it fell clear on its own. Zakio and his mother would be able to feel the use wherever they were, stomping around in the banquet hall. I couldn't have cared less. They knew where to find me.

My blood sang softly with the reverberations of the magic when I pulled Wahara's son inside. It was musty and smelled like mops badly needing a wash, and if he minded, he was smart enough not to show it. I'd learned a long time ago not to take dalliances up to my chamber after one of them made off with a priceless royal heirloom. I hadn't gotten any pickier, but at least I'd gotten smarter with the location selection.

One would have guessed forethought to be a trait valued in the heir to the throne.

Wahara's son huffed out something of a gasp, as if trying to form words. Words? He'd probably try to do something phenomenally useless, like give me his name, so I grabbed his face and kissed him soundly. A sour burst of *niyun* wine sat on the corner of his lips, leftover in his haste to follow me from the celebration.

Our elbows bumped a few times as he engaged fully, the drawback of having such encounters in pitch-dark closets. My shoulder smacked into a wooden mop handle when he pushed back. It burned a bit when my back hit the wall, but he kissed with the sort of reckless passion that usually came from living in repressed households, and I liked the contrast. He even had enough muscle on him to hoist me up against the stones, which let me wrap my legs around his waist and lock my ankles against the dip of his lower back.

His hand slid beneath my shirt to trail across the skin of my waist, like he was going to dip lower beneath my silver-studded belt, and that was when the door to the closet flew open. The sudden burst of torchlight burned so jarringly I squeezed my eyes shut.

Wahara's son dropped me like a stone, and my ankle turned in my stumble to keep upright.

"Get out," my father growled. I opened my eyes again, just in time to see the young man trip over his own feet in his hurry to obey, looking like he might soil himself.

My father's sudden appearance had startled him so badly he'd bitten my bottom lip, and it throbbed.

"I really need new hiding places," I said, hoping my tone came out light. "But sadly, the third-rate wine didn't do much to expand my imagination tonight."

"Have you no shame?" my father asked, low and dangerous—at least it would have been if he had anyone else to give the crown to, or if he didn't know I could kill him with the flick of my hands. Sometimes, I wondered if he was so angry because he hated me or feared me.

On darker nights, I suspected it was both.

"I guess you already know the answer to that," I replied, though I had to avert my eyes so my father couldn't see the traitorous sheen in them. The corners pricked, but I wouldn't let the tears fall. Crying wouldn't make him love me.

I'd learned that lesson before I learned to write my name.

My father stiffened for a long beat, his whole body then trembling with barely controlled fury. "You will destroy everything I've built, everything I've created."

"What, you mean the constant skirmishes with our neighbors?" I asked. "The towering import taxes levied as warnings? You've created nothing but a kingdom so isolated that when we starve to death on the mountainside, you'll have only yourself to blame."

"And when do you have time to study foreign policy? Before or after your nightly romps with the noble boys?"

I laughed, and it sounded horrible. "You might be surprised how much attention I pay, Father. Or are you disappointed?"

"Disappointed that this is what you do with yourself, yes."

"Give it up," I snapped. My bottom lip still hurt, and any possible amusement from the night had been chased off. The light-headed euphoria from the wine had faded away, leaving behind a persistent ache in my temples. All I wanted was to collapse in bed and forget the way this terrible evening had ended. "I'm all you've got unless you still think my magic came from *your* side of the family."

His scowl deepened; I'd hit a well-worn nerve.

"Still dreaming of finding your own latent abilities?" Rattled, I couldn't resist the jab. "Alas, Father, they would surely have manifested by now. And it just so happens that the only person who did carry those quiet genes is dead. So, either you and I have to come to another arrangement, or you can deny me the throne and find a way to live forever."

If I hadn't been so unnerved and sticky-tongued, I might have noticed how something changed in his features then. But despite all evidence to the contrary, self-preservation had never been my strong suit.

"You're drunk," he said, as though he'd stumbled across new and life-changing information.

"Not anymore. Though it would certainly help this conversation."

His fingers tightened around the thick wood of the closet door, turning his knuckles white. "I expect to see you in my study tomorrow morning, where we will discuss this with clear heads."

"Let's make it afternoon, so I can sleep off this hangover."

He didn't answer, which I took as agreement, and stumbled through the hallways and staircases to my chamber. The hearth was bare and cold, but I welcomed the chill. I didn't bother summoning a servant to light the logs before I sagged onto the mattress.

I was asleep before I registered closing my eyes.

THE SUNLIGHT—AND my throbbing headache—woke me the next morning.

My mouth tasted sour, my tongue thick. I hadn't bothered to shed my banquet clothes before falling into bed, and they were likely rumpled beyond repair. Changing into something else took a long time with the pounding behind my eyes, and it was late by the time I finally managed to leave my chamber.

My father was, as promised, sitting in his study with parchment scattered across the dark cherry desk. I could make out only enough to know the papers concerned numbers, probably the royal accounts. I'd be surprised if the crown wasn't hemorrhaging money with all the fines and taxes the neighboring kingdoms had levied. People tended to do that when they were abruptly cut off from promised import supplies by isolationist behavior. Still, my father found enough silver coin to throw banquets in his attempts to marry me off. I wondered where that wealth came from.

I remained standing despite the open chair, just to be annoying.

"About last night," my father began, sitting back and lacing his fingers together on his lap.

"A wonderful time for all involved," I said.

"I may have been too hasty in choosing my words."

That startled me. An apology? I could count on one hand the number of times my father had apologized to me, and none were in the last ten years. Thrown, I couldn't think of anything to say, which he took as encouragement to continue.

"If you are so against the idea of marriage—"

"I'm against *your* idea of marriage."

"—then I'll refrain from any further attempts in the next year."

My head spun. "Until I'm eighteen?"

"Until then," he agreed.

I'd never dreamed of getting so lucky, especially given how I'd anticipated a barrage of lectures and ire, walking into the study that morning. My body was responding too sluggishly and painfully to truly focus, but hope lit up within me, a beacon announcing my desperation for everyone to see. Even my fingers were tingling with it, as if I'd brought it about with magic. The buzzing in my limbs convinced me it was all real.

I'd be free of the parades of nobles' daughters, the long nights of making inane conversation. I'd be free of endless silk dresses and long speeches espousing on virtue and beauty.

Perhaps finding me in the closet with Wahara's son had been the final straw for my father's regard to my reputation.

"What's the catch?" I asked and swallowed hard.

"Keep your head down, and just maybe we'll find a better use for you than banquets."

"Agreed," I said, swiftly so he couldn't take it back once he rethought the plan. "Nothing for a year."

He smiled, the expression tight. "Now leave me to my work."

I was happy to comply. Out of the study, my legs turned to water beneath my weight. I sagged against the wall, heaving, so overwhelmed by my good luck I could hardly breathe. It was staggering how much lighter I felt without that weight shackled across my shoulders, and my lungs burned with relief.

My fingers ghosted across my lips, recalling the frantic kisses of the night before, and my steps held a distinct spring as I walked away from the room.

IN HINDSIGHT, IT was all so much clearer.

I never bothered to lock my chamber door—the servants needed access to start the hearthfire in the long winter months and bring up breakfast. Whenever I got up to anything truly sordid, I left enough clues to alert the servants and keep them away, and besides, I hadn't used my chambers for that purpose in months. If anyone came for me, I'd figure they'd use magic, and I'd know they were using it well before they arrived at my bedside.

Even the day before my eighteenth birthday, I wasn't worried. My father had stayed true to his word, and there hadn't been a single matchmaking banquet since our agreement. Maybe the relative peace had lulled me into unassuming calmness, or maybe it had been my father's good humor.

Whatever the case, I didn't suspect a thing when they came for me.

The door creaked, enough to wake me, and then a rag pressed against my mouth. The concoction they used smelled strong and slightly sweet, immediately jellying my limbs. When I tried to speak, I couldn't get a sound past my lips. My body wasn't my own. I was at the mercy of my captors.

As they dragged me down the hall, I wanted to laugh, and I wanted to cry. Without access to my magic, I had nothing. The hands on my arm pinched tight, as if only out of spite, and I knew who it was even before I saw his profile through the slits of my heavy eyelids. Zakio must have been elated that he'd finally gotten the chance to wage his war against me.

They put me in a room without a fire, so cold my fingers shook. I could only catch snippets of the conversation around me as I bobbed in and out of the hazy stupor they'd drugged me into, but it was enough: I knew what they were going to do. They were going to use my magic like a conduit, a copper rod channeling a lightning strike.

They were going to use my magic and leave my body a hollow shell to house it.

Of course, they waited until my birthday to go through with their plan. It was one thing to make someone a slave, but quite another to do so to a child.

It was ironic, at the end of all things. If I'd had control over myself, I would've laughed. After all, I'd planted the thought in my father's mind, hadn't I? I'd told him he'd either have to learn to live with me or get rid of me.

I just never believed he'd choose the latter.

Part Two

Chayd

three years later...

Chapter One

THE KNOCK ON the door came just as he finished refilling his quiver. Tatsu froze, blood running cold. He put his hand on the leather pack for stability before he was able to oust the lump in his throat. His house was too remote for anyone to simply stumble across it, so whoever it was had meant to arrive. As the air in the small house hung still and heavy, his hand slid to the uneven table with the broken leg he'd never gotten around to fixing, fingers finding the familiar and well-worn hilt of his skinning knife. It was sharp enough to take apart a jack hare. He hoped it was also keen enough to defend himself.

He took a few steps toward the noise, his feet unconsciously finding their way around the long, loose floorboards. He was almost to the door when the knocking came again, impatient. The new round of knocking was paired with a female voice. "Tatsu?"

The anxiety left his body in a rush that felt like the hot sting of Chayd's summer against his skin, months too early.

"Alesh?" he replied and opened the creaking wooden door. "What are you doing here?"

His first thought was that she had to be injured, sick, or something worse. After all, it had been a long time since she'd last bothered to travel all the way to his hut in the inner woods. But she appeared to be in one piece, her hair worked back into three simple plaits, and she seemed no worse for the wear. Irritation surged through his chest.

Knowing she'd been fine but not taking the time to visit made her sudden reappearance cut deeper.

"Please," she said and, at once, he knew. Alesh wouldn't journey to his doorstep for any other reason. She needed a favor.

He had half a mind to shut the door right in her face, his insides still untangling themselves from tight knots, but movement flashed behind Alesh's shoulder. Ral lingered behind her, digging in the constant scourge of weeds growing in front of the house without any care to the dirt embedding itself under her nails. The young woman was laughing at Tatsu's wildflowers. Her light-brown dress fabric, marking her as *enol*, or baseborn, was already streaked with smears of mud.

He didn't close the door, but he didn't edge it open any further either.

"Hear me out." Alesh had the good grace to flinch when Tatsu snorted.

"Isn't that all I've ever done?" he asked.

"I need your help."

Help was not a word that came easily from her, though Tatsu guessed they had wildly different definitions of it. *Help* to him meant aid and a friendly ear and someone present, offering suggestions and finding solutions. *Help* was nothing Alesh had ever allowed him to do.

"The last time I tried to help you..." he warned.

She slammed the door so forcefully the ripples shook Tatsu's arm. "Listen, this isn't for me, you know. I can't leave her alone, and I don't have anyone else."

Tatsu peered over Alesh's shoulder again. Ral had gotten a handful of the reedy flowers and pulled them up by the roots, laughing with delight at the white tendrils she'd exposed. When Tatsu's gaze flickered back to Alesh, her dark eyes were focused on him, narrow and unflinching.

"Please." The second time sounded much less like a request. She knew she'd already won him over.

Tatsu sighed and called out, "Ral, would you like to come in?"

Ral complied, though she left a trail of dirt behind her as her movement loosened the clumps that clung to her skirt. She might have gotten taller. She was taller than Tatsu, at least. She seemed happy in the house, and Tatsu tried to keep half his attention on her as she moved around, in case she got her hands on the extra snares in the corners. If he had known a houseguest would show up, he might've done something with the place.

"It's only for a few days," Alesh promised. "This is the safest place I could think of. I mean, who's going to come way out here? I have some business I need to attend to—"

"Other people's possessions, you mean? Or is there a new line of criminal mischief you've found that pays better?"

She frowned. "That's not fair at all, and you know it."

"Do I?" Tatsu asked. "How could I know it, when the last time you bothered to show up here and tell me you were still alive, the first snow had just fallen?"

Her face pinched tight, mouth hard, before it slackened again in defeat. She sighed, equal parts exasperation and resignation, and ran a hand through the few dark strands of hair hanging wild and wavy around her face, too short to plait back.

"Look, can you...spare me the whole spiel?" Her gaze sank and stayed on a spot near the entrance where the beams of the house were embedded deep in the dirt. "I promise you can lecture me all you want when I come back to pick her up. But for now, I really need to go, and I don't have time for this."

Tatsu leaned against the door. Behind him, Ral had discovered the utensils for cooking and was excitedly going through them all, copper spoons and mugs clanging against one another. Alesh stood slumped on his doorstep as if the weight of the world hung on her shoulders, hobbling her. She seemed smaller than the last time he'd seen her, under the same sky and a moon tinged with red. He thought about saying something, something like *stay*, but the times they'd shared had long since passed between them. There had been too many winters and too many summers. The word died on his tongue.

Instead, he nodded. "Fine. But only for a few days."

"Thank you." Alesh's mouth twisted up into a rueful smile. "She's learned to count to a hundred—you should ask her to demonstrate for you. She loves showing it off."

Behind them, as if in agreement, Ral banged Tatsu's ladle against his big iron pot, the sharp crash echoing.

"I will," Tatsu replied.

Alesh tucked a bit of unruly hair behind one ear. "It won't be long."

"No," Tatsu agreed. "It never is."

HE WAS AT home in the woods.

It didn't matter how many times he walked through the same stretch of thick-barked trees, he always found something both calming and new: a bird's nest stretched across branches, an anthill at the foot of upturned roots. He could find his footing in the darkest corners of the forest, rain or shine. A few motionless moments with his eyes closed, ears keen, and he knew which animals were slinking around him, eager to get lost in the shadows away from his snares.

The daily chores through the trees were made more difficult with the addition of Ral. While she was cheerful and bright, Ral didn't care much for keeping her footsteps quiet. Hunting, it seemed, was out of the question until Alesh returned. Ral seemed to enjoy moving through the seemingly never-ending green of the trees, even if she did march through while trying to alert every creature to her existence. The tall trunks of the trees expanded overhead into a splay of branches and coarse leaves with notched edges. The farther away from the cottage they went, the more the woods around them changed, darkened, and grew thicker with pines and the sweet smell of their needles.

Chayd might have *physically* owned the woods, but Tatsu knew their *soul.*

"Ral, let's find some berries for dinner," he suggested, and she followed, singing a song composed of more guttural noises than actual words. She trailed her fingers along the leaves as they passed. The loss of hunting frustrated him, but his traps would feed them well enough if they could find something to supplement the catch.

It had rained the night before, and the ground was still wet with the aftermath. Tatsu's boots sank into the dirt as he pushed his hand against one of the trunks and waited. This area of the woods wasn't known for being rich with edible berries, but he had a feeling something sprinkled the ground nearby. It had been a long time since he'd checked, and the odds were in his favor.

Overhead, a raven flew as they walked, screeching out its song in sporadic bursts. In the mud, the remnants of the forest's night scene remained, half buried beneath fallen leaves and creeping ground vines. Tatsu could see tracks from a long-gone deer and the erratic path of a rabbit escaping its owl predator. He noted all of them as they trekked. Even if he couldn't go after the deer with Ral, its existence signaled the possibility of this area being good hunting ground in the days after.

He found what he'd been searching for within the hour: a cache of berries, plump and red, clustered on the branches of a bush. The plant crept up like a thief around the side of one of the weaker, crooked trees, barely holding on to its place in the forest.

"Ral, come look," he said, kneeling to capture a few of the juicy berries between his fingertips.

She knelt beside him, face open and excited.

"So pretty," she murmured, reaching for the splashes of red, bright against the backdrop of green. He picked a few from the branch, the juice splashing on his skin and running down his fingers and held out the burlap pouch he'd brought with him. Ral had other ideas, however. She insisted on depositing all the ones she picked into her skirt, which she'd pillowed out over her folded knees. As they collected as many as they could, staining their hands maroon, she laughed and laughed, and Tatsu couldn't help laughing with her. When she stood, she managed to keep most of their bounty within the fabric, though he knew there'd be no helping the red stain.

If they cut back east toward the Turend Mountains, Tatsu could check the rest of his snares, set up around his usual circuit. He let his fingers rest loosely on Ral's wrist, smearing her skin with some of the berry juice. He started for his location, saying, "One final check and then we'll go back, all right?"

She didn't protest, though her steps were as loud as ever through the underbrush.

His traps had collected an abundant bounty. Two hares and a ground squirrel, all relatively fresh and untouched by the raptors that made their nests overhead. He tied his catches up by the legs and swung them over his shoulder, one by one, carefully resetting the wires and triggers disguised by the long grasses around bumpy tree roots. Finishing the last one, he stood, pleased with how the day had gone despite everything. He turned, expecting to find his companion already snacking on her berry haul.

Ral, however, was gone.

Tatsu turned and then turned again, all the way around, and saw only the tree trunks he knew by heart. Ral was nowhere to be seen. How, he cursed, could she have disappeared so quietly when all day she'd scared off his game? To slip away in the woods while he was otherwise engaged... Tatsu darted forward before he stopped again, crouching and attempting to calm his racing pulse. He knew the woods and she didn't. He pressed his fingers into the drying dirt and closed his eyes, allowing the scent of the still-moist mud and dead leaves to wash over him. When he opened his eyes again, there in the mud were the tracks left and the leaves bent as she'd passed them by.

He took off in the direction her trail led. In his haste, he dropped one of the hares, and while he was loath to leave it, Ral came first. The predators in the trees didn't bother him, but she was unarmed and vulnerable, and the closer they moved to the cliffs, the closer they came to the territory the wolves liked to patrol.

"Ral!" he called, sharp and almost angry.

He lost her trail and, after a wild moment, found it again, bolting forward like a vole evading a falcon. He was moving quickly, and he swerved too close to a low-hanging branch. Its bark made contact and stung against his cheek, but he didn't even bother to wipe the blood away. He kept moving until his lungs burned and his hands shook. Then, all at once, he burst out of the tree cover at the side of a cliff, overlooking the mountains stretching out like rocky roots protruding from the ground.

Ral stood with her skirts whipping around her body. The berries were strewn across the grass in front of her, a bloodstain on the green, forgotten.

"Stop," she said. She looked frightened, but she wasn't giving him an order. It took Tatsu a few steps to see what she was talking about.

The mountains were dying.

Not the cliffs themselves, of course, but the vegetation on them. The steep sides had once been lush and green, pines forming stripes of year-round color constant even when autumn came and dyed the other leaves gold, but instead of bright swathes of color, everything was dead. What little was left of the trees had darkened to almost black, limbs twisted over one another and hunched down toward the soil. It wasn't just a small section, like a victim of a tree blight, but the entire slope of the peaks. The angry brown continued as far as Tatsu could see until the life stopped along the uphill climb of the mountains themselves.

The sight shocked him so much he stumbled back a step before he caught the real horror of it. A line had formed in front of him in the grass, nearly perfect between the withered blades and the still-living green of the rest, just near the edge of the cliff. The ghastly contrast of colors continued along the divide until the clearing ended and the mountain sloped steeply downward. The dead grass swept into the valley, and the green continued back into Tatsu's woods.

"What is this?" Tatsu whispered. "What's happening?"

Ral whimpered, weak at first and then more forceful. Her hands clutched the sides of her head as she sank into the grass and the remnants of the berries.

"Scary, scary, scary," she repeated. "Bad! Stop, stop!"

"Ral." Tatsu reached for her, nearly missing her shoulders because her shaking was so violent. "Ral, stop! Come here. Let's get away from this."

She allowed him to lead her back into the relative safety of the trees. Once they began to put distance between the border of decay and themselves, her condition seemed to better, but Tatsu couldn't purge what he'd seen from his mind. Those mountains had once been a thriving ecosystem. If that line meant what he thought it did, it was only going to expand farther and farther, reaching his woods and devouring them whole. If that wasn't bad enough, he didn't think the forest would be able to stop it.

Beyond the trees, beyond his snares and traps, Chayd's capital of Dradela sat directly in the path of the unnatural destruction.

The birds were chattering above them on their walk back to the house, but the warning roared against his ears, a white noise of fear and dread that silenced everything else.

RAL REMAINED SILENT as Tatsu made dinner. Sometimes, she simply sat motionless, staring at nothing on the floorboards, and other times, her eyes darted around the room as if taking stock of invisible enemies floating above their heads. Tatsu wasn't sure what to do about it. The miles and miles of dead forest wouldn't leave his mind either, even as he skinned the newest prizes from his snares and cooked them in a rich, starchy vegetable broth until they were tender.

When he served the concoction to Ral in a slightly cracked clay bowl, her gaze finally met his. She didn't take the offered bowl, though, so he set it on the table in front of her and seated himself across from her, feeling equally queasy about his portion.

"I know what we saw today was very…strange," he said, stirring bits of the meat around with his wooden spoon until they stuck to the sides. "But you do need to eat something, so please, try and eat a little?"

Her eyes flitted across the table, from the bowl to the spoon, and then she wrapped her fingers around the utensil.

"What do you think all of that means?" Tatsu asked.

"Bad. Scary," Ral replied around the spoon. Her dark hair, which always fell in loose waves around her shoulders like a young girl's, fluttered against her collarbone. As she ate, a bit of the stew escaped from her spoon and splashed across her chin. Tatsu grabbed a towel and dabbed at the rivulets for her as her eyes tracked his movements. Her smile stretched watery and wide when he finished, and he could manage only a weak smile back.

"It *was* scary," he agreed. "And you know what the scariest part was?"

She didn't answer, but he didn't expect her to.

"I think that dead part is coming this way. What would happen to me and these woods?"

Ral grinned again, spooning bigger bits of the stew into her mouth. "Yummy. Like this food."

For a while, Tatsu studied her. She'd been small for her age when younger. It was a reaction, they'd said, to the plague that had struck during her infancy and kept her mind from growing up with the rest of her. Despite being older, she'd always trailed behind Alesh in height, year after year. Eventually, she'd sprouted up, tall and willowy, like a tree that had finally found the sun. She was every bit a woman now, with the brown coloring native to Chayd. Her skin, next to Tatsu's, was a warm, rich sepia.

Self-conscious, Tatsu pulled his arm back, absently rubbing his skin as if he could darken his own to match. Ral, oblivious, only smiled at him again through mouthfuls of dinner.

"Eat up," he told her, even though he pushed his own bowl aside, appetite lost.

When they were done, he cleaned up everything with the big pot of warmed water and let Ral sit on the floor. She liked playing with the old odds and ends that never seemed to make it out of the house. The wooden carvings in the shapes of animals caught her attention, along with the scraps cut free when he was making new fastenings for his sheath and quiver. She stayed clear from the boots in the corner, though, and Tatsu was glad for it. The boots were covered in dust so thick it hid the leather in a mottled white shroud. They were the last things in the house his father had touched before he died.

Tatsu didn't have the strength to move them.

The keening noise sounded from the center of the room as he was almost finished washing. When he turned, Ral was shaking her hands in front of her, eyes wild and white, darting from side to side.

"Ral?" Perhaps she was seizing.

He reached for her but never made it—the thud and smack against the door stopped them both cold. For a second, there was nothing, and then, barely audible from the other side of the wooden panels, came a low groan of pain.

Tatsu ran to the door and threw it open to find Alesh bleeding all over the doorstep.

"Tatsu," she managed, and that was it before her eyes rolled back in her head, strength fading, and she pitched forward into the house and his arms.

Chapter Two

SHE WAS HEAVY when he caught her, barely able to keep her knees and knuckles from hitting the floorboards. Tatsu's knees buckled, and he grunted, though somehow, he kept them both somewhat upright.

"Ral," he ground out between clenched teeth. She was upset and rattled, still flopping her hands on limp wrists in the air, but she moved to his side and reached for her sister, enough to help balance the dead weight. "Help me get her to the bed."

Somehow, they did. Alesh left a trail of blood on the boards beneath her, but it wasn't as much as Tatsu had initially thought. Dark splashes of it had soaked into the side of her brown shirt. The flow, however, had ebbed. The red spots on her arms and face, while no doubt painful, would blossom only into vivid bruises within a day or two. Whatever spark had kept her awake to make the journey through the trees to Tatsu's house had clearly disappeared.

He pushed aside the fabric of her stained shirt, which was so sticky it tugged at her skin. Tatsu whispered an apology, even though she had drifted far beyond hearing it. The wound appeared clean, which was something good, at least, and not terribly deep. The knife had gone in and missed hitting anything other than veins and skin, and the blood had already begun to clot. The air left his lungs in a painful rush.

"Ral, I need you to take this cloth and press it against the red part." Tatsu guided Ral's hands where he wanted them. Her fingers were shaking and there were tears on her cheeks, but she did as instructed. When he removed his hands from hers, she held absolutely still aside from her terrified, shuddering breaths.

"Good," Tatsu breathed. "Just stay there."

He went to the water pot and set it over the fire. Already, the tightness within was relaxing, soothed by familiar, useful tasks. He'd patched up worse wounds on his father before the age of fourteen: the time the man had nearly been taken down by a lone wolf that had strayed too far from the pack, and twice when the traps they'd been setting malfunctioned during placement. Still, he didn't want to take any chances.

A sewing kit sat collecting dust on the cluttered shelves hanging near the fires, and Tatsu grabbed it. Sterilizing the needle in the flames didn't take long.

By the time he returned to Alesh's side with his tools, Ral was shaking harder. Her shoulders were slumped over in a miserable arch.

"Help, please," she whispered. Tatsu reached for her hands and pulled them away from Alesh's injury. Getting another look at it helped—he was sure the wound wasn't dangerously deep.

Once Ral had sat back, she turned her face up toward him. "Tatsu, help?"

"Yes. I'm going to help her."

He cleaned the wound with the warm water and terrycloth. Once the water grew pink with blood, he hunched over and peered close so he could stitch up the skin in a neat, even row. It was easier than working on himself. Even so, when he'd finished, his back was screaming from the unnatural bend, and his hands were stiff and trembling. Against Alesh's brown skin, the stitches were hardly visible. Her chest was rising and falling in rhythmic, if shallow, breaths, and Tatsu allowed himself to sit back and steady his own breathing.

"Why?" Ral asked, her voice small.

He couldn't think of anything to tell her. From his kneeling position on the floor, he stared at the angry red, staining the remnants of Alesh's shirt. Her black hair remained braided and wrapped with cord, but a tumble of the waves had fallen free and were hanging off the side of the bed. When he still didn't have an answer for Ral after a full minute, he moved to wrap his fingers around her skinny wrist.

"I'm scared," Ral said, and her shoulders shook.

"Me too," Tatsu admitted.

THE FLOOR WASN'T the most comfortable place to sleep, but Tatsu doubted he would have gotten much rest anyway. His neck ached from the awkward curve in which he'd first managed to doze off for perhaps only half an hour, and after that, he couldn't get his mind to calm down enough to drift away again. He stared at the boards of the roof above them. Cracks had long since begun splitting the wood grains and splintering the panels. He'd once known them all and had named them, creating elaborate stories for them, back before Alesh and Ral had been part of his life. Back then, his father had been the only one around.

In the dim light of the candle, the same cracks seemed foreign and far away, unreachable.

He sighed and turned over. Looking beneath the bed, there was a layer of dust that had accumulated on the floor, which should have bothered him much more than it did.

"Tatsu?" came the weak voice from above.

He pushed his weight up onto his elbows so quickly he banged both joints against the floor and winced from the resulting jolt up his shoulders. "Alesh?"

Scrambling to his feet, he found her with bleary but open eyes, registering and following his movements.

"You're awake," he said and instantly felt stupid for doing so. "I mean, we were worried about you."

"Ral?" Alesh rasped. The right side of her face was starting to take on a green tint, no doubt the precursor to the widespread bruising she would soon have. It seemed to impede her speech a bit, as though moving her jaw sparked new flashes of pain.

Tatsu checked over his shoulder to take stock of Ral's sleeping figure on the floorboards. "She's fine. We're fine."

He knew Alesh well enough to decipher the look of relief that flashed across her features, no matter how swollen and inflamed they were. Her eyelids fluttered closed as she breathed, perhaps to steady herself. When her eyes opened once more, her gaze seemed stronger.

"Alesh," Tatsu started, and part of him, a part he didn't quite recognize anymore, wanted to reach for her shoulder. An unblemished and uninjured bit of skin was visible between the tattered remains of the shirt she was wearing. An old memory stuck in his throat, bitter and rotting. "What happened?"

Her mouth screwed to the side a bit, evasive. "Job went bad."

"You show up on my doorstep, bleeding and almost unconscious," he started, and then, with a pang of guilt when he saw the way she flinched, softened his voice to finish. "I think I deserve a little more than that."

The lines at the corners of her mouth deepened. She must have been feeling a bit better, because she turned her head to the side to stare at the knots in the wood of the cottage wall. She was quiet for a long time. If Tatsu hadn't been able to see her eyes, still open and fixed upon nothing, he'd have thought she'd fallen back asleep.

After what felt like an eternity, she said, "You know you're the only person I can really count on."

Tatsu didn't answer, mostly because he wasn't sure how. Alesh straightened her neck, looking directly at him with inky shadows on her skin flickering and dancing from the candlelight. "And I know I don't really deserve that, after everything."

"Stop," Tatsu said, halfhearted at best.

"You know it's true." She sighed. "And I'm sorry."

Staring at Ral's form, half-covered by a threadbare blanket unraveling on one edge, Tatsu tried to ignore the familiar sting. "You always were."

"And that's what always made it hurt so much."

They sat in silence for several long minutes, listening to the constant hum of the insects outside. Alesh's return had brought up long-dormant feelings and old pain he'd been trying to ignore for years. The cottage squeezed in, too small for the three of them as they remained trapped in a strange waltz of tiptoeing around the past.

"Alesh," Tatsu tried again, his voice low, "what happened?"

Resigned, her head lolled to one side again against the fibers of the pillow. "Guards showed up on the job and got most of the hands. I managed to get away, but not before one of them got a few hits in."

It was likely, then, that the colors languidly brightening on her face were from trying to flee rather than being the aggressor, which made Tatsu feel a little better.

"The whole thing was strange, though," she continued. "They had an entire company. They must have been tipped off, because why else would they have so many guards for a routine trade inspection?"

"You think someone sold you out? From the inside?"

She was halfway into a shrug before the pain of the action registered. She stopped quickly, and it took a while for her body to relax again, her face pinched. "Or else we were being watched."

"You need to get out."

Alesh laughed, harsh and barking, and this, too, appeared to be painful. "You know I can't. They'll come after me. And Ral. They've got too much on me to let me go now. They'll kill me before they let me go."

"At this rate, you're going to die anyway," Tatsu shot back, blood heating. "What good are you to Ral if you're killed pulling some stupid job?"

Alesh didn't answer him but held his gaze. There was a lot there, murky in the depths, and he couldn't quite get a handle on it all. But somewhere in her eyes, buried beneath the pain and walls used as a shield, he liked to believe a twinge of affection remained. The long burned-out embers of what they used to have settled between them. Stung, somehow, and too tired to muddle through, Tatsu wrenched his eyes away.

"I'm not apologizing," he mumbled.

"I didn't ask you to. I deserve it."

"I'm still allowed to care about what happens to you."

Her fingers were cool when they threaded through his. "You're good like that."

He snuck another glance at Ral, who was snoring softly. Hopefully, the dreams flitting through her head shined brighter than her reality. "What was the job?"

Alesh seemed surprised by the change in topic, pausing with pursed lips before answering, "Smuggled goods from Joesar. I'm not really sure what it was—potions, maybe, or poison? Something in glass bottles. The distributors weren't particularly forthcoming with details, but I could hear the glass clinking as we moved it."

She sighed when she saw the dark look on Tatsu's face. He pulled his hand free as she said, "Look, I know. I...I'm trying to be honest. You asked me what I knew about it."

"Well, bringing poison into the city isn't exactly something I'd be proud of," he said.

"Neither is watching my sister slowly starve to death," Alesh snapped, cheeks flushed with ire.

Tatsu sighed, staring down at the calluses on his fingers. "Here we are again."

"Yeah," Alesh whispered. "Seems familiar."

She didn't say anything else, and Tatsu couldn't force an apology past his lips, so they sat in silence until they both fell into an uneasy, restless sleep.

TATSU WOKE EARLY, briefly comforted by the song of the birds outside the house, the same trills every morning bringing the sound of home, of stability. He moved around the extra blankets and Ral sleeping on the floor to get his knife and his boots and laced up the latter with practiced efficiency. The air outside was cool, but not cold—the kind of spring breeze that nips at cheeks but invigorates steps. After a night of stale air in the house, Tatsu welcomed the chill, and he sucked in a few deep lungfuls. Splotches of spilled blood had pooled at the entrance to the cottage, and he rubbed the toe of his boot against one of them, making a mental note to clean it up later in the day.

Weaving through the trees refreshed and grounded him, as did finding his almost invisible snares in the weeds springing up flat near the exposed roots. He ducked under branches scraping across the grass. More himself again, Tatsu's mood had lightened by the time he returned home with his catch and a pouch full of herbs. He even found his houseguests awake when he got through the door.

"Still up and moving early, I see," Alesh said with a smile from the bed. She was sitting up against the wooden headboard, which was a positive sign. The bruises on her face and left arm were intensifying, but when Tatsu approached to check her injury, he found a clean wound free from infection. The edges he hadn't sewn seemed to have already begun to knit themselves together.

"Breakfast!" Ral exclaimed with a bright peal of laughter and a clap of her hands.

Tatsu's stomach growled in response. The stress and energy of the previous night had burned through his stamina stores.

"Ral?" he asked. "Want to learn how to skin a hare?"

Despite giving the animal a pat on its unmoving head before they started, she seemed to take to the task with relish. He modeled the motions before giving her control and found she was a natural at getting a clean slice with all the fur removed. She didn't even seem concerned by the blood settling on her skin.

As they divided the animal and strung it on the spit over the fire, Alesh said, "I'm sorry that we'll have to be here with you longer now, the both of us."

"I don't mind," Tatsu told her, and he wasn't lying. It was nice, in its own way, to have people with him whom he felt comfortable around. Having another person to talk with made the days go by quicker.

"Still," she replied, "I hadn't meant for either of us to be here this long."

"There might be a hit out for you if your gang was betrayed. They don't seem like the sort to just let someone go."

She fell silent, observing Ral and Tatsu work. "No," she finally agreed, and her voice had lost most of its edge. "I suppose you're right."

They ate in companionable ease, and Ral was eager to help Tatsu clean up, for which he was grateful. But once they'd finished stacking the clean bowls and plates on the rickety shelves, she started to back away, grabbing bits of her hair and tugging on the strands with hard, anxious little noises coming from her throat.

"Ral," Alesh said before Tatsu could respond. She didn't sound concerned—she sounded *scared*. "Ral, what is it?"

It was the second time Tatsu had seen Ral behave in such a manner in only a matter of days. His gut twitched in warning as his belly constricted. Something tried to connect in the back of his mind where he couldn't quite reach it. Then a knock sounded at the door, just like when Alesh had arrived, only this one was a pounding, incessant and authoritative.

"Open this door by order of the queen's guard!" came the angry shout from the other side, shaking Tatsu's resolve as much as the knocking shook the walls. Alesh's panicked eyes met Tatsu's, and her mouth opened to resist, maybe, or to tell him not to open the door. But there was nothing either of them could do, and he knew he didn't have a choice.

He'd barely edged the wooden panels apart before the guards were storming in, pushing him aside and heading right for the bed. They went past the distraught Ral, who was still half crying in fright. Even in the low light, their gold-plated armor seemed to sparkle like the sun—hard and bright and impossible to escape.

"You are hereby placed under arrest by order of the queen on the counts of smuggling, resisting arrest, and injury to a member of the royal guard," said the first one, a big, stocky man with the cropped Chayd beard that seemed to be in fashion lately. "It is for your own good not to get in more trouble by saying something stupid."

Alesh didn't have any time to protest before the other two guards were dragging her up and out of the bed, onto her feet, which weren't steady and didn't seem quite able to support all her weight. Her toes slid across the wood a bit before she straightened, her face ashen.

"How did you find me?" Alesh asked through clenched teeth.

"One of your 'associates' gave you up." The first guard sneered as he leaned toward her. "When you weren't in the shack you call a home, we asked around. Your addled neighbors kept mentioning some cottage out in the woods. It took us awhile to find it. Who in their right mind would live all the way out here?"

"She's injured. She shouldn't be standing," Tatsu said, and he instantly recognized his mistake. The head guard rounded on him next, towering impossibly wide.

"You are also under arrest," he said.

The room spun out of control as Tatsu's vision swam. "On what charges?"

"Harboring a fugitive," the guard sneered, "and failing to turn her over to the queen."

"Stop it! It's not his fault!" Alesh cried.

She started forward, maybe to help Tatsu or to push back against the men. But her body couldn't quite handle it, and she pitched forward onto the floor, barely managing to catch herself before hitting the boards. The guards dragged her back up to her feet even as she cried out sharply in pain. She seemed to have smacked the bruises on her face again, but her wound, Tatsu was relieved to see, hadn't reopened.

"Don't do this," she continued, blood dripping from the fresh cut on her lip. "It's not his fault. I came here and—"

"Go ahead," the big guard said to Tatsu, ignoring Alesh completely. "Add resisting arrest to the charges. It's always a good day to bag a *Runonian*."

Alesh gasped in sympathy. Tatsu turned his head away to let the guards clamp the iron shackles around his wrists. If only he could melt into the floorboards to get away. Unable to leave, trapped in shame, his ears burned. It had been a long time since he'd been around people who didn't already know him. To have the long-simmering hostility between Chayd and Runon shoved in his face—a rivalry he had nothing to do with, stemming from a mother from a kingdom he'd never known—was more than he could handle. His mind shut down, blocking out everything around him. Shoulders slouching dejectedly, he didn't resist any further, even as the guards manhandled him to the front door.

Behind him, Alesh did the opposite and fought against the guards' hold on her.

"She can't stay here alone. She's not all right on her own!" she said over and over. As the men pushed her past the entryway anyway, she called back over her shoulder, "Ral! Ral, stay here! There's food. You can eat for a while. Don't run away. Do you hear me?"

Ral was weeping and didn't answer. She stood frozen as the two of them were hauled away.

"No, you can't leave her alone!" Alesh cried out. "*Please!*"

Tatsu tripped on the way over the front stoop, over the dried bloodstain. His last thought as the men shoved him away from the only home he'd ever known was that he wished he'd gotten the time to clean it up.

He didn't think he'd be coming back to get the chance again.

"Ral!" Alesh kept screaming, her voice raw and vulnerable. "Ral! Just stay here! Stay alive! I'll come back for you; I promise!"

Chapter Three

BY THE TIME they reached the end of the woods at midday, Tatsu's shoulders were in agony. The shackles on his wrists demanded his shoulders be slumped forward, and the pain of it bunched beneath his neck, throbbing in time with his footsteps. Beside him, Alesh was crying. Tears streamed down her cheeks and dripped onto the ripped collar of her shirt. The shirt, tattered and bloodstained, hung in large swatches wide enough to cover most of her skin. But when the breeze picked up, the fabric billowed out behind her, exposing the aftermath of his stitching handiwork. Every few minutes, she would strain against the shackles on her wrists with frustrated growls, though it was a lost cause. Her arms were littered with angry red splotches, the extent of her success, and she didn't pay them much notice. Tatsu kept quiet, afraid more of the immediate retribution than the sentence waiting for him upon reaching their destination.

When they'd started walking, Tatsu's thoughts had flitted around in a panic. Yet, leaving the forest, the only thing his mind seemed able to settle on was wondering what Ral would do by herself with no one to help her. He was so unsettled by the gnawing worry, he lost his footing as the last gnarled roots faded away into an even field, speckled with willowy grass and reddish rocks. Chayd's dry, clay-strewn plains covered most of the kingdom's land and flattened out further beneath the capital of

Dradela. He'd walked this path many times, but never had it felt so foreboding.

Dradela was Chayd's largest trade hub. Home to most of the artificers and distributors, it served as a central cog in the gears that kept the kingdom running. The nobles lived in grand estates near the palace, and if a traveler saw only those, they would think Chayd overflowing with riches. The majority of the fields were kept outside of Dradela's official jurisdiction. In the poor farming districts, rows of trees yielded dates and palm oil, which were heavily exported across the sea beyond Chayd's southern tip.

The nobles in Dradela kept large gardens, blocking them off with walls of white sandstone topped with sharpened pikes to keep the undesirables out. They kept their own schools and their own bathhouses. They would have kept their own roads if they'd been allowed. According to the nobles, there were "the wrong sort" of people within the city. Those sorts lived near the edges, where the houses were bent so far inward with age, they nearly toppled. There were no gleaming white stones in the Iah district, only uneven planks secured with rusty, leftover iron and muddy streets that always stank of too many bodies close together.

Alesh lived in the Iah district.

Tatsu never liked to ask too much about it. As soon as he broached the subject, Alesh would clam up, face contorting with shame or regret or something else entirely. But she hadn't always lived there. Once, her parents had owned a small shop. They hadn't been particularly well-off, but they kept their own textile business and sold to the nobles. Alesh had hated it. She once mentioned that her father had talked about apprenticing her to a neighboring merchant instead, to get her away from the dyes and chemicals. Tatsu wondered if part of her shame at the memory was her own inability, when she'd been younger, to appreciate the decent life she'd had. Tatsu's father had traded almost exclusively with Alesh's parents for textiles, and, once or twice, Tatsu had visited the shop in his childhood. His memories included the pungent aroma of simmering dyes kept bubbling over fire pits.

After her parents died, Alesh and Ral lived in Tatsu's cottage, under the watchful eye of his father, but it had only been temporary. Without her parents and their good standing, there was no chance for an apprenticeship. Citizens in Dradela without prospects could find only unscrupulous work to get by. Alesh had been young, but not young enough to ignore what she had to do. Finding darker lines of work in Iah proved no trouble. In fact, it was very easy to get into Iah—it was just that precious few ever seemed to make it back out.

During Tatsu's childhood, the capital had been a place of fear and distrust for him, but over the years, Dradela lost much of what had once made it so intimidating. Tatsu traded only with the outlying vendors and traveling merchants, the foreign caravans that journeyed to Chayd to sell their exports. He interacted only with those he already knew and had formed a mutual trust with. By avoiding the interior, the secluded estates, and the laborer's taverns, he scarcely ran into anyone who didn't know him at least by sight. It helped to take the edge off, anyway, and he could avoid strangers leaning in to gaze curiously at his gray eyes.

"How odd," a Chaydese trader had commented during his childhood. "Like silver, but not quite. Didn't get the full brunt of his mother's genes, did he?"

It took until late afternoon for them to make it to the city gates. As the guards pushed them roughly into the first streets that led into Dradela, Tatsu's heart sank further. In the center of the city lay the palace, surrounded on all sides by the sprawling sandstone walls of the wealthy estates, which sparkled in the sunlight. The well-trodden pathways that eventually narrowed into uneven alleyways seemed threatening in a way they hadn't for a very long time.

Mimicking Alesh's earlier struggles, Tatsu strained against his shackles and only really succeeded in digging one corner into the soft flesh of his lower arm, making him wince at the sudden pain. They quickly moved off of his regular trade routes and into the interior bulk of the city. Away from the trade hubs and seasonal caravans, he knew no one. The faces on the street began to blur together as people, fueled by morbid curiosity, gawked at the parade of criminals. A spectacle: that was what they were. A cautionary tale being marched past the good citizens to remind them to keep in line or face the consequences.

All eyes were on them, and it made Tatsu's skin shiver with agitation, tiny sparks of discomfort skipping through his arms. A textile worker's gazed tracked them with raised eyebrows, her fingers stained permanently purple from years of contact with the dye. A stonemason paused from carrying a shoulder yoke to stare at them. A couple of noblewomen took shocked steps backward, the braided coils of their dark hair glittering with jeweled pins. He'd spent years trying to avoid being the object of amusement, and he ended up surrounded by it anyway, labeled as a miscreant.

Tatsu tried his best to keep his head down, hoping to shadow his eyes with the low tilt of his gaze, but no matter what, the lighter skin of his exposed arms gave him away. Around him, the whispers and murmurs rose above the constant din Dradela always seemed to hum with. They reverberated between the stone walls and tented trading stands.

The guards turned a corner too quickly, running into a young boy pushing a wheelbarrow far too large for him. The wheels creaked and skidded across the packed dirt, and then the barrow followed, overturning and dumping its contents—palm nuts in mesh sacks—across the road. Several sacks and the boy's knee split in the fall, and the group stopped so abruptly Tatsu ran into the head guard in front of him. His nose skimmed against the back of the man's metal chest plate, and his cheek made contact with the aging leather straps.

The errand boy squealed, eyes darting between the mess of his wares and the soldiers in the glinting armor who were blocking his path.

"Watch where you're going!" the big guard snapped. They tried to pick their way through the scattered nuts now rolling gently toward the edge of the road.

From Tatsu's side, a noble with gold rings woven into his beard said, "*Feas.*"

It felt like a physical slap. His cheeks burned, and his throat swelled. He couldn't possibly put his head down any lower and manage to keep walking, not with the guard hauling one arm above the other and his hands still shackled behind his back. His feet were still trying to find the clear path between wobbling palm nuts, but his lungs deflated when their tiny spectacle started to move quickly again.

The debacle with the errand boy seemed to give Alesh a renewed burst of energy. She bucked up against the guard, and for a moment, Tatsu was terrified she was trying to break free and make a run for it. When she merely jerked her arm out of his grasp, wincing in pain, his stomach settled again. The last thing they needed was for her to add more to their list of crimes.

"Where are you taking us?" she demanded, cheeks still shining with the tracks of shed tears.

"Keep your mouth shut," the big guard ordered, "unless you plan on giving us more ammunition to use against you."

"We deserve to know!" she argued. "Where are we going?"

The guard turned around, one thick black eyebrow raised high. He gave her brown clothing a perfunctory once-over before he said, "Even common street thugs know what happens to people caught breaking the law here. I would guess that's where we're going, wouldn't you?"

"No." Alesh sounded out of breath. "No, not there, not—"

"Criminals don't get much of a choice," the guard holding Tatsu told her. As if he was somehow personally affronted by the entire exchange, he gave Tatsu's body a shake. It rattled his bones all the way up to his teeth, which chattered against one another, his face still hot with anger and shame.

"We're not criminals!" Alesh exclaimed, but the guard was uninterested in conversing with her further.

They continued to move through the streets, and the sun had sunk deep to the horizon by the time they moved into the noble estates, where the walled gardens looked more threatening than serene. The onlookers were not curious like the traders and merchants had been, but disgusted. Tatsu saw one woman sniff in disdain behind her hand, a string of sea pearls clasped at her wrist. The streets were wider and in better condition. No refuse lay thrown to the side, left to fester in the afternoon heat. Only a few shops could be found within the noble district, but all of them catered to luxury products: indigo fabrics to match the royal fashion, expensive jewelry to show off disposable wealth, and pricey, imported spices that had crossed the Turend Mountains in long caravans.

They were very near the palace, with its tall spires reaching up into the blue sky like hands held together in prayer, and it had never looked quite so menacing. The wide windows, unblinking eyes, refused to look away from them on their march, and the arched entryway blocked out the sun, casting long, stretched shadows across the ground.

"You can't prove that we did anything wrong!" Alesh continued.

"Save it for the sentencing," the head guard said, laughing.

"Stop it!" Alesh struggled hard against the shackles and the guard, though she had no chance of freedom with the fresh wound still in her side and their position so far from the city gates. "I have to go back to my sister. You can't take me there! Stop it!"

As the palace loomed before them, sliding closer and closer, Alesh's fight against her restraints doubled. Tatsu saw his freedom and his woods slipping farther and farther away. He would have given nearly anything to be back in the trees again, with the smell of the pine needles and the bright green of new buds arriving every year after the last mountaintop snowfall beyond Chayd's borders.

That freedom was gone, and its absence throbbed mournfully in his chest. Alesh twitched violently, and her shoulder bumped against his as she sidestepped the guard again to fall into one of the others.

"Let me go, please! Listen, my sister, she can't be alone. She'll die without me. You have to let me go back to her! Please, *listen*!"

Tatsu's steps echoed his pounding heartbeat as they reached the palace gates—huge pillars of stone that towered over them, etched and marked by years of wind. They made a hard left, circling one of the pillars, toward the structure that stood next to the palace. The black walls of Aughwor Prison rose even darker in the palace's shadows. Known as the last stop for anyone who'd managed to catch the ire of royal law, all actively feared the place, even the merchants at the outskirts of the city.

Seemingly unaffected by the dismal atmosphere, the guards pushed them up the shadowed steps. Tatsu stumbled again, lost in his own misery and despair, and then Alesh hunched down next to him with flashing eyes and flushed cheeks.

"Fight them!" she hissed. "Dammit, Tatsu, why won't you *do* something?!"

He didn't get the chance to answer. A rough hand around her throat yanked Alesh back up, her subsequent cry of pain sharp. With each step, she resisted. Escaped hair from her braids had knotted into clumps. Despite the blood on her arms from the rubbing of the iron bindings, she jerked against the guards even as they shoved her into the impossibly big hall making up the prison entryway.

All along the walls of the entryway stood pillars that mirrored the ones outside, except for the impassive faces carved into the white stone. They looked like judges ready to decide the fate of those who walked between them. Perhaps they already had. Tatsu tried to push away that unsettling thought as their entourage made its way to the end where a small, balding man sat at an unimpressive desk.

"Nothing was scheduled today," he said sourly without looking up from the papers he was scribbling on. The lot of them were strewn across the surface of the desk.

"Book them," the head guard ordered and pushed Tatsu forward so far his hips banged against the hard edge of the wooden desktop. "Or do I have to do your job for you?"

The jailer threw his hands in the air, finally looking up. "And will you build me another prison to put them in as you do that? I suggest you march them straight back out and help them return whatever coin they stole to the pockets they nicked it from before—"

He stopped abruptly, standing up and leaning in. It seemed he'd noticed Tatsu for the first time, and his eyes, black as coal and just as hard, squinted at him. His piercing gaze was as bad as the bystanders from the market, although, to the jailer's credit, he at least didn't say anything out loud. Cringing, Tatsu tried to pull away, but even then, the scrutiny lasted far too long. When the jailer finally straightened, his face had smoothed into something unreadable.

"Crimes?" he asked, tone maddeningly neutral.

"Unproven," Alesh spat, and one of the soldiers swatted at her cheek.

"Against the crown," the head guard replied. "Do you need the full rundown now, or will that suffice?"

The jailer flicked his hard eyes between them and then said, in the same unwavering, bored tone, "That's enough."

"No!" Alesh cried. "You can't put us in here without justification!"

"Actually, I think I can do whatever I want. You will be held here overnight, and your sentencing will be tomorrow." The jailer's voice was infuriatingly mild. He began rummaging through the papers on the desk, apparently trying to find something of great importance. When he couldn't, his face melted into a deep scowl. "You will have the great pleasure of your charges being read to you before the queen and her court. At that time, you can plead however you wish."

He paused, glancing at her, and added, "I highly suggest that you plead guilty, for that will be the verdict the court finds regardless of your stance."

"This isn't fair," Alesh whispered, but her eyes were wide with fear.

The jailer nodded at Tatsu. "You. You're Chaydese?"

"Yes, I am," Tatsu vowed, mouth very dry.

He got a disdainful snort in reply. "Not that it matters either way. You'll be tried and imprisoned here the same as everyone else. Aughwor Prison does not discriminate."

He seemed to finally find the paper he was looking for—a list of names, in varying hands and splotchy ink. He nodded again, gesturing to the paper, and handed Tatsu a worn, ragged quill.

"Write your name. This will be what they use tomorrow when handing you your final sentence."

Tatsu's hands were shaking when he pressed the nib to the paper. There would be no getting out of the prison once the ink bled his name into the parchment. By signing his name, he was effectively pleading guilty. It took him a second to even figure out how to draw the letters as his head pounded out an angry, anxious rhythm in time with his heartbeat. It echoed loudly in his ears, blocking out everything else.

The air felt heavy when he was finished, and the jailer made Alesh do the same.

"Holding cells are full," the jailer told the guards, rolling up the paper they had signed, smudging the ink in fading lines across the page visible even on the other side. "They'll have to bunk up tonight in the main blocks. *E* for the girl, and *C* for this one here."

"Wait!" Alesh cried, but one soldier was already tugging her to the right, to a wooden door reinforced with metal bars. Her heels dug into the stones, but she had no grip at all. Her boots and body simply skidded across the floor. "Tatsu! No, wait!"

"And do try to pick a cell where they won't get killed this time," the jailer said, sounding tired. "We need the prisoners alive for the proceedings tomorrow."

Chapter Four

C BLOCK WAS a hellhole Tatsu never could have imagined, and he doubted any of the other areas were any better. Even without the stench of bile and urine hanging heavy and unrelenting in the air, the lack of windows and sunlight and the conditions—sometimes up to five men in a single cell, nearly on top of one another—were appalling. The shuffling gait of his resigned footsteps as he was led through the stifling quarters sounded in tandem with the groans and cries of the prisoners, an offbeat song of hopelessness he couldn't avoid focusing on. Aughwor Prison was a life sentence none of those men would ever see the end to, and Tatsu realized he had joined them as they hit the halfway point in the corridor. His legs froze, stiff with awareness, before he was pushed into one of the cells. The door clicked shut and locked behind him.

There were only two other men in his cell, a tiny box of iron bars already closing in around him. A Chaydese man with a rotund belly and a long, curling beard leaned against one wall, and a barely visible, light-skinned bundle of knobby limbs and impossibly thin appendages curled up in the corner.

"Take a seat," the Chaydese man huffed, and Tatsu couldn't tell if the offer was made in jest or dry humor. "Join us in our suffering."

Tatsu did sit, but only because he was afraid his legs would give out from under him. His hands were still shaking, and no amount of twisting them together seemed to help stave off the trembling. The stones against his back were cold, but at least it gave him something to focus on other than wondering if the man curled in the far corner was still alive. The harsh shadows in the place afforded him a bit of privacy, and he let himself sag back within the blackness.

"What are you in for?" the Chaydese man asked. "Pickpocketing? Trying to swindle a member of the high court?"

"Treason," Tatsu whispered. His lips were painfully dry. Even when he ran his tongue over the split, puckered skin, they stubbornly remained so. "Harboring a fugitive."

There was a great guffaw of laughter that, again, had a hint of malice to it. "A little slip like you? Picked the wrong person to play hero with, I suppose."

"How long do people stay here?" Tatsu asked, looking through the bars to the other cells, some so full that arms were dangling loosely out between the bars like landed fish.

"How long?" his cellmate repeated, and his voice darkened. "Forever. Until they find a better use for your corpse. Maybe as fertilizer for the queen's vineyards."

Tatsu forced down the knot of fear that had lodged in his throat. "The queen?"

"Prison's full," the prisoner said, shrugging. "There's no room, but they keep bringing people in. The queen is ordering the guards to come down hard on crime. They've doubled all the patrols. The only way she can prove her strength in ruling, I'd wager."

Tatsu risked another glance at the silent ball of a man in the corner, but he couldn't hear anything from him. If he *was* dead, then Tatsu could only hope someone would come sooner rather than later to dispose of the body. His Chaydese cellmate across the way shifted, and iron clanged against stone. The others were bound in shackles, while Tatsu remained free. He inquired about it while subconsciously rubbing at his wrists, already raw and burning.

"They don't snap those on you until after your sentencing," the Chaydese man told him. "Didn't tell you much about prison operations, did they?"

"No."

"Never heard anything at all about Aughwor?"

"Not much," Tatsu replied, and then, feeling like something more was necessary, added, "I live in the forest."

"That'll do it," the man said in agreement. "Not many folk live that remote. Bet you don't get into the capital much."

Tatsu didn't bother to confirm the hunch. Something pushed against his back, and then movement sent shivers down it. He lunged forward and whipped his head around, his instincts prompting him to at least *see* the danger. But it was only a rat, rooting around for scraps. His panic had landed him in the center of the space, where the last bits of gleaming sunlight were making their way through the high-set barred windows at the top of the cell.

The Chaydese man laughed, hard and sharp, and said, "Don't mind him! He's a friend of ours, always—"

He broke off very suddenly when Tatsu looked up, meeting his gaze.

"*Feas*," he wheezed. "Your eyes."

It was the second time in less than a day. Tatsu hastily shoved himself back against the wall. Rat or no rat, the shadows were better than being ogled in the light like some kind of fancy toy. He pulled his knees up close to his chest and wrapped his arms around them, burying his face in the loose bits of fabric. He was suddenly very glad he wasn't wearing the brown, which would serve to mark him as a pauper. Because the trees didn't care much for social standing, he'd always followed his father's routine of buying imported fabrics from the caravan traders instead. In Dradela, even behind prison bars, the crushing weight of his unique situation overwhelmed him.

"Well," his cellmate said, distinctly unkind, "guess you should get to know our *other* houseguest here."

He jerked his head to the side, toward the far corner as he spoke. Then he began ignoring Tatsu entirely, focused outside the cell bars to the hall. As Tatsu's pulse quickened, the man curled in the corner began to loosen himself from his ball shape. He was not so dead after all, although that didn't give Tatsu any relief. It took a full minute, at least, before the man leaned forward enough for Tatsu to see silver eyes under jet-black hair in the dying light. Runonian.

His pale eyes reflected the sun's fading light just as much as a polished ring might. From decades of silver mining, the stories said, though no one ever questioned how years spent underground surrounded by unprocessed metal would create such a radical change. The Runonians had never bothered to further explain, at least not that Tatsu knew, and besides, Runon had closed its borders years ago. Few got in and out any longer—legally, anyway.

Tatsu wasn't sure he'd ever seen true Runonian eyes before, the reflective glint both striking and unsettling.

The prisoner said something in a language Tatsu didn't understand. When Tatsu shook his head, he repeated, this time in Common, "Thought you said you lived in the forest."

"In Chayd's forests," Tatsu replied, quietly. "I don't speak Runonian."

"You'll find it affords you no better courtesy to admit that." The man smiled, revealing a mouth full of yellow-brown teeth.

They slipped into silence for a long, long time, and the hall and all the cells filled with an oppressive darkness with the setting of the sun. The only light came from the torch sconces flickering near the double doors, resulting in a tense, eerie atmosphere. Most of the other prisoners also quieted after night arrived, but a few began wailing forlornly. The sound lingered and carried as it bounced between the stones, impossible to escape from.

"Are there other foreign prisoners here?" Tatsu asked, desperate for something to distract him from his own thoughts.

At first, he feared his cellmates had drifted off to sleep.

"Some. Why not?" his Runonian cellmate finally replied. "Keeps the thugs off the street, doesn't it? But they don't seem to care much for our conditions here. Doubt they'd care much for me either way, but the others...well."

Someone down the hall was coughing, a sickly sound echoing thick and wet.

"That word he used earlier," the Runonian man continued, voice low. "I don't know it."

"It's old Chaydese," Tatsu said. "People don't speak it much anymore. It's all Common tongue now."

There was a shift against the stones, of fabric being dragged down. "What does it mean?"

"Outsider," Tatsu whispered and pressed his head against his knees.

BY THE MIDDLE of the night, the prison brimmed with the sound of snoring and deep breathing. Tatsu didn't know how any of them could sleep in the dank cells, but he supposed with no other options, it became natural to the prisoners. His own body too jittery, his mind racing with apprehension, Tatsu sat with his back against the cold stone wall, listening to his cellmates snort and roll over. He took stock of the rats slipping between the bars with tiny nails clicking against the floor. His stomach growled, but hunger afforded him no distraction.

Straightening his legs felt good after so long, but his muscles protested the move. Getting his body to respond to his commands took longer than he'd have liked to admit. He stood, taking care not to wake the others. Reasonably sure they were asleep, judging from the rhythmic breathing surrounding him, he didn't want to take any chances. The moon beamed full and shining and streaming in through the windows, leaving sectioned squares of hazy white-blue on the stones and setting alight the dust particles in the air.

The moonlight winked in and out as both a blessing and a curse. Seeing the glow reminded Tatsu of his forest, and his breathing calmed—until he remembered he'd likely never see his woods again. Then all it did was dredge up an unquenchable ache in his being. Outside the window, the stars dotting the sky seemed so far away.

The window hung much too high for him to reach, and even if there had been stones sticking out for climbing, his Runonian cellmate had curled asleep in front of the wall housing the opening. Tatsu stretched his legs as best he could with such limited walking room and then settled to the floor again. At least he could see the stars, if nothing else.

A few times, a horned night bird flew past the opening, blocking the moonlight with its long, outstretched wings. When it called out its song on the second pass, Tatsu closed his eyes to imagine himself back in his cottage and hearing the same creature outside. He was there with Alesh and Ral, cooking dinner—

Ral. His eyes opened, blood growing cold. Ral, alone in the woods. There were enough dangers without the line of decay creeping ever closer. She had no one else to turn to, and certainly no one else who knew of her plight.

Looking back up at the moon, Tatsu let the full wave of frustration and remorse take hold of him, and he knew he wouldn't be getting any sleep that night.

AUGHWOR PRISON WOKE with the dawn.

With heavy, itchy eyes, Tatsu watched the men around him rouse. Morning brought out the worst in them; coming back to the reality of confinement had to be jarring. More than one scuffle broke out when prisoners rolled too close to one another. In the cell only two spaces from Tatsu's, a fight broke out so violently it shook the iron bars all the way to the far wall. The shouted insults and curses were barely discernable over the noise, especially after all the other prisoners joined their voices in. The altercation ended with a thud, and the shouting died out. Tatsu kept waiting for the guards to come in and check up on them, but none did. They were content to let the prisoners cull out the numbers on their own.

Knowing that a man struggled to draw breath in a neighboring cell was more unsettling than the nighttime hours had been.

It wasn't long after the sun rose that the guards finally came with breakfast—cold rice consisting of more mush than grains, hard to get down and even more difficult to keep there. The break of the new day set Tatsu's nerves on edge, constantly wondering when the soldiers would arrive to take him to the palace for sentencing.

As it turned out, he didn't need to wait very long. Just after the meal, they came for him with clanging steps.

"You," the guard said as he opened the cell door and nodded in Tatsu's direction. "Get up and follow me. You've an appointment at the palace."

From another cell, a howl of wild laughter rose, and Tatsu tried to ignore it as he climbed to his feet. He wasn't sure if the sound was aimed at him or the loser of the earlier fight. They put iron around his wrists again, and the metal shocked his system cold. He let himself be led out through the doors where the air didn't burn when it made contact with the lungs. Leaving the prison should have felt like a relief, but the truth was told in the pounding of the guards' footsteps around him. He would go nowhere but back into one of those cells, no matter how he pleaded in front of the court.

He was so lost in his own thoughts as they marched through the line of twin pillars that he almost ran into the person stopped in front of him. It took another moment to recognize the dark hair and dirty, bloodstained brown linen.

"Alesh," he said under his breath. Anger flared within, bubbling under the skin, but when she turned, the marks on her face had finally emerged—angry red welts across one side, streaking up past her eye, swollen and purpled. Anything he might have said disappeared, forced back to the secret pit inside him.

She seemed happier to see him. "I wasn't sure they would send us here together."

It wasn't only them. Another prisoner stood beside them, a burly man with more muscle than clothing who glared at them without blinking. The three of them were ushered into the main entry of the palace, though no farther.

Despite the circumstances, the palace was still impressive enough to nearly take Tatsu's breath away. Ornate, curved arches dipped from the roof, sliding farther into marble covered in paintings and patterned fabrics. The walls sported brightly painted murals, all scenes from Chaydese stories and legends. He'd heard once from a trader that a single vase from the palace was worth more than a local farmer made in an entire year. He suddenly understood what she had been talking about.

"Cheery," Alesh said.

Their bulky companion's expression pinched. Upon closer inspection, he was missing his right ear. "Better than being in the cells."

"Aren't we going straight back?" Tatsu asked. "This is just a formality."

"Nothing here's a formality." The man shifted, and the iron on his wrists pinged. "Guards threw me in here three weeks ago and never bothered to yank me out before now."

Tatsu's stomach roiled. "Three weeks without a hearing?"

"Got one now, don't I?"

Tatsu's eyes slid to meet Alesh's. She tipped closer and lowered her voice when she said, "We were brought in yesterday."

"They must like you," the man said, one thick eyebrow rising.

"Or the opposite," Tatsu mumbled.

"Come," a guard said, grabbing Tatsu's arm and tugging him forward. He turned to say goodbye to Alesh, to say something, *anything*, and found instead that she was being escorted in with him. Footsteps echoing, they stumbled to the middle of the receiving room.

The queen of Chayd herself was seated in the forefront.

Tatsu had never seen her before. He'd been in Dradela only a few times, and none of those had corresponded with the holidays in which she rode through the public streets. He'd heard of her beauty and assumed the same was said about all ruling monarchs, but looking at her, the words rang startlingly true. Her thick black hair twisted up in ornate knots, some of it cascading down in braids with royal-blue ribbons woven through, a sign of her status. The gold hoops adorning her ears matched the gold of the crown on her head, both studded with round, red rubies. Embroidered sashes draped her body, all dyed blue or purple, and some with gems and jewels sewn to the silk itself. Tatsu had never seen such finery. All at once, he was ashamed of the dirt latched to every stitch of his pants.

She nodded at them to approach as one of the guards read off their names in a booming voice.

"You have come here today as the basest of citizens, as criminals facing arrest," she told them, her voice grander than Tatsu had expected. "I am told you have already seen the inside of Aughwor Prison and the cells within. When criminals here plead or are found guilty, that is where they spend the rest of their meaningless, miserable days."

There was something strange at the end of her sentence—a hanging in her tone, an opening to continue. Tatsu glanced at Alesh, who appeared to sense it too. Why the quick sentencing for them, but such a long wait for their companion? Hundreds of bodies were piled into Aughwor. Why weren't more of them present in the receiving room?

In front of them, the queen rose from her throne. Raised high, at the center, she was certainly the most important figure. It took her moving for Tatsu to realize that behind her stood a semicircle of others, all wearing inky robes that kept them blended in with the shadows. The queen motioned to several guards near the side of the room.

"Leave us," she commanded.

In the resulting shuffle, Tatsu risked another glance at the figures behind the queen's golden throne. They were *mages*. He could see nothing of their faces beneath the heavy hoods pulled close over their heads, but he knew the mages covered their hair as a sign of deference to the queen. Their appearance made a striking contrast to the queen's elaborate hair coils and the nobles' imitation of it beyond the palace walls. From the line of mages came a thin pulse of energy, just enough to set his nerves on edge. Tatsu's palms grew slick.

Then, quite suddenly, the queen sighed.

"We are in a crisis," she said, and she looked younger, softer. She appeared less rigid with duty and more like a woman simply trying to keep her kingdom afloat. "And I am going to give the three of you a choice."

Alesh inhaled sharply at Tatsu's left.

"As you know, the ongoing conflicts with Joesar and Rad-em have left us with only a fraction of our naval forces intact." The queen approached them, taking small, controlled steps down the marbled stairs. "We have very little by way of a standing army and are already losing the lives of our young men in the skirmishes on the sea.

"Diplomatic relations with Runon have deteriorated in the last decade. By closing its borders, Runon has cut us off from desperately needed imports, yet now, facing shortages of their own, they wish to expand their borders. I have kept Chayd from succumbing to Runon's unrelenting demands for more land only through luck and long-owed favors, but I can do so no longer. Runon has created a weapon we cannot match, and if we fail to stop it, the entire kingdom will fall."

"What are you talking about?" the other prisoner asked.

"What does this have to do with us?" Alesh added.

The mages started moving forward, coming out from behind the throne. The air in the room stretched, like a bowstring pulled and primed for release, and the hair on Tatsu's arms stood up. The hooded figures looked vaguely threatening, robes plain and devoid of gems or embroidery, and their hands clasped uniformly behind their backs. The queen seemed unfazed by their presence, as did the small clusters of noble advisors to either side of them. Trapped, Tatsu couldn't quite pull his gaze away.

"There is a magical energy device located in their capital of Yuse," the queen said, ignoring their questions. "Its purpose is to drain the surrounding lands of their life force to feed itself. Because we have refused to surrender our lands, Runon will bleed the kingdoms around it dry while it alone prospers."

"That's not possible." Alesh's face had grown ashy. "There's no way to do that. They'd never be able to get something like that working."

"It already is," the queen told them. And Tatsu knew what he had seen the other day with Ral in the forest, where the trees had been withered and dry, and the brush had died, brown and useless. He knew what was creeping its way into Chayd, devouring everything in its path. An involuntary sound worked its way past his lips, even as he tried to force it down.

The queen looked at him, dark eyes hard and fierce. "You've seen it."

As the others looked at him, shocked, he managed to sputter, "In the mountains, north of the woods. Everything is merely...dead. As far as I could see across the peaks."

"And it will continue south until it swallows Dradela and the rest of the kingdom whole," the queen said.

"Gods," Alesh whispered. "If the land is gone and useless, everyone in Chayd will..."

"Starve," the queen finished for her, and then, as if amused, she amended, "At least the ones that survive the initial bloodshed of the resulting panic."

A murmur went through the crowd of advisors. Tatsu couldn't make out any of the words, but their expressions were hostile. The queen shot them a glare and they quieted, though their features remained twisted. Something rumbled within the court, placing Tatsu on wildly unsteady ground, unable to find the safe path out.

As the weight of the situation sank in, the prisoner next to Tatsu laughed humorlessly. "You brought us here for a reason. So, what exactly is the choice you mentioned?"

The queen drew herself up to her full height, regal in her shimmering sashes with her chin held high as her loose braids tumbled down her back.

"I have told you what will become of Chayd should this weapon continue to function. So, I am asking you to go to Yuse and steal it."

Chapter Five

THERE WAS A long, oppressive silence before any of them spoke again, and then all of them began talking over one another at once.

"There's no way to get into the castle in Yuse and steal it," Alesh argued, her forehead furrowed, eyebrows high. "It's magic, it's important, and it's going to be heavily guarded!"

"That's assuming we even make it into the castle," the male prisoner interjected after her, "and I wouldn't wager a single *omn* on us even getting that far."

The advisors were arguing too. With the queen's proclamation, they'd divided, turning on one another and shouting with wild gestures. They didn't seem any happier about the idea than Tatsu, and without him knowing anything of noble politics, their anger felt even more dangerous. The undercurrent of tension and hostility ran deep in the receiving room, like an ocean wave ready to drown them all the second it crashed onto the shore.

The only people who remained silent were the mages. The line of them stood perfectly still.

Rattled by the nobles and deeply disquieted by the motionless mages, Tatsu asked quietly, "What happens if we refuse?"

It cut through the din without him meaning it to, and the queen's head snapped toward him. "You remain in Aughwor for the rest of your days to serve out your sentence."

Tatsu glanced at Alesh, her jaw tight and protruding as she bit down on her bottom lip. It didn't seem like much of a choice. Just a single night in the prison had been too much for Tatsu to handle, and spending an uncountable number of weeks there would be a fate worse than death.

"You have all been chosen for your individual skills." The queen's words were bordering on approving, but her eyes were hard.

But they'd only just arrived. What if they hadn't? What if Alesh had turned down the smuggling job, the entire situation averted?

The queen smiled, the expression anything but pleasant. "It is perhaps ironic that the things that condemned you to prison in the first place are the very abilities we need."

She nodded toward the male prisoner. "Brund, you are a drunken bully, but your skills in combat are unparalleled. How many noses have you broken since you were arrested?"

Brund shrugged. "In total, or merely at morning ration distribution?"

"You—" The queen's gaze swept to Alesh, for apparently Brund's answer required no further comment. "—the thief girl. You got away from my soldiers."

Alesh shrank back a bit, but she said nothing.

"We will need you to find the exploitable weaknesses in Yuse's castle to get the group inside."

"And me?" Tatsu asked, though he tried to bite back the words.

He would have sworn, if he didn't know better, that the queen was smiling when she finally looked at him.

"You will guide them to Runon without being detected," she answered, "through the woods and the wilds. Don't you isolate yourself in those same trees, avoiding human contact? It ought to be easy to find your way north through them."

An uneasy stone ached within, but he tried to uproot his hesitation with a reminder of how terrible the past night inside Aughwor had been. Given that the queen had ordered most of the guards out of the room prior to making her request, he assumed the mission was known only to the high court; though by their fervent discussions, clearly not all of them agreed with the decision. An unspoken demand hung in the air, tangible in the space between Tatsu and the queen. *Refuse this, and you will never be given the chance to speak of it.*

Glancing again at the court advisors, Tatsu could make out at least three daggers in hip sheaths. They would never make it back to Aughwor if their answers were no. They were unlikely to even make it past the door of the receiving room.

Would they die instead on Runonian pikes?

"How *will* we get in?" he asked. "Alesh is right. We'll never get past the defenses for something like that."

"You will be escorted by one of my mages," the queen said and held her arm out wide to one side, sash sparkling in the sunlight streaming through the room's painted glass. At her invitation, a young woman on the far left of the mage's half circle stepped forward. "She will explain to you the specifics of the mission."

The queen let the silence grow until it reached unbearable heights and then said, "I will ask only once for your response. The danger is nothing compared to Chayd's precarious existence. This duty is for your kingdom. Your future is in your own hands now."

Brund apparently did not need any further time to think. After all, he'd had weeks in Aughwor. "I'll do it. It's better than rotting away in some cell."

Alesh met Tatsu's gaze again, her answer clear. Fear reflected in her eyes, wrapped around something that might have been relief. He knew her thoughts strayed to Ral, because so did his. The knot of worry over Ral's fate pulsed where it sat lodged between his lungs.

"So will I," Alesh said, her eyes still locked on Tatsu's, and his fate was sealed.

"All right," he echoed, as if he'd finally decided, when in truth, there could never have been a different answer.

BEFORE HER DEPARTURE in a swirl of silk, the queen had ordered them into a small room just off the receiving hall. Lit with tall tapered candles and colored with tapestries hanging on the walls, all depicting old scenes of valor and glory that Tatsu couldn't place, the compact chamber quickly became stifling, especially when several court advisors came in with them. Four guards immediately took up posts at the far doors. Their faces gave away nothing.

The mage picked by the queen also followed them in and introduced herself as Leil. Her face was round beneath her mage hood. Sometimes, when the fabric pulled back with her gait, the shimmering of a deep blue scarf tied around her hair peeked out, contrasting with the rich brown of her skin. She led them to the white stone table in the center of the room.

"The queen had her strategists plan out the attack for us," she told them and gestured at the parchment spread flat across the tabletop. The sleeves of her robe pulled back a bit to reveal two wide gold bracelets fit snugly around her wrists. Tatsu started backward. They looked like *shackles*. Restraints made of gold and missing the chain linking them, but shackles, nonetheless. So caught up in staring at the metal, which disappeared quickly back beneath her sleeves, Tatsu nearly missed what she was saying. "Should you require anything for the journey, you are to ask either me or the guards here, and it will be found for you."

"I still don't understand how we're going to get into the palace," Alesh said.

It did feel an awful lot like a suicide mission, which didn't sit well. Tatsu leaned over the table to see the paper, and the others followed suit.

"We will begin by going through the north woods to the Turend Mountains, avoiding the trade route," Leil said. She let her finger slide across the parchment—an inked map with tiny, intricate lettering. Tatsu's heart fluttered at seeing his own woods depicted in watered ink. "After that, we will—"

"No," Tatsu interrupted. Leil looked surprised as her head shot up, and she fixed her large eyes on him. "I mean...we shouldn't go through the mountains."

"Why not?" Leil asked.

Tatsu shook his head and pointed at the gray space on the map. "It's faster to go through the Weeping Forest. And carrying enough provisions and equipment to get us through the mountain paths would be nearly impossible. It would more than double our time."

The other three seemed to evaluate the projection on the map together.

"The Weeping Forest is difficult to navigate," Leil said, sounding hesitant, one fingernail tapping out an uneasy rhythm on the table. She bit down on her lip, enough to pucker the skin, before continuing. "It's so easy to get turned around, and there are no path markers to help point the way."

"I can get us through," Tatsu told her.

She seemed unconvinced. "It's outside our jurisdiction." She glanced up at one of the nobles standing by the back wall, and something unspoken passed between them.

"So are the mountains." Tatsu frowned. "And I'm telling you, we'll never make it across Turend. I've seen the decay the queen spoke of. It's headed right up the peaks. Where do you think the displaced predators have gone? That's wolf pack territory."

He was afraid, for a breath, he'd gone too far, but if he had to choose his manner of death, he might at least give them all a fighting chance. Leil and the advisor conducted a strange, secret conversation without words. Leil's soft features broadcasted her hesitance. There were too many factors that Tatsu didn't understand at work within the small room. As he waited, Leil's fingers continued their nervous tap on the tabletop, but then her shoulders relaxed and the creases in her robe disappeared. She nodded.

"All right. We go through the Weeping Forest."

Alesh leaned forward to prop her chin on her hands, elbows squeaking as they slid across the table. "That still puts us in the capital and at the mercy of Runon itself."

"So, if we aren't killed by the wolves, we'll be taken out by Runonians," Brund added.

"We have a contact on the inside," Leil said. "He's an informant who's been working as a servant in Yuse and the castle for six months. He will meet us in Yuse at the rendezvous point and guide us into the castle undetected."

"Lucky," Brund grunted. "Did he sell out?"

"No." Leil leveled him with a steely look, the first real show of strength she'd displayed. "He was placed there to gather information. We do have a few Runonians working for us."

It was obvious she struggled to keep her gaze from moving as she said that, but she couldn't seem to help her eyes darting at Tatsu. He dropped his gaze to the map and focused on the rough edges of the parchment. At least if his eyes were downcast, their color was harder to see.

For a long stretch of time, the air felt suffocating.

"And then?" Brund asked.

Leil pulled out another, smaller roll of paper and unfolded it. "Our informant has also supplied us with the locked doors and guard locations. Once we are inside the castle, we proceed directly to the room holding the siphon."

"The mages will be guarding it," Alesh said. "They're not going to let us *take* it."

"Our plan, as such, involves no direct confrontation," Leil said. "A small number gives us a much better chance at getting in and out unnoticed."

"And if we *are* noticed?" Brund asked.

Leil's expression hardened. "Well, that's what you're for, isn't it?"

She was remarkably unthreatening to be a mage. If Tatsu had seen her in the noble estates without her signifying robe, he'd have guessed her to be a wealthy merchant's daughter or part of a court advisor's family. As she carefully refolded the roll of paper, Tatsu tried not to fixate on her hands and the golden bracelets on her wrists. Her fingers could weave magic and alter the world—at least, he assumed they could.

Tatsu had to admit he didn't know much about magic.

He stiffened when she looked up at them and asked, "Let's discuss what you'll need in preparation. We should begin to collect all of the essentials now."

As the meeting drew to a close, and Leil was finishing the list for the palace guards, Tatsu asked, "Was it your wish to be part of this mission?"

"I am here to serve my queen, however she commands," Leil replied with an answer that really wasn't an answer at all. The sides of her mouth pinched slightly, however, and Tatsu thought perhaps that was truth enough.

"Are you from Dradela?" Part of him wanted to know about this strange, mystical entity. Part of him simply wanted to delay his return to the dank cells of the prison.

Leil looked surprised when she met his eyes. "I—no, I'm not. I was born in a village by the seaside. My father is a fisherman. I came to the palace when I first displayed my magical abilities. I was only ten. My family remained there, in our village."

Her tone turned bittersweet near the end, so Tatsu continued, "Do you miss them?"

"Yes." Her mouth curved up into a sad smile. "I miss them very much."

Tatsu looked to Alesh, but she wouldn't meet his gaze. Her face was pained and taut, and she glowered down at her boots.

"But," Leil said, seeming to shake herself out of her reflection, "I am happy to serve my kingdom. I am pleased I can assist my queen."

She left no room for further conversation and summoned the guards to escort them back to Aughwor.

TWO DAYS AND two seemingly endless nights in Aughwor later, Tatsu found himself with the odd quartet at the edge of Chayd's plains. Their packs were full and slung over their shoulders, and the others wore guarded expressions, as if not to allow anyone too close. Alesh was the only one Tatsu actually trusted not to use his exposed back for target practice, and the reality of that didn't help with his growing apprehension. Being outside again without having to look at the blue of the sky from behind thick iron bars was wonderful, but even the warmth of the sun on his face felt significantly cooler from the weight of the implied debt it held.

He knew better than to assume that his obligation would end with the successful retrieval of the siphon, yet his only option was to do as he was told. The whole thing put a sour taste in the back of his mouth.

Alesh, shoulders sloped with the weight of her pack, moved beside him and nudged his shoulder with her own. "We're ready when you are."

He turned to face the group. Behind them, the city of Dradela rose up in jagged, sloping peaks in the still-pink morning sky. Already, the trading caravans were arriving and setting up their tents along the outskirts, and the stalls spilled out beyond the sandstone gates into the plains. A handful of figures were moving, specks of black against the yellow horizon.

"We're moving through territory that's not Chayd's," he began, "but it's not Runon's either. It's sparsely populated, so we shouldn't encounter many locals. But just in case, stay behind me at all times so we have a chance of remaining out of sight."

He looked to the group for confirmation. Brund shrugged halfheartedly, Leil just nodded, and Alesh gave him a somewhat watery smile, clearly forced at the corners.

Not knowing quite what to do next, Tatsu said, "Well, then...let's go."

They stayed on the road as the sand-and-dirt plains gradually melted away into knolls of grass, and then Tatsu took them northeast. There were two small farming settlements along the way, but neither was more than a small cluster of shabby, well-worn barns and houses, and the inhabitants didn't pay them much mind. Grazing pastures lay golden before them, fields of rowed trees promised a yield of dates later in the summer, and the air smelled of slightly damp leaves and sweet, ripening fruit.

The landscape began to change, rolling and shifting into hills as they made their way into the trees: sparse at first, with lonely, single trunks curved from the wind's lashes, and then more, until they were weaving through the wide-spaced pillars of green and brown. The sun made a high arc across the sky and began to dip below the uneven, tree-filled horizon line.

They were near his woods when Tatsu stopped them for the night. He busied himself with setting up the fire and tents, finding it easier to let his mind wander when his hands were moving through memorized, practiced actions. His muscles felt comfortably used, tired without being painful, but his mind was buzzing.

Alesh was doing the same, readying her bedroll, but her movements were stiff and jerky, as if her mind flitted elsewhere. He kept her in sight, out of the corner of his eye, as he distributed the salted meat and slightly stale bread. He continued as they settled in for the evening and the moon rose high above the trees. Something felt off about her expression, carefully schooled into neutrality.

His eyes were heavy, but he stayed alert and awake until he heard the scuffle of her boots against dirt and loose pebbles. Tatsu pushed himself up on his elbows and shifted his legs one at a time, quietly, until his eyes had adjusted enough on her form heading for the denser trees just beyond their makeshift camp.

It was probably only her experience in sneaking through treacherous places that kept her from crying out in surprise when he grabbed for her arm.

"What are you doing?" she hissed, voice shaking, and Tatsu pulled her into the trees to which she'd been heading to avoid waking the others. When he thought they'd gone far enough, he stopped.

"That's what I should be asking you," he whispered. "Where were *you* going?"

"I'm *leaving*." Her words warbled with frustration, the outline of her face and the whites of her eyes dim in the cover of the trees. "I'm going to find Ral. She's alone out there, and I've got to find her!"

He'd figured as much, but he was still glad to hear the admission of it.

"Then I'm going with you," he told her. "We should start back at my place. If she's smart, she will have stayed put where it's relatively safe."

It was difficult to completely see Alesh's expression, but he had a good guess what it would be. Ever since childhood, Alesh wore gratitude vulnerably and openly, easily readable.

"Tatsu—"

"Don't. I care about her too. I'm not going to let anything happen to her."

They were still near enough to the others to make him nervous, and he wanted to get moving. The light of the stars and the cover of darkness would help them to make it to his cottage without being found, though after that, he didn't know where they could go. He pushed the thought from his mind and focused on Ral. One thing at a time.

"Do you think she's stayed at your place?" Alesh asked.

"I don't know. But it's the best place to start."

They began moving quietly through the underbrush toward the thicket of trees. There were few sounds of animals around them, except for the shuffling of a mole somewhere in the tangled weeds on the forest floor. Tatsu steeled himself for what they were doing—deserting during a royal duty—and ran smack into a large branch dangling in the air.

A split second of confusion—the branch hadn't been there only moments earlier, had it?—and he stumbled backward. It took him a moment or two to regain his footing, and that was when he realized the branch wasn't dangling from the trees at all. It was hovering in the air in front of them.

"No," Alesh whispered and bolted forward before Tatsu said anything.

Another branch rose up from the ground, even as Tatsu tried to move around the others in the dirt. The air grew thick and sticky with something—something impossible to see even as it slid across his skin. Alesh was a few steps ahead of him when several roots lifted up from the ground. Her boots caught between them, and she tripped, lurching forward. She caught herself with her hands but didn't have enough time to get moving again before several vines snaked out from the bushes and wrapped around her ankles. The creeping plants created an effective restraint.

"No!" she cried, smacking her hands against the ground, but all movement was useless. Vines found Tatsu's legs as well, rooting him to the spot, and they were solid and strong when he struggled against their hold.

He turned just as footsteps behind them sounded, crunching on dried leaves and twigs. Leil and Brund emerged from the shadows.

Leil's hands were in the air, fingers splayed, and understanding clicked into place. She was manipulating the plants to stop them. Brund moved directly to Alesh, his gleaming war axe held ready in both callused hands.

"Don't," Alesh began. She sounded defeated.

"We won't go anywhere." Tatsu raised his hands in surrender. "Don't kill us."

Leil's face had creased with anger. "We should kill you! Traitors stealing off in the dead of night to try and get away!"

"We weren't," Tatsu said. "I swear; we were just trying to find her sister. She's alone, and she might be in danger."

The branches abruptly fell from midair, crashing through bushes on their way to the dirt, and Leil dropped her hands. The fury on her features, however, didn't dissipate as quickly.

"You would call that *not* leaving?" she asked. "You gave your word to your queen that you would complete this mission. The sentence for even planning desertion in the royal army is hanging, and for confirmed traitors, the punishment is far worse."

"We weren't..." Tatsu failed to find the right words. "We weren't leaving to desert the mission. We need to find her sister."

Brund cut away the vines with his axe, freeing Alesh, though he looked like he wanted to use it for a different purpose. His allegiance to Leil was surprising, but it shouldn't have been. Their promised freedom came in the form of a successful retrieval, and who was Tatsu to expect loyalty from a man he'd just met? The betrayal stung, though, as if he'd hoped for more.

"You probably should have thought about that before you got arrested," Leil said. The anger began to melt away, replaced with something that looked very much like resignation. She was probably calculating how great the odds of success would be with only herself and Brund. "Do it again..."

"And I go for your throat," Brund promised, leering in close to Alesh's face.

Alesh shrugged him off. "Get away from me with that thing."

Leil led them back to the camp, with Brund taking up the rear, and Alesh's expression remained blank, impossible to read. She stared at the ground and the toes of her boots, shuffling her feet as if caught between wretched and resentful. She refused to look up, even when goaded by Tatsu's elbow, trying to get a reaction.

When they sat again on their bedrolls, something shimmered around the camp. A few seconds later, and a net of fallen branches and sticks encompassed the area, reaching up toward the sky. Only a small hole opened at the top, with the stars visible beyond it.

They were clearly not going to get another chance to get away.

Alesh, sulking, wrapped her arms across her chest as soon as she lay back down and refused to speak. Brund also fell into slumber quickly, but Tatsu's pulse continued to race, keeping his nerves alight. After a while, it was only Leil and himself awake.

"Why didn't you stop us from running by paralyzing us or freezing our legs?" he asked quietly to the woman sitting opposite the smoking fire pit from him.

"I can't do that," Leil said. She leaned forward and poked at the burning branches with a long, slender stick. "I'm only a *haem*."

The word clearly had some kind of significance. Tatsu felt uncomfortable when he said, "I don't know what that means."

She was clearly put off guard by his statement. "All mages are organized into groups by what they can do. Haven't you seen us during the festivals in Dradela?"

"I live in the woods," Tatsu said, "and I...avoid festival days in the city."

When she looked at him, he could see she wanted to agree it was probably for the best, but propriety won out. He was glad for it.

"And your parents never told you anything?" she asked. "Surely they could not allow you to be so far from Chaydese society. Everyone must contribute in their own way."

Tatsu shrugged. "I never knew my mother. My father died ten years ago when I was fifteen. He never told me anything about magic, and we lived in the woods for as long as I can remember. I stayed there after he died."

"Your father was...?"

"Chaydese," Tatsu replied, cross. She took the answer and didn't say aloud what it really meant, that his mother had clearly provided the Runonian influence.

"Well—" Her gaze settled on the network of branches curved around them, her face pensive. "Not all mages can do the same things. We are born with a connection to the living earth, which is where the power manifests. The lowest magic ability is sensing, which all mages can do. It allows a mage to sense things such as the level of nutrients in soil, for quality, and the amount of life left in plants and animals. They can also sense magic being used. Mages that can do only this are called *laom*."

She gestured at the sticks held in the air. "I am a *haem*, in the group above *laom*. We can move things, provided they are not too heavy, and manipulate simple plants and organisms. Our power runs deeper because our ties with the land are stronger."

Leil sighed and dropped her hands. Again, she seemed strangely morose, and Tatsu couldn't put his finger on why. "But humans are far too complex for *haem* to control."

"Are there mages who can control organisms like humans?" Tatsu asked, and he was afraid of the answer.

"Yes." Leil's gaze blazed, full of something he couldn't describe when it met his. "They are called *soelm*."

The conversation was causing his stomach to tighten. "Are there many *soelm* in the world?"

"None in Chayd," Leil replied. "We have no one that powerful."

Tatsu swallowed hard. The truth was he already knew what the answers were going to be. Somehow, in his bones, he knew it all before he spoke. Still, he had to ask, "Are there *soelm* in Runon?"

"Yes," Leil said again.

So, they were walking into a situation even more dangerous than Tatsu had imagined it to be, with a mage guide who couldn't possibly be expected to defend them. Was that why the nobles in the Chaydese court had been so divided? The chance of success was impossibly small, but then again, Leil was the only member of their team the queen would mourn. Criminals were expendable resources. Tatsu settled back a bit, distracted by thoughts of mages controlling his body to make it do whatever they wanted. Perhaps this was why his father had never spoken of magic. Living removed from it and not knowing about the power lurking in the world certainly kept the mind lighter.

He remained lost in his own thoughts when, across the embers, Leil moved to lie down.

"Try not to worry about it too much," she suggested. "We have more important things to focus on before we even get there. Her majesty would not have given us a mission she did not believe we could succeed with."

Tatsu stared at her over the dwindling smoke, unsure if she was reassuring him or herself. He wanted to voice but couldn't seem to: *You are walking us into death with far too light a step.*

THEY ROSE EARLY the next morning and made good time before midday. The summer air had just begun to creep in, and within a month, the green plains would be mottled from the blistering Chayd heat. But for now, most patches of grass were the bright green of new life with spots of yellow, the last remnants of the winter fading away.

Brund kept carefully at the back again, as if he expected them to try to run once more. Tatsu thought maybe he should be angry with the other man as a fellow prisoner, so keen on keeping them together. But he couldn't be; Brund's freedom was also on the line. A failed mission promised no sanctuary for any of them. Tatsu might not like it, but he understood why the huge man was keeping with Leil.

The same could not be said for Alesh, who continued her sullen silence well into the afternoon.

"I'm sorry, you know," Alesh said, breaking the quiet. She looked over at him with shielded eyes. "It's my fault that this happened to you."

In a way, it was true, but it still rang hollow. "I don't really blame you," Tatsu told her. "It feels wrong to think everything was your fault."

"Isn't it?"

"I opened the door. I let you in. And I knew what you'd been doing."

She kicked a bit at some loose dirt with her boot. Her motions were slow but smooth, which meant her wound was healing enough to allow for it. She hadn't complained about the pain, though Alesh had never been one to let that sort of thing show.

"Everything went so wrong," she commented, voice low. "The whole job, it was...a mess. And it just keeps getting worse."

"Worse than us?" Tatsu asked, intending to keep it light, but the words came out a bit harsh.

She snorted, a half laugh. "I knew what I was doing when I ruined that. I *knew* what you would say, and I knew it would end...everything. But I felt like it was what I had to do, in my gut. I knew it was worth losing you for."

She looked at him again, hair hiding her face, and he could see a shimmer in her eyes.

"I'm sorry," she repeated. "That's probably the worst thing I've ever said to you."

"It's not." Though Tatsu couldn't actually think of anything that could compete with it. His tongue stuck to the roof of his mouth, dry and swollen.

Alesh sighed, forlorn. "I don't have that anymore, that resolve. I don't know where it went."

"It'll be okay," Tatsu told her. Unspoken, the follow-up *she will be okay* hung between them, and both statements felt weak.

"I really am sorry, though. We could have been...well, who knows what we could have been."

Tatsu shrugged. "You'll find someone else someday."

"If we live through this. But I'm more worried about you."

Tatsu tripped over a large rock embedded halfway into the dirt and hopped a few times to keep his balance. "About me? Why?"

"You're too happy to isolate yourself in the woods! Getting you to come into town is a constant struggle. What are you going to do, live alone your whole life?"

"Maybe." He'd thought of it, of course, but forever had always felt ages away. "Maybe not. Who knows?"

"How are you ever going to meet anyone that way? At least a companion would make for good company."

Tatsu laughed. "That's awfully diplomatic of you. A 'companion'?"

"Well, it could be anyone." Alesh frowned. "You wouldn't really care if it wasn't a woman, would you?"

A moment, and Tatsu replied, "No, not really. I suppose it doesn't matter, but I assumed most people felt the same. Have you always known it about me?"

"I've suspected," she said and genuinely smiled for the first time all day. "You're surprising like that. Some details are deal-breakers for you, but they're the smaller ones. Things like this, you're unbothered by."

They drifted into silence once more. She frowned as she stared down at the leather of her boots, already dirty from the dust and grime of the road.

"Why are we here?" Tatsu asked.

Her head rose. "So, we don't have to go to prison, of course."

"No, I mean—" Tatsu shook his head, trying to clear his thoughts. "—why send us? Criminals? Why wouldn't they send soldiers, or advisors, or anyone who hasn't been arrested? They can't trust us. And many of the nobles were displeased during the queen's reception."

"Because no one will mourn us," Alesh said. When Tatsu opened his mouth to argue, she cut him off with a wave of her hand. "It's true, though. When soldiers die, there's a march through the city to their homes to honor them. I've seen them on their mourning parades, and I've seen the families wailing in the streets. But for us, there would be nothing. No one would even notice we were gone."

She glanced sideways at him and added, "You've never seen it since you hide away in your forest. It's awful to witness."

But Tatsu wasn't entirely convinced. On one hand, it didn't *feel* like a trap, though the good ones never did. But it didn't feel completely right either, and he couldn't figure out how to describe their position between the two, hanging useless and vulnerable. The absence of a tickle at the back of his neck signaled he had no reason to fear attack from Leil or Brund. He thought about telling Alesh what Leil had revealed about the mages in Runon but thought better of it. He didn't want to add to her worry. She had enough on her mind.

He sighed instead. "It just feels...wrong."

"Well, let's focus on getting it done with as soon as we can," Alesh said. Worry laced her tone, and the same thing coiled in the bottom of Tatsu's stomach.

A minute later, Alesh stumbled over several pebbles, her foot sliding out from under her, and she nearly fell. Tatsu shot his hand out to grab her arm, to steady her. Then, when she seemed steady again, he started to slide his grip free.

She grabbed for his hand as he moved it away, and her fingers lingered in his a little longer than necessary. The touch felt different, somehow, after everything, but Tatsu squeezed them anyway, clinging to the bit of comfort they gave. He hoped the feeling would last long enough to help get them into Runon.

BY THE AFTERNOON, they had arrived at a dense section of trees, the outskirts of his woods. The trees were easy to navigate through even though Tatsu didn't know them as well as he did the ones by his cottage. As the terrain shifted upward, climbing steeply at their left into the sharp peaks of the Turend Mountains, it became clear they were approaching Chayd's border, and the relative safety of their journey neared an end.

Just as they reached the border, his senses flared to life. He stopped, concentrating, trying to figure out the buzzing beneath his skin.

"What is it?" Leil asked.

Tatsu didn't reply. He placed a hand against the closest tree trying to suss out the source of his unease. Closing his eyes, he breathed in deep lungfuls of air, one after another, and waited. He stretched out with his awareness. This landscape was his home, and he knew it like a brother. He knew the way the land shifted, and the brush grew, and the way the tree leaves filtered the sunlight down onto the spindly weeds.

He couldn't pinpoint the discomfort, and neither could he shake it.

"I don't know," he answered, hand falling back to his side. His throat burned, as if he'd eaten a burr. "There's something."

"Are we close?" Brund asked.

"Yes." Tatsu strode forward again without another word. He thought perhaps he could shrug off the sensation, but it intensified as they continued on, becoming a deeply disturbing knot in his belly.

Minutes later, Leil gasped in alarm behind him.

"Something's wrong," she said with a hand to her head, as if her head hurt fiercely. "Something's very wrong."

A few steps closer, and it became clear.

The Weeping Forest lay before them, looming and wide. The name had come a long time ago from the particular nature of the trees with their low-hanging branches and long, vine-like leaves that scraped against the ground. Tatsu had been to the forest a few times before on hunting trips with his father, and he fondly recalled the peculiar smell of the trunk-growing moss, but this—this was not the forest he remembered.

Instead of lush green hanging from the branches like curtains, only black remained. The trunks of the trees looked so dark they appeared burnt, twisted and gnarled into impossible angles, and the vine leaves were no longer there at all, instead, replaced by decaying webs of what used to hang. The webs stretched across the darkened branches like amphibian skin pulling between splayed toes. And the smell...

Tatsu ducked his head, even though it did nothing to help him escape the stench of rotting, putrid compost.

"Gods," Leil whispered, muffled from behind the hand held against her mouth.

The Weeping Forest had been drained.

Chapter Six

THE WRONGNESS OF the forest trembled. Deep in Tatsu's bones, rattling and dizzying, the *off*-ness of it seemed to moan in agony in front of them. No breeze ran through the remains, but the branches twitched regardless. Toward the middle of the forest, a fog had settled low to the ground, and after a moment, it became clear the swaying of the woods was no optical illusion—the trees *were* moving.

With thin branches that reached out like fingers toward them, the Weeping Forest begged them to enter.

Leil's skin had taken on a gray tint, and she took a step back with her hands pressed against her mouth.

"Oh, no, I don't—I don't believe—it's not—" She seemed unable to finish a single thought, eyes wide and glassy white.

"What happened?" Alesh whispered. "What *is* this?"

Tatsu didn't know how to answer. Pressure lodged in his chest, pressing tightly against his lungs, making it hard to breathe. The reality of what was happening began to set in, though grasping the full horror of it was impossible. The queen had been talking about this. He'd seen it from his woods, in the rolling peaks beyond Chayd's bounds, and this was Chayd's future if they did not succeed. An unnatural coolness rolled from the trees, hitting the exposed skin of his forearms and raising goose pimples across his flesh.

He turned to Leil, still babbling out fragments of nothing to herself. "What happened?"

"It's empty." Her fingers clutched at her head. She dislodged the outer hood of her robe, and it fell back, revealing a snugly tied scarf wrapped around her hair. "But it's not—it's not dead. It's *hungry*."

A chill ran down Tatsu's spine. He dreaded going through the Weeping Forest now, but they'd already come so far, and the necessity of timeliness had become extremely apparent. Each day they delayed, the siphon devoured more land. Tatsu took a hesitant step toward the trees and the shadowy underbrush lingering beneath them, and when nothing immediately jumped out at him, he took another. The scent of decay made his skin crawl, but he could deal with the discomfort, if that was all it ended up being.

"What are you doing?!" Alesh cried out. She moved for Tatsu's arm and missed, fingertips grazing the fabric of his tunic sleeve. "We can't go in there!"

"It's the way to Runon." Tatsu kept his eyes on the gnarled trees, just in case. "It's our only option. We *have* to go through."

"There are other ways," Leil said, voice low. "The mountains—"

"And how will we get there?" Tatsu cut her off. "Double back and add a week or more to our time? This is the fastest route to Yuse."

Leil's eyes darted in his direction before skipping away again. "The Shyreld, then. It's less than a week's journey from here, and we could avoid..."

She fell quiet, though he couldn't read the expression on her face, and she pulled her hood back on with trembling hands.

"Avoid what?" Alesh asked.

Leil sniffed, turning her head away from them. "There were rumors of High Mage Zakio of Runon destroying the nomadic tribes in the Shyreld recently, but I don't know how much of it was truth."

"Rumors like that and you don't know if they're true?" Brund growled.

"There could be many reasons for the tribes disappearing from contact," Leil shot back. "And the queen is not inclined to believe rumors without proof to back them up."

Tatsu only half listened. High Mage Zakio was surely one of the *soelm* Leil had told him about. But, to connect that amount of power with hunting down nomadic tribes... Staring at the near-dead woods in front of him settled his stomach more than continuing with that particular thought.

"It doesn't matter," Tatsu said. "We'll go this way. We can't afford to lose the time."

Truthfully, his voice sounded a lot stronger than he expected. He was fighting a losing battle against the fear rising cold through his body. The goal of their journey beat against his back, driving him forward, even though he dreaded entering the trees. His job remained to get them to Runon, and he would.

As he moved slowly into the trees, Tatsu closed his eyes. Nothing was as it should be, and the change made it difficult to focus on the things he was searching for. But he tried anyway. He relaxed his shoulders as best he could and slowed his breathing, though the stench of the forest caused his breaths to hitch. Around him, the branches seemed to groan—like whispers against his ears, things he wasn't sure he wanted to understand. The forest closed in, oppressive and dangerous, but within that weight, the erratic pulse of life continued, though faint and no more than a shadow.

He opened his eyes and said, "Come on. Follow me. And nobody touch the trees."

They started in slowly in a frightened line with Tatsu at the head. Carefully, he measured each step, half-afraid the decaying soil would fall away somehow beneath his boots, but it seemed stable enough. Although the grime was full of dead leaves and the remnants of what the forest used to be, dissolving into muck, they had no trouble with the ground itself. Within the forest's confines, the rotten air congealed, and it took all of Tatsu's resolve not to press a hand to his nose to block it out. There were smells he could identify and some he never wanted to be able to, and all of it swirled together, trapped beneath the branches and souring further.

Leil seemed to be the worst off. Every few minutes, she let out another strangled half cry, all seeming to be ripped out involuntarily. Being able to sense whatever life was left had to be excruciating. Nothing but death surrounded them, but the pulse continued, fluttering beneath Tatsu's skin, and if he'd had the ability to cut to the core of it... The smell of rot and decay was enough without its sticky residue clogging up his awareness. Leil's mind had to be a tangled mess. When Tatsu looked back over his shoulder at her, she had hunched over with her arms wrapped around herself.

He didn't want to stop and cost them even more time, so he slowed a bit and drifted back, closer to her.

"You told me you could feel the land," he said softly. "What do you sense here?"

It somehow seemed like the wrong question because she glared at him, though the expression lacked bite. "You don't want to know."

"I need to get us through here," he said, "so, yes, I *do* want to know. I need to know what we're walking through."

She was quiet as they ducked beneath some of the webbing that hung low, curved and ragged. Finally, she answered, "We knew about the siphon, of course, through reports by our scouts on the outer borders, but we didn't know the specifics. We couldn't possibly imagine the scope of what it means. It's not only that it drains the life away, like we thought. It leaves a tiny bit, just enough, so that what's left is...desperate. It's as if the land has been starved for weeks and then left, and now it's trying to find anything it can use to feed itself."

Tatsu glanced at the branches over their heads, blocking out most of the sunlight with their black bark. "So, it's...alive?"

Leil didn't answer. All her silence did was add to the discomfort already buzzing in his veins.

They walked for a long time in quiet. In the decay, Tatsu couldn't tell how far they had gone or how long it had been. Everything seemed to blend together in a blur. Without the angle of the sunlight or the color of the sky, he didn't know how long into the day they'd walked, or when they should stop. His feet dragged, and his arms hung heavily at his sides as if part of the siphon had remained in the woods and was now trickling into their own bodies.

Brund tripped over one of the exposed roots that jutted up from the dirt.

He didn't completely fall, but when he listed to the side, he instinctively threw his hand out to catch himself on the tree next to him. In a moment so quick it was like a flash, the tree *reacted*.

Like the petals of a flytrap, the branches closed into a ball, scooping him up in a fluid motion with such force that his axe, which had been strapped to his back on a leather harness, fell clattering to the ground. The air sparked with shocked surprise as, for a breath, nothing moved, and then Alesh screamed and staggered backward. The trees near the one holding Brund began to creak and groan sideways, their branches extending out like hungry fingers trying to grasp a piece of a meal. From within the bone-like cage, Brund shouted over and over. His noise sounded startled at first, and then, as the seconds ticked on, it became a terrified, pain-filled screech that made Tatsu sick.

The tree was devouring Brund.

Wrapped around the branches, the webs expanded and shifted until they covered him completely in a putrid cocoon that rippled like jelly, like a balloon made from entrails. Tatsu reached his hand back to his bow without thinking, and he let an arrow fly, but it bounced harmlessly off the branches curled across the sphere of webs in protection. He couldn't do anything to the thick bark, and even if he managed to get an arrow through, he was more likely to hit Brund than a weak spot in the tree.

The space between Leil's hands flashed bright. It was as if she'd finally remembered in her panic that she could *do* something, but even the bits of rotting earth she levitated from the ground seemed ineffective against the grisly sight.

"Do something!" Alesh cried. "Help him!"

But there was nothing else that Tatsu could do. His arrows were useless, and the other trees were moving to create a wall they couldn't even hope to get through. The screams from within the rubbery confines ended abruptly with a wet gurgle, and Tatsu wrenched his gaze away, squeezing his eyes closed, wishing he could block out everything happening in front of him.

The forest went still, leaving only Leil's ragged, sobbing breaths.

"Oh, gods," she gasped. "What—*how*—"

The woods had fallen into an eerie quiet much worse than the frenzied motions of the devouring trees.

Tatsu sucked in a deep lungful of air that did absolutely nothing to steady him. None of them could stop staring at the spot where Brund had been—or still was, depending on technicality—and Tatsu wanted nothing more than to leave the wretched place.

"Come on," he said and grabbed for Alesh's shoulders, hauling her back up straight. His lungs and throat burned. "Come on; we move. We have to keep moving."

Alesh fell very quiet, but she didn't fight Tatsu and moved away from the tree. It had stopped swaying, and while the branch-cocoon remained, no sign of anything stirred within.

"He's dead, he's dead," Leil repeated over and over, and Tatsu reached for her too, to drag her out to a safer distance. She pulled away from him and started toward the tree, as though she wanted to try to get Brund's body out. Tatsu only just managed to catch her before she made contact, yanking her backward.

"Don't touch it!" he hissed. "You'll only end up the same way!"

Her face was streaked with tears. "But we have to perform the death rites for him."

Tatsu shook his head. There was clearly nothing they could do, not even to get what remained of Brund out of the tree. He wasn't even sure how he found his voice. "Let's go."

"He's *dead*," Leil said again with more force. She looked at him with eyes full of anger, and Tatsu understood. He thought about the day his father died, and how long it took for him to find the strength to move the body. He thought about how many hours he'd stared at the worn and weathered skin of his father's face, willing the man's eyes to open. He remembered how waxy and false his father's fingers had become, how foreign against his own. Leil's worldview had just radically shifted.

"Yes," he said, because he knew they couldn't stop. They had to keep moving. The woods had already proven that, and they were tempting fate by stalling. Hundreds of trees remained, all caught in the same veil between living and dead. "And we will be too, if we stay here. Keep walking and stay behind me."

As he finally got them going, he added, "And don't *ever* touch the trees."

BRUND'S GRUESOME DEATH was more suffocating than the Weeping Forest, and Tatsu wished he could shake it off as they walked. He didn't completely trust his senses to guide them in the right direction. They were the only thing he'd ever truly been able to trust, and they were failing him. With the oppressive atmosphere hanging over them, his thoughts got lost in the whispers and sighs of the trees above. He shook his head and tried harder to focus, which only served to intensify the murmurs.

They had to get north. The sooner they were out of the trees, the safer they would be. It was as if the trunks and webs were spying on them, observant of where they were and how quickly they were going. Had he not seen firsthand what they were capable of, he'd have dismissed his wariness as nonsense. But after...underestimating what the siphon had done to the woods would clearly spell the death of them all.

"This is all wrong," Leil said sorrowfully, and Tatsu had to agree.

"And if we don't get to Yuse, this is the same fate that we'll all share."

She gave him an unreadable look but said nothing in response.

They moved beneath the canopy of waxy webs stinking of rot until Tatsu didn't notice the smell any longer. His nose had numbed to it. Orange bits of light filtered in from overhead, and with the sun setting, they'd have to spend a night in a forest of trees wanting to eat them whole. The thought of remaining in the woods sent shivers down his spine, but no other option presented itself.

The compass in his hand pointed them through the trunks, but as he followed it, something pulsing beneath it all became apparent. He stopped, careful to keep them in the center of the woods between the stooping, tangled branches, and tried to stretch out with his instincts. Something loomed in the middle of the festering death, something living—a smell he hadn't sensed since they'd entered. It was the smell of life, and he wasn't sure if he trusted it.

The others huddled near him, their fear palpable.

"What is it?" Alesh asked, almost a whisper, and she was so close her breath tickled the back of his neck.

Tatsu didn't answer. He looked at the compass needle they needed to follow. Going farther into the trees would do them no good, and it would only add to their travel time. And yet...

The scent of life stood out from the fog of decay like a beacon, strong and clear and impossible to ignore. The whispers coming from the trees goaded him to go after it.

He turned to the right, shoving the compass back into his satchel.

"What are you doing?" Leil sounded alarmed, but Tatsu ignored her, instead attempting to focus on the pull tugging at his abdomen and beckoning him forward. He led them east, careful to find a path that allowed them room to move through the gnarled trees lying in wait. Each step was slow and deliberate, as the upturned roots in their way had nearly disappeared in the ground-hugging mist. He wasn't sure what he was doing, or what he thought he was going to find. Certain that the more time they spent within the forest, the more dangerous the situation would become, he still pushed on.

"Tatsu, where are we going?" Alesh caught up to him and pulled even, ducking low to avoid one of the blackened branches stretching out above their heads. "Your face looks strange. What are you thinking?"

"There's something here." He was frustrated he couldn't explain more.

Alesh's features wrinkled into a frown. "What do you mean 'something here'? Look at this place. Anything here is going to be as bad as the forest itself! Why would we want to go *toward* it?"

Tatsu shook his head. He didn't understand it, and he didn't want to voice it. The trees in front of them were shrouded in a deeper fog, the mist clinging to the bark of their trunks. He slowed further, trying to keep his footsteps cautious in case the dirt shifted beneath them. It seemed his senses were leading them into a denser part of the woods, and he didn't like that. It wasn't safe without space to avoid the trees, and Brund's fate still echoed through his head in time with his pounding heartbeat. Memories of the other man's death screams caused his throat to constrict.

"I don't know," Tatsu said to Alesh, "but I just—"

He stopped with a jolt. The forest in front of them had abruptly ended, falling away to reveal a clearing heavily shrouded in more of the gray mist. The trees curved in a somewhat lopsided circle, but an obvious glade nonetheless, with a flash of movement in the middle. His body seized and he froze, breath catching painfully until he made out the outline of the form seated there: a human figure, kneeling in the rotted grass, with hands held serenely in her lap.

It was Ral.

"*No*," Alesh gasped. She moved forward with a jerk, as if she couldn't quite control her legs in her shock. "Gods, no, how—?"

She tumbled forward, almost falling before she made it to Ral. Her hands shook when she threw her arms around her sister, heaving a sob that started as a burst before it faded into nothing. Ral, for her part, never lost her blissfully blank expression, though she did hug Alesh back. Watching them rang surreal, bouncing between relief and confusion.

"How…?" Alesh asked again, pulling away to look Ral over for injuries. There didn't seem to be any, and Ral indulged her sister by allowing the inspection as Tatsu and Leil crossed the clearing to where both women knelt.

Alesh's eyes flicked up at Tatsu when he approached. "I can't find anything. She seems fine. I don't think she's hurt."

"How did she get here?" Tatsu reached out to grasp Ral's shoulder, and she beamed at him through the tangled mass of her loose hair. "Did she follow us?"

"Happy!" Ral said, which explained nothing.

Something inside had released upon finding her; the worry that had grown and bubbled in him dissipated in a sudden loss of energy that left him bone-wearingly tired. The same thing was there on Alesh's face as she moved her hands to her sister's cheeks and put their foreheads together, breathing deeply as if to steady herself.

"It's a miracle that she made it so far without something attacking her," Tatsu said.

Alesh sat back very suddenly on her heels. "We have to take her with us!"

"It's dangerous, we're heading towards the enemy, and this isn't a sight-seeing—"

"It's not any less dangerous here!" Alesh cried. "We're in the middle of some kind of dead forest with trees that *eat people*."

She stood, bringing Ral up with her, who didn't seem to mind. The bottom of Ral's brown dress had matted with mud, but other than that and the twigs caught in the bird's nest of her hair, she was relatively unscathed—an enigma. Tatsu gave her another hard look, trying to find something that would explain things, but there was nothing.

"Ral?" Alesh asked. "Do you want to stay with us?"

"Yes!" Ral smiled at Alesh and then at Tatsu. Not smiling back proved impossible. Alesh turned to Tatsu and Leil, shoulders squared.

"She comes with us," Alesh said with an arm thrown protectively around Ral's shoulders. "That's it. I'm not leaving her here to this nightmare."

Helpless, Tatsu looked to Leil, but the mage was staring at Ral with a furrowed brow. The sash tied across her hair had slipped onto her forehead and was now peeking out beneath the shadows of her hood.

"I don't know what else to do," Tatsu said.

"I suppose she'll simply have to join us," Leil said. "Can she be quiet?"

"Of course," Alesh snapped, bristling.

Tatsu thought of Ral's stomping through his woods, and then the silence when she'd run off, and privately agreed with Alesh. Ral could be quiet when she wanted to, but he was never sure when those moments would arrive.

Leil crossed her arms over her chest. She looked tired again, with lines on her face that might not have been there earlier. She still appeared rattled from their encounter with the hungry trees, though it seemed she was trying to hide it as best she could. Her fingers trembled, even when they were pressed into the thick folds of her robe. "Then it's our only option. We have to keep going. The queen is counting on us, and we can't lose any more time. The longer we take, the more this unnatural destruction expands."

In the clearing, Tatsu had a better look at the sky, even with the fog. There were a few more hours of daylight, at most, and they were too far from the border to make it before nightfall. His initial hunch had been correct; they would have to stay. The glade seemed safe enough, if Ral had waited there, and as good a place as any to make camp, particularly because staying to the middle allowed them to remain a good distance away from all the trees.

The vulnerability shone clear in Alesh's face. "Tatsu?"

"We'll stay here for the night," he said, "and Ral comes with us in the morning."

At the sides of the clearing, the trees sobbed.

THEY TOOK SHIFTS keeping watch, though Tatsu found sleeping in the Weeping Forest to be difficult. Several times during his shift, he thought he heard something shuffling in the woods beyond the clearing, but he was never able to actually see anything. Discerning which sounds came from the trees and which didn't got tangled up with the rot and his thundering heartbeat. The whispers from the forest itself didn't lend themselves to rest, and his eyes ached dully when the morning finally came. Sluggish and heavy, he pushed himself upright.

From the drawn faces of his companions as they also rose and readied their packs, he gathered he was not the only one who'd had trouble sleeping.

"I had nightmares all night." Alesh sighed, shrugging on her bag. "This place makes me uncomfortable."

Tatsu decided not to tell her, or Leil, about the things he'd thought he'd heard in the woods. He kept his senses on high alert, scanning the clearing from left to right every minute or so to check they were still alone. The hair on the back of his neck stood up.

"How far are we from Runon?" Leil asked.

"A day, maybe, if we travel fast," Tatsu answered. "If not..."

Leil's voice sounded stronger than she looked. "Then we make it quick."

Alesh grabbed a bit of bread from her pack—the last of it that would keep without molding—and tore off a section to hand to Ral. The young woman bit into it, and for a second, she looked up to meet Tatsu's gaze. There was something infinite in her eyes, captivating; her face was unreadable for a pause, and when Tatsu began to worry, she grinned, lopsided and wide.

He wasn't sure, but he wondered for the first time if they were taking care of her or if it was the other way around.

"Want eat?" Ral asked him and offered him some of the bread.

Tatsu smiled thinly and gently pushed her hand back. "You can eat it, Ral. I'm not really very hungry."

He could have sworn that the trees actually *laughed* at that.

"I'm not either." Alesh shuddered. "Let's just get on with this."

She started ahead with Ral at her side, and Leil hung back, studying them.

"She won't slow us down," Tatsu said, trying to discern what the look on her face meant.

Leil shook her head. "It doesn't matter. Alesh will bring her anyway. So long as she doesn't keep us from our goal, having her with us is fine."

After a period of silence, she glanced at Tatsu, her features drawn. "She must be important to you, your thief friend."

"What do you mean?"

"Just that she was worth being arrested for." Leil hugged her arms close, and the gold bangles on her wrists glinted in the morning sunlight.

Tatsu's blood went cold. "How do you know that?"

"Oh." Leil paused. "Well, I heard it during your sentencing, of course."

She started ahead, quickening her pace to meet Alesh and Ral at the edge of the clearing, and Tatsu stared at her retreating figure. The trees stood waiting with their webbing, stretched and veiny, but it wasn't the woods that suddenly seemed threatening.

Tatsu didn't remember the queen announcing their crimes in the receiving hall.

Chapter Seven

THE SUN MOVED behind clouds early in the morning and stayed there, which made the Weeping Forest even darker than it had been the day before. Tatsu wanted to get to Runon as fast as he could, but the danger of missing a step between the trees couldn't be understated, so he slowed his small group even further. They made miniscule progress before what he guessed was midday, and their creeping pace kept Tatsu's nerves on constant edge. He kept trying to stretch out with his senses to read what little of the woods he was able to. All he could discern from the trees were the constant low mutterings as the branches shifted and sighed.

Ral offered nothing in her expression or actions that gave away how she came to be in the forest, or how she got there unharmed. When Alesh asked her about it, she merely smiled.

"Was she born this way?" Leil asked under her breath, drawing close to Tatsu's side.

"No," Tatsu replied. "She got sick with a fever when she was very young. It lasted for weeks. They said it kept her brain from developing. Now she's like this."

Leil fell quiet, looking thoughtful. "She feels strange."

"Strange?" Tatsu's chest pinched tight. "She's not going to hurt anyone. I've known her for most of my life."

"That's not what I meant," Leil said. "I don't know what it is, but she feels almost like magic."

Ral, oblivious to their murmurings, was gazing up at the tree cover with open fascination.

"You mean she can use magic?" Tatsu asked. Had Ral been capable of something like that, wouldn't it have manifested much earlier? She had a knack for being in the right place at the right time, but she'd never shown abilities like the ones Leil had. Tatsu didn't know enough about magic to be certain.

Leil shook her head. "No, that's not it. I can't work out what it is."

"Maybe it's nothing," Tatsu offered. He hoped so, anyway. The last thing Alesh needed was Ral to be found to have magical abilities and taken away to the castle. She'd never forgive herself for losing her sister to the crown, no matter how high the reward.

"Maybe." Leil sounded dubious. "Fever, you said? She's lucky to be alive."

Tatsu swallowed hard. "Not everyone seems to agree with you."

"Hey," Alesh said, and both of them started. A wave of hot guilt ran through Tatsu, but when he turned, Alesh wasn't looking at him at all. She was looking ahead at the fog hanging low between the trees, her mouth turned down. "Did you hear something?"

They all stopped. The silence had become so heavy it was almost palpable. The whispers of the trees had disappeared. At some point behind them, the branches and webs had ceased their waving, and the stillness of them felt worse than the movement had. Tatsu peered ahead but couldn't see anything. Still, they waited, with the sensation of unease growing. With the ragged, frightened breathing of Leil next to him, Tatsu took a hesitant step forward and winced when twigs snapped beneath the heel of his boot.

"Listen," Alesh whispered.

Tatsu was about to chastise her for scaring them all, and then he heard it: a low shuffling noise, like weight dragging over dead leaves and withered weeds. His muscles tightened involuntarily. Behind him, the others shifted closer, and Alesh's fingers touched the back of his arm.

"Tatsu," she said, in a hitching, hushed tone. "What is it?"

"Stay behind me," he told her, and all of them. Anything living within the Weeping Forest in its current state had to be dangerous. He slowly reached over his shoulder for his bow, sliding it out of the leather strap with practiced quiet even though his hands were trembling. The mist, too thick, prevented him from seeing the source of the sound, but the noise crept louder, and the echoes moved directly toward them.

Skin-tingling heat flared up to his left, and out of the corner of his eye, dead branches swirled, lifted up from the ground by Leil's magic. They floated in front of her like a twisted shield.

He scarcely dared to breathe as they waited, the dragging shuffle echoing in his ears.

The wolf appeared as a dark shadow in the fog. Tatsu could identify the creature from its shape, only something was very wrong—the lines were off, with too many angles and misshapen limbs. Its movements were jerky and strange. Tatsu slid his hand back for an arrow, fingers brushing the feathers just above the nock, and withdrew it in one fluid arc to notch in his bow.

"No one move," he hissed.

The wolf—or the creature that used to be a wolf— emerged from the fog with sunken eyes the color of blood and a growl rumbling in its throat. Nothing more than a sack of mangy fur, the skin stretched taut over hideously curved bones. As it drew nearer to them, Tatsu saw that two of its legs were malformed, one shrunken and curved on itself, and the other badly broken. The thin, white bone jutting out of the animal's joint was sickening, but the muscles that had pulled up around it were worse. The wolf paused, stalking them in a game it knew it would win.

Whatever had twisted the Weeping Forest had drained the creatures too. Tatsu hadn't seen anything their first day in the trees, and he'd assumed all the living beings within the woods had deserted it or perished as the drain advanced.

The reality of it was much, much worse.

"Leil?" he whispered.

"I don't know." Her voice shook. "I can't feel it. It's like it's not really *there*."

As the growling increased and took on a more urgent tone, Tatsu slowly aimed his arrow at the wolf's throat.

"One," he breathed, preparing to count up, and then the creature lunged.

He barely got the arrow in flight before he dove to the side, grabbing wildly for Ral's sleeve to take her with him. They hit the ground as he remembered they needed to stay clear of the trees, and it was only luck that kept them safe. One of the branches reached down for him as he scrambled back and away, the mangled webbing dragging across the ground. As he rolled and tried to ready a second arrow, Leil swung the floating branches and hit the wolf in the side. Between Tatsu's first arrow and the harsh smack of the bark, they stole a few moments as the creature stumbled.

Tatsu spun up on one knee and aimed the second arrow, releasing the string. There was a whimper of pain before he could identify the fletching sticking out of the wolf's hide. The weapon should have drawn blood or brought the creature down, but instead, the animal failed to react to the impact. The arrow stuck in the decaying flesh without slowing the wolf down.

Leil shouted something Tatsu didn't understand and whipped her hands out to the sides, sending her wooden shield forward at the wolf's snout. The branches hit squarely, and Tatsu had enough time to aim his third arrow for a direct hit in the creature's left eye.

As the wolf pitched forward, its growl nothing more than a low moan of pain, Alesh darted forward in a flash and sliced across its belly with her dagger.

It shuddered once and then lay still, and the pounding of Tatsu's heartbeat was so fast it made him dizzy.

"What," Alesh gasped, taking a large step back but never taking her gaze off the unmoving body, "was that?"

"It was a hole," Leil said. "Nothing. Like it shouldn't even have been alive."

Like the surrounding trees, the wolf had hungered desperately for any life it could find. Tatsu didn't want to approach the creature, but if that was the sort of thing they'd have to face again, he'd need the arrows. He pulled all three out of the wolf and wiped them swiftly on the dead grass and the bottom hem of his shirt, but little blood had splattered onto the wolf's head. The creature hardly bled, and all there was gleamed so dark it appeared black.

Repulsed, Tatsu quickly stepped back from the corpse. Ral moved forward with her hand outstretched as if she wanted to touch it.

"Don't," Alesh snapped and pushed Ral's hand down. "It's not safe."

"It's not safe here either," Tatsu reminded them. The forest remained silent, but other life-drained creatures most likely hunted in the mist. The trees and fog might be concealing their shapes as they lay in wait, just like this one had been. Tatsu was itching to keep moving. It was almost a relief when the trees resumed their ominous whispering.

"But you don't see it," Leil continued, blubbering into her hands and unable to tear her eyes away from the wolf's broken body. "This isn't—this isn't right. It's *sick*. I've never—this is unimaginable. We didn't *know*—"

Tatsu pulled her back a bit, though hesitant, afraid in her hysteria she might also try to get near it. "There's nothing you could have done for it."

"Don't you understand?" She whirled on him. "It was a walking corpse. And it's going to happen to all of us next!"

"No, it won't," Tatsu said. "At least, not if we keep moving."

"We shouldn't—" Leil started, and her mouth snapped shut as her face colored.

When she didn't continue, Tatsu prompted, "We shouldn't *what*?"

"We need to get to Runon," Leil mumbled at the ground. "The queen is counting on us."

Tatsu was lost by the turn in the conversation, but more than anything else, he needed Leil to pull herself together. He thought of the mountains past his own woods, where the drained line had been days earlier. Maybe it had already consumed his hunting grounds, destroying the trees and brush he'd grown up in. Thinking about his woods turning into something similar threatened to freeze his legs in place, but he tried to push the inkling aside.

"Come on," he said, and Alesh looped her arm through Ral's to keep her close. "We have to get out of here. The only thing we can do is get to Yuse and stop the siphon."

"We should perform the death rites." Leil had resumed staring at the wolf's body, but Tatsu was pretty sure she was talking about Brund.

"Move," Tatsu barked, his mind still on the haunting image of his own woods turning sinister. "Before I make you."

BY THE TIME night fell, he felt bad about snapping at Leil; she looked miserable as they walked. She was visibly rattled and had experienced something with the fallen creature and the woods he couldn't understand.

She retreated inside herself for a long stretch of time before Tatsu was able to slow down to walk next to her, resigning himself to trying to keep their ragtag group in one piece.

"Look," Tatsu began. "I know it must be hard for you. All of this, I mean. It's a big change from spending all your time within Dradela."

"Chayd needs us to save everyone," Leil murmured in reply.

Tatsu frowned. "It does, but this is bigger than just us, and the queen had to know that. You must know her well, considering you live in the palace now. Does she really think we'll succeed?"

"She has to," Leil said. "She is...determined. It's hard for her. There have been so few ruling queens, and everyone assumes she can't be as strong as a king would be. She's only trying to do her best by her people."

"And is she kind?"

Leil paused for several seconds before answering, "She is fair."

It didn't really answer his question, and her decisive tone implied the end to the exchange. Though Tatsu lacked her senses, he knew it must have been difficult for Leil, but he wasn't entirely sure what he should do.

They still hadn't made it to the edge of the Weeping Forest by the time the sun dipped down in the sky, so they had to stay another night within the forest.

The trees curled their branches and sighed as Tatsu found a clearing large enough to set up their sleeping rolls. Leil sat on the ground and roped her arms around her legs, pulling her knees in close to her chest. When she ceased moving after that, Tatsu thought it best to let her be.

"I don't like this," Alesh said, spreading out her blanket. Brund's pack had been destroyed with him, and they were short one after having picked up Ral—Alesh would have to share hers again with her sister. "It doesn't feel right to stay here now that we know those things are out there."

"Staying here is a better option than trying to continue through the trees in the dark," Tatsu told her, though he, too, was struggling with the discomfort of remaining where they were. He didn't like the idea of sleeping within the woods again either.

Alesh's eyes darted to the side, making sure she could see Ral, who was seated in the center of their little camp and humming to herself.

"How did she get here?" Alesh asked. Tatsu couldn't tell if the question was aimed at him or at no one at all.

"She was at my house when we...left," Tatsu said. "Maybe she came from there."

"How? Look what's happened to us, and we've only been here for two days. Who knows how long she arrived here before us."

His eyelids drooped too heavily to work out the mystery of it all. "She's not hurt, and that's the important thing."

"Is it?" Alesh's eyes were hooded. "She's always... been like this. She's always done things that were a little off, but this is the first time that..."

She trailed off, staring down at her palms.

"Sometimes, I think she can see things that I can't," she whispered after a moment of silence. "Like she can see what's going to happen later."

Tatsu sighed. "I can't give you any answers, Alesh."

She looked defeated when she nodded, shoulders slumped forward. "I know. Sometimes, I don't think that anyone can."

THAT NIGHT, TATSU dreamed.

He dreamed he was back in his house, his father's house. Around him were the familiar pieces of his childhood: his first skinning knife with the notched hilt and the old linen straps he would use for his legs in winter. But the images were hazy, like they were just out of his field of vision and he couldn't quite focus on them to clear the scene. He tried to move to his old rickety table when a knock sounded against the dream door.

He knew who stood on the other side before he answered, but Alesh's face was drawn when he swung the heavy wood open. He knew that look because he'd never be able to forget it.

"Tatsu, I'm sorry," she started.

"You knew what you were doing," he heard himself say, and he remembered this too. "You knew what was going to happen because of it."

"I didn't." She shook her head so hard her dark braids fell free and flipped over her shoulders. "I never would have done it had I known—"

In reality, the moment had remained lodged in his mind for months, and in the dream, the pain sprang up anew. "People were going to get hurt. You knew that. And Hesch had always been kind to you, to both of us. He was one of the only real friends my father had."

"Tatsu, I'm *sorry*. I never meant to hurt—"

Tatsu turned his back on her, and instead of the interior of his house, he saw only the Weeping Forest. The memory ended. The trees waved their branches as if they were beckoning to him, leading him deeper into the darkness at the heart of the woods. It was night, but there were no stars. The sky above the trees hung like a black void of nothing. He moved toward the trees, and they parted for him. With each step, the trunks of the half-dead giants slunk back, until he was walking through a path peeled away for him.

He kept moving, and when he turned to look over his shoulder, both his cottage and Alesh had disappeared. Gazing into the forest before him, he thought he could see ripples of movement. He froze, fearful of another encounter with a wolf, dangerous even in his dreams, but the figure was upright and walking with purpose.

"Ral," Tatsu called out.

She only giggled, turned, and took off farther into the dark woods. Tatsu tore after her as fast as he could get his legs to go, but they felt strange and heavy, and he had trouble picking up enough speed. Ral stayed stubbornly ahead of him, a bit of her hair flying like a banner behind her head, her delighted peals of laughter echoing through the forest.

"Ral!" he tried again, to no use.

All of a sudden, the Weeping Forest ended. Instead of Runon, there was a cliff, sheer, dropping straight into an abyss. Tatsu tried to stop, but he couldn't quite halt his movement in time. His arms pinwheeled as he tried to keep his feet from forcing his whole body over the edge. He thought he'd made it, and then he tipped forward and fell into nothing.

It woke him with a start.

"Tatsu," Alesh said as he sat up and tried to steady the frantic rhythm of his blood and breathing. "It's your turn for watch."

"Yeah." He looked over at Ral, but she was sound asleep.

Alesh leaned in, peering at him. With the light of their single lantern, she was mostly shadows. "Are you okay?"

"Yeah," Tatsu repeated, though he couldn't seem to shake that final, heart-wrenching sensation of falling.

WHEN MORNING CAME, Tatsu knew which way to go.

He kept his senses outstretched as they continued north, but they encountered nothing like the wolf-creature from the day before. The woods were quieter too. Tatsu could catch only tiny snippets of the whispers that seemed to fade in and out of existence. Something had changed, though he didn't know if it was their defeat of the woods' guardian or something else, something deeper.

But they were close, and he kept moving them ahead, until the blackened, twisted trunks stopped, giving way to a rocky terrain punctuated by short, squatty coniferous trees. They'd made it out of the Weeping Forest, and Runon stretched in front of them, all the way to the mountain peaks on the far horizon.

The breath he hadn't even realized he'd been holding escaped his lungs in a gasp.

They were well away from the roads, and nothing sounded nearby. He hoped they could stay clear of most of the settlements by sticking near the mountain line where the soil contained too many pebbles to be of much use. Just like in Chayd, the population stuck to the cities and the more fertile grounds.

Still, even the undesirable land in Runon was a beautiful sight after the gloom of the woods. Tatsu's legs threatened to collapse in relief, but he settled for a short break with his head between his knees. His muscles were still jittery with lingering, leftover fear; his abdomen ached with the aftershocks of it.

Leil *did* crumple to the ground as if her legs simply couldn't hold her upright any longer, her robes a puddle of dark blue around her.

"We made it," she said as she pushed her headscarf back from the low point at which it had settled on her forehead. "I didn't think we would make it out of there. I've never...I've never felt anything like that before."

"What now?" Alesh asked. "According to the queen's maps, Yuse is farther north. And we have to meet up with that informant once we're inside the city. How do we even know where to go?"

Tatsu waited for Leil to respond, but the woman seemed entranced by the simple, normal soil beneath her hands and knees. When she failed to reply, he looked to Alesh, who shrugged.

"We shouldn't wait long," she said. "We're very exposed here."

"Agreed," Tatsu replied. The lack of trees near the hills offered them no cover. He wasn't familiar with Runon's terrain, but the kingdom kept a steady stream of exports in a round, red fruit called *niyun*. *Niyun* grew only in a few areas within Chayd, and only in the deeper parts of the forests because it needed shade to get plump and sweet. Tatsu was willing to bet the woods would dramatically increase as they approached the capital, and they would find wild-growing fruits to help supplement their dwindling food stores.

The forests would also give them enough shadows to sneak through, provided they avoided any foragers.

Tatsu looked at Ral, and she gazed back, features open. Slowly, her face split into a smile, softer than her usual grin and curved slightly at the corners.

"Go," Ral said.

Yuse was not far. Tatsu took one more breath, heady with the satisfaction of being free from the Weeping Forest and its nightmares.

"Go," he agreed.

Chapter Eight

AS THEY WALKED along the rocky outskirts of Runon territory, the terrain began to change. Runon's landscape had traditionally been tough to cultivate because of too much elevation and too little nutrients in the soil. Instead of the pebble-strewn hillsides that Tatsu had expected, green grass covered the entirety of the plains. The colors were impossibly bright as clusters of trees began to appear in greater number.

The trees dotting the grass stretched straight and tall, and when the small group moved past the trunks, the branches brimming with leaves laughed. They kept to the woods as best they could, but whenever the trees gave way to clearings, darker spots of settlements came into view. The fields there were halfheartedly fenced in and flourishing, comically heavy with their yields. Sometimes the ground disappeared entirely beneath the tangles of green vines, hanging low with fat, round fruits. Even at the height of summer, Runon couldn't have had such good fortune with outlying farms, not even with perfect temperatures and an absence of destructive storms. The abundance was unnatural, jarringly so, artificially bolstered with pilfered life.

He wondered which parts of it were from the Weeping Forest, its life energy stolen and repurposed to fulfill Runon's own needs.

He wondered which parts of it were from the mountains beyond his woods.

As they walked by the trees, packed with perfectly formed leaves, something twinged behind Tatsu's ears. When he focused on it, he realized the trees were singing—a low hum, melodic until it faded with a contented sigh and then, seconds later, started back up again. One of them reached down and grabbed for Tatsu's hair, giggling. The weedy undergrowth bent slightly as they passed as if watching them. When they moved away, the plants straightened once more.

It was incredibly disconcerting. The Weeping Forest had been twisted, hungry, and horrifying, but this—this was unnatural, and just as unsettling. Whatever the siphon had done here existed well outside the laws of nature.

Tatsu kept them as close to cover as he could, and with the overzealous growth, he easily found places where they could slip quietly through the shadows of the trees. The thick groves they wove through smelled strongly of pine. The aroma clung to the fabric of their clothes, making Leil sneeze several times, and stepping around the fallen cones was more difficult than moving deeper into Runon's lands. Tatsu tried to ignore the twigs that caressed soft needles across the fabric of his clothes as he passed underneath them.

They stopped at nightfall and set up their tent. Although Tatsu knew the danger had significantly lessened outside of the Weeping Forest, he still had trouble sleeping. He kept his senses on alert but never heard more than the rustling of nocturnal animals and the odd songs of Runon's newly vigorous trees. Even the grass beneath his bedroll was lush and spry, sliding through his fingers as he ran a hand through it. It was the healthiest grass he'd ever seen, without a single brown blade to mar its uniformity.

And absolutely all of the life was stolen.

He tried not to think about his woods and how far the drain had expanded into his trees. The siphon could have progressed quickly. For him, it had been a week, but for his woods, their doom might have already arrived. He pressed his face against the coarse blanket and willed the images away. There was nothing he could do to help his home until they reached Yuse, and he needed to be as focused as possible. When sleep still refused to come, he sighed and rolled over, staring up at the bits of stars visible through the leaves above them.

He thought about his woods until the sun rose back over the skyline.

They kept moving the next day, growing closer and closer to Runon's capital. As they approached the kingdom's center, more villages dotted the landscape. Tatsu kept them to the trees, but the villages were still there in the distance. Farmers worked the fields, shin-deep in the sitting water of the rice paddies, and by the forest's edges, foragers carried linen sacks tied across their chests. By the afternoon, there were too many villagers, making it difficult to continue escaping detection. They were also too close to Yuse to be able to move during the day hours, so Tatsu stopped them early for a rest before setting off again after sundown.

"As we get closer to Runon, we will need to gauge our time carefully," Leil told them, breaking off bits of dried jerky to chew on. "It is planting season now for the summer crops, which means many of the court mages will be busy tending to the land."

"You're saying they'll be out of the castle for much of the time," Alesh said.

Tatsu didn't voice his question: does this include the *soelm*? He feared the answer.

"And the festivals to ask the gods for good fortune accompany this," Leil added. "There is a great deal of activity in Runon revolving around the seasons. We should be able to meet up with our informant without our movements being noticed."

"We travel at night," Tatsu told them. "We could never pass for Runonians, and there's no way to disguise it."

The look Leil leveled at him betrayed nothing. "*You're* Runonian."

"Not enough," Tatsu shot back, stung. "And it will only draw more attention, not less."

Leil didn't press the issue. Instead, she said, "Once we reach the city, we meet up with our man. He has a way into the castle and will provide us with shelter."

"What about the defenses?" Alesh asked, as if she'd known Tatsu's earlier thoughts.

"We should not run into the mages themselves if we follow the plan laid out by the informant. We'll bide our time and use the opening."

Alesh shot Tatsu a hard look, lips pursing, but said nothing.

Leil turned her gaze to Ral as she continued, "Will she be a problem?"

"She's *fine*," Alesh snapped. "She's not stupid. She understands what she needs to do."

"I never said that she was," Leil replied, "but your very freedom rests on this mission being successful. More than that, all the lives of Chayd hang on us removing the magical drain."

Alesh turned livid, fingers clenched into furious fists. "I'm not leaving her behind, so don't even think about asking."

"I'm not certain we can sneak into Runon's castle and have her with us." Leil's eyes darted from side to side as she spoke. "I let her come this far because we couldn't leave her in such haunted woods, but this is serious. There are dangerous people here."

She was wringing her hands in front of her stomach. Tatsu had seen the same behavior from her in the palace when they were looking over the infiltration plans; again, she appeared to be waiting for someone to give her a signal to continue.

"Stop talking about her like she isn't sitting right here!" Alesh cried.

Leil's expression clouded further. "Would she be able to reply if I asked her directly?"

Tatsu was on his feet seconds after Alesh—she was up and diving, with her hands clawed and ready to grab at anything she could find. He managed to swing an arm under hers and across her middle to pull her back, several steps away from Leil, although it took him a few tries to get his hand over her mouth. After all, daylight still shimmered around them through the leaves, and they were deep in enemy territory.

"Stop it!" he hissed. "You'll bring them right to us!"

Alesh spun in his grip, face contorted with anger. "You heard what she said!"

"It doesn't matter what she said! Alesh, calm down and think about this a moment. What's going to happen to Ral if we get caught sneaking into the castle?"

She had no response for that, growing silent, fury written on her features. It seemed to have turned inward, and Tatsu understood. None of her options were good ones. One wrong step would doom them all.

"I promise she'll be fine," Alesh finally said through clenched teeth. "And if she isn't, you can blame me for it. But I'm not leaving her behind again. So, it's both of us or neither of us."

Tatsu looked at Leil, who didn't react right away and then finally nodded, clearly reluctant.

Alesh yanked herself out of Tatsu's grasp. "Let me go."

"I was only trying to—"

"You didn't stand up for her. You didn't stand up for *me*. You always do that."

Tatsu fell back on his heels a bit. His cheeks burned. "That's not fair."

"Gods, Tatsu," Alesh said, eyes angry and narrow. "For once, take a stand about something."

She stalked off to where Ral was standing, near the singing trees, leaving Tatsu with heated cheeks and trembling fingers. When he gulped air into his lungs, her comment formed a lump that stung the whole way down. He'd only been trying to keep the peace, because if their group fell apart, so did the future, yet her pointed words echoed with betrayal. He'd taken a stand once, hadn't he? He'd stood his ground, and they'd both paid the price for it.

Alesh pointedly ignored both Leil and Tatsu for the remainder of their rest.

MOVING THROUGH THE darkness provided relief. The full moon afforded them light enough to continue walking, and though Tatsu was initially concerned about being seen as the trees fell away leading up to Yuse, there were few people out past sunset. As he relaxed a bit, the tension in his shoulders loosened.

One of the trees caressed his cheek as they passed, a tender slide of leaves against his skin. It sent shivers down his spine, reminding him of things yet to come.

"The mages in Runon," he said to Leil. "I need to know about them now."

"You mean the *soelm*," she replied. "There are two in Runon—High Mage Nota and her son Zakio. Nota is the most powerful mage in Runon's court. She and her son are a fearsome force, even from just the stories that find their way to the court's ears."

"You spoke of Zakio earlier." Tatsu tried to remember her exact words. "You said there were rumors of him attacking nomadic tribes. Why would he do that?"

Leil turned her head away, her face now hidden by her hood. "Because some mages are corrupted by their powers."

"Everyone can be corrupted by power. But that doesn't explain why a mage would be allowed to do something like that."

"The king of Runon is...weak," Leil said slowly. "Though I know only what is said within the palace walls. He visited Chayd once, many years ago, before I was taken from my village. He is angry that Chayd controls the fertile banks near the sea, while Runon is left with the rocks and hills that yield fewer crops."

Tatsu glanced at the trees overhead with their unnatural humming. "The queen said he was demanding more land."

"And he will take it, if he can," Leil supplied. "High Mage Nota has been in the Runonian court for years. She is a powerful influence on the king and is suspected to be the source of his demands. She has collected much freedom for herself and her son."

"Nota and Zakio," Tatsu said. "What can they do?"

Leil glanced at him furtively, and the corners of her mouth turned down. "*Soelm* have the deepest connection with the earth's energy. They can sense it, move it, and manipulate it—even complex creatures such as humans can become weak under their power."

"You've never mentioned them being able to create anything," Tatsu said.

"They cannot. Even to mages, the power of creation lies solely within nature. Even *soelm* cannot create fire or ice from thin air. They must have access to it, and then manipulate it, just like *haem*."

There was a small measure of comfort in knowing his nightmares of mages bringing down lightning and storms on his head were impossible.

"But Nota is powerful," he said.

Leil nodded. "She is extremely powerful. *Soelm* have enough power to control multiple aspects at once, without draining the mage's reserves. Well-trained mages can quickly manipulate everything around you, which is what makes them so dangerous."

"If they're this powerful, we can't possibly expect to defeat them."

"We will not go up against them directly," Leil said. "The seasonal festivals are a show for the king and the court, and they will likely be required to be present, especially with their social standing. Mages as high profile as Nota are not allowed to be absent from that."

"You claim that your spy can get us into the castle," Tatsu said.

"He will." Leil bristled. "We have the maps he provided and the entrance he will use. The siphon continues to function, even with the mages otherwise engaged with duties, which means it does not require them to be nearby to control it. We will find a window of time when they are not present to slip inside."

Tatsu couldn't put a name to the unease hanging over his shoulders, nor a reason. Whatever he was looking for, Leil didn't give him anything more to go on. She sighed, features drawn and pinched.

"The gods don't favor those who take what is not theirs," she added. Tatsu assumed she was speaking of the too-healthy crops and whispering trees and was inclined to agree.

"I suppose they don't," he replied, but the pressure persisted, a twisting stone inside him.

THE THIRD DAY, it began to rain. Unlike the summer rain near the coast in Chayd, the water falling from the clouds in Runon was significantly cool. The droplets quickly soaked through the fabric of their clothes, causing the material to stick to their skin like a damp cocoon. As they shivered beneath the happily sighing tree leaves, Tatsu was aware he'd made a gross miscalculation in underestimating the elements.

They couldn't afford to stop moving. Miserable, Tatsu pushed them forward through the trees, but the combination of the cooler night and their soaked clothing slowed their pace to a crawl. He was fearful of starting a fire in case the smoke gave them away, but by midnight, it was unavoidable. By choosing a nook nestled in the mountains that held traces of animal habitation from seasons past and nothing more recent, he hoped the stone overhang would help conceal their tracks.

The group huddled around the fire with outstretched hands, waiting for the flames to dry their clothing.

"Are we still on schedule?" Tatsu asked.

Leil frowned, the image of the flames reflected in the gold encircling her wrists. "The festivities will last for a week, which gives us a bit of time. We had hoped to arrive before it began, but even if we do not, we will still have a small window as it continues."

"You're sure?" Alesh pressed.

Leil didn't look entirely convinced, but she nodded anyway. Her eyes darted to Tatsu's face again and then at the fire.

Tatsu turned to Alesh and shrugged. "Then we keep going once we are mostly dry. I don't think we have any other choice."

"It doesn't seem like it," Alesh said, and one corner of her mouth twisted down. She reached for Ral's hand and added, "Are you drying off?"

Instead of answering, Ral spun completely and threw her arms around Alesh's shoulder, burying her face in the ends of Alesh's damp braids. It clearly startled Alesh enough that she took a step backward, away from the flames.

"Ral?" she inquired and hesitantly touched her sister's back.

"Sorry," Ral replied. Her voice was muffled against Alesh's shoulder, but Tatsu could still hear the soft whimper accompanying it. "So sorry."

Alesh's eyes went very wide. "Ral? What are you talking about?"

"So sorry," Ral whispered and then went silent, and none of their additional encouragement could prompt her to speak again. Alesh patted Ral's back, but her eyes, when they met Tatsu's, were glittering with worry.

THEY REACHED YUSE two long nights of walking later, after the rain had stopped.

By the time they arrived at the outskirts of the city, Tatsu had grown tired of the constant chattering and giggling of the trees. It was too hard to tell if they were being followed, or if the brush whispered as they passed by, and his head ached from trying to keep his focus where it needed to be. The roads leading to Yuse from the farming outposts were dotted with soldier guards, so Tatsu took them up around the side from the fields that melted into clusters of houses. They moved slowly, with caution, to avoid waking any of the occupants and sounding the alarms.

They entered Yuse at night, with the moon merely a sliver in the clear sky above. The slants of the roofs were broken up by rounded corners and facets, some carved into shapes and animals, and behind the roofline, the rocky slopes of the Great Mountain Range rose up into the stars. Yuse seemed to be built shorter than Dradela and lacked the brightly colored trading tents that always occupied the sandy pathways out of Chayd's capital. It felt detached and quiet, with only a few hanging lanterns to light the cobbled stone paths. Between the imposing mountains behind and the cool stones curving into somber roads, Yuse offered little warmth to travelers.

It made sense, then, given how much they'd shut themselves off to everyone else years ago, long before the siphon had begun.

Tatsu and his companions moved quietly through the shadows into the cramped alleys between the buildings while trying to ignore how the cooler breeze made their skin prickle. The air smelled of incense and spiced meat dishes, wafting through the slits in the shuttered windows, and it made Tatsu's stomach growl. Where Dradela was a city of sand, built on stacked stones, Yuse's buildings were comprised of wood panels and tiled clay roofs.

The houses were built close to one another, leaving only small pathways between them. Only a few people moved on the roads, even at night, though they all walked with purpose. Tatsu was grateful for the traditional mountain-farming shoes the Runonians wore, smoothed leather lined with fur and soles punctuated by iron darts. They made tiny, rhythmic clacking noises against the stone pathways. It wasn't difficult to maneuver his group to avoid being noticed, listening for the telltale clicking and sliding covertly up against the side of the buildings. Alesh pulled up her hood to hide her features, though Tatsu wasn't sure it made much of a difference. The shadows hid them all well enough.

As they moved through the outskirts of the city toward the informant's location, which was situated near the center of town, Tatsu tried to take in his surroundings as much as he could without lowering his guard. If they needed to leave quickly, they'd have to remember the quickest and easiest way out. To his left stood a tavern, marked with a sign he couldn't read but windows he could gaze into. Men were sitting around fire pits with small clay cups heating on thin boards above the flames. The scent of the warmed liquid reached outside, a spicy concoction smelling of anise and cinnamon. Beside the tavern was a market, closed for the night, with an empty wheelbarrow and a worn-looking counter beneath the notch-covered windowpane.

When they passed a house with slightly open windows, snippets of conversations, all in Runonian, filtered out. It reminded Tatsu of his cellmate in Aughwor as they ducked low beneath the shutters and crept slowly across the path around the lights.

"Do you speak Runonian?" he asked Leil under his breath, once they were out of range, but he received only a shake of her head in response.

At the next corner, they were met with the strong smell of meat cooking once more—goat legs on dowels of wood and kept over a fire inside one of the buildings. The front of the shop was missing a wall and sported only a short, waist-height rail made of rusted metal. Behind it were the spits of meat, still slowly cooking, although the owner didn't seem to be present. Tatsu's stomach rumbled again. The meager rations of dried jerky and fruit they'd carried with them felt like a cruel jest compared to the delicious scents. Tatsu's mouth watered with desire, but he kept his legs moving.

The next building was a metalworking smith, and there were amulets and bracelets made from twisted silver held under panes of glass in the window. Tatsu *did* pause there, but only because the shimmer of the metal surprised him.

"Sorry," he said when Alesh and Ral nearly ran into his back. "I haven't seen silver like this in years."

"I haven't seen it since before...well..." Alesh paused, shrugging a bit. "You know."

"Before Runon retreated in on itself," Tatsu supplied. The biggest known silver vein ran through the Great Mountains Runon was situated against, and with the lack of trading, silver imports in Chayd had tapered off into practically nothing. But that hadn't been what she was talking about. Alesh's face grew stony when Leil looked at her in question, and she refused to elaborate. Denizens of the Iah district were seldom humored in fine jewelry stores.

Tatsu started walking again, trying to leave the awkwardness behind.

They moved among the wooden houses until the city began to change, and Leil took the lead. The buildings became smaller and older, their uneven roofs crumbling at the edges. Just the smell of the area—unwashed bodies, stale air, and rotting food—told Tatsu they were in the slums of Yuse. They might as well have been in Iah; the houses looked different, but the feeling of misery was very much the same.

It seemed for all its stolen energy and life, Runon could not be bothered to help the poorest of its citizens. The pulse of despair in the dirty maze of alleys stood out in sharp contrast to the vibrancy of the life-gorged foliage they'd witnessed outside the city walls.

Leil led with a step far too confident to be genuine, and Tatsu hung back, observing. In one of the wood-paneled houses, tattered curtains hung out through broken shutters. Inside, there was nothing but blackness and a low, throbbing wail—the sound of exhausted sobbing half-muffled by the dingy linens. The sound echoed in his ears even after they had crept past the building.

During their journey, he'd been so focused on Runon as the enemy that he forgot to think of Runon as its people.

The odor grew stronger as they moved deeper between buildings. Leil stopped them in front of a house indistinguishable from the rest, save for a broken lantern with one red-painted corner hanging out front. That, it seemed, was their sign.

She rapped on the door three times in quick succession and then, after a pause, twice again. It took a minute for the wooden door to creak open, and when it did, the walls of the building shook so violently Tatsu was half afraid the entire thing would collapse in front of them.

"Quickly," the man inside told them and ushered them all in.

The interior of the house appeared just as shabby as the outside, with cobwebs strung between the higher rafter beams and dirt strewn across the floor. When Tatsu moved farther in, he stumbled where the floorboards curved down in a slant. But clay bowls and dishes littered the table in varying stages of cleanliness, and it helped to put his mind more at ease. No turncoat would invite foreign traitors into his real home if he intended to turn them in.

The man, clearly Runonian, introduced himself as Akao. He had a long, thin face and faint dark circles beneath his silver eyes. His clothing was well worn but traditional—long but thin linen sleeves and loose-fitting pants tucked into his thick-soled leather boots, the whole of which Tatsu hadn't seen in a very long time, and only at second-hand trade carts.

"I'm glad to see the four of you made it safely," he said, and Tatsu risked a glance at Leil, who didn't seem keen to correct the assumption they were the same four who had set out from Dradela originally. Maybe it didn't matter.

"Thank you," Leil replied. "We are ready to prepare for the infiltration of the castle."

She mentioned nothing of their troubles in the Weeping Forest, so it seemed their informant didn't need to know about the status of the lands outside Runon's borders.

"I expected you to take another three days to get here," Akao said. "The seasonal festivities have not yet gone into their full schedule, and it's too risky to get into the castle before they begin. The castle will not be empty enough to get you inside unseen."

"How long will it take?" Tatsu asked.

He received a long, level stare from their new host. "Until I am confident that you will not jeopardize my position or be caught within the walls. Until then, you stay here and out of sight. I can't possibly explain your presence if the guards catch sight of you."

Leil's mouth was set in a hard, drawn line, but she didn't argue the order. "Then I suppose we have no choice but to wait inside."

Akao shrugged a bit and gestured to the grimy floor behind them. "Make yourselves comfortable. I can bring you a little food and ale, but if I don't report to the castle for my shifts, our cover will be blown."

The fire in Tatsu's blood pumped wildly, too strong to dampen. Remaining in the house for days would be maddening, but Akao was right. They would stand out too much. Tatsu didn't like the idea, but he trusted their judgment enough to agree with it.

As Akao went to the rickety upper level of the house, every footstep shuddering the walls below, Tatsu settled in for a long period of waiting.

THE NEXT DAY passed slowly, minutes stretching into hours, and hours ticking away into the rising sun. They continued to sleep during the day to be ready for the night raid and spoke only in hushed whispers. If anyone walking outside heard Chaydese coming from the house, their position would be compromised.

Remaining in the house without access to the outside was the worst of the torture. Tatsu might as well have been back at Aughwor, staring at the clouds through a window he couldn't climb through. He longed for the clean open woods outside his cottage, where he knew both the best and worst of the land. In Yuse, he trod on unsteady ground.

Trying to keep himself busy and relatively quiet, Tatsu sharpened both his blade and Alesh's, using long, slow strokes to keep the noise down. He went through his quiver of arrows and redid the fletching on several. A few of the seams were coming loose on Ral's skirt, so he and Ral worked together to stitch it back up, borrowing Akao's mending kit. Keeping busy felt good but did little to hasten the passing of time in the cramped quarters.

The second day was even worse. Tatsu's muscles were itching to stretch. He took to slowly walking the floor, maneuvering around the boards that creaked loudest, but it was hardly enough. By the time the second sunrise began filtering vivid orange light through the boarded windows, he feared he would go mad.

Akao returned that morning with already purpling bruises on his face and a long cut across his cheek.

"What happened?" Leil cried, jumping to her feet with so much force the dirty table shook against the floor. Her hands moved toward Akao's head, but he slipped out of her reach, eyes glued to the floor.

"Zakio," he mumbled. Tatsu assumed he was embarrassed, until he realized Akao's lip was swollen and puffy.

Leil stepped back, eyes wide and glassy, one hand going up to touch against her throat with shaking fingers. "Does he know about us?"

"No." Akao continued to stare at a dark spot on the far wall. "I was washing one of the floors in the castle, and Zakio tripped over the bucket of water. He...*punished* me for thoughtlessly leaving the bucket where he could run into it."

Shoulders unclenching, Leil tried to reach for Akao again. Tatsu looked to Alesh, whose face had set in angry lines.

"Does this happen often?" Alesh asked.

Akao shrugged and started up the stairs. As he retreated, he moved through one of the bright streams of morning light, which colored the bruises and swelling to such a harsh hue they nearly mimicked bloodstains.

"Tomorrow night, they will be out of the castle for the celebrations," Akao told them. "That is our window, and we can't afford to get distracted."

"That didn't answer my question," Alesh said, and her frown deepened.

Akao sighed. "It doesn't matter. Being revered at the festivities emboldens the mages. Zakio is enjoying his privilege."

He disappeared into the second level and the door, full of insect-eaten holes and more a symbol than an actual barrier, slammed shut behind him. After a long creak of the floorboards and the thudding of boots, there was no further noise from his room.

Tatsu turned to the others as Alesh wrapped her fingers protectively around Ral's wrist.

"That's disgusting," Alesh said. "People like that are filth."

A distinct unease permeated the room when Tatsu sat back down. Alesh busied herself with repairing a small hole in her pack, back curved over the leather she was working on. Ral leaned in a bit, eyes shining.

"Scary man," she whispered. She pressed her index finger against the tip of Tatsu's nose and then laughed. Before Tatsu could question her further, she turned to Alesh's workspace and pushed her hands in to help.

Tatsu moved to sit next to Leil, who was staring up at Akao's closed door as if lost in thought.

"If all mages can sense living energy, what are you getting from the trees in Runon?" he asked.

When she stayed silent, he added, "If you'd rather talk about Zakio and Nota..."

"It's...not something I can explain well," Leil replied, eyes darting to glare at him for a second before resettling on the grimy floor. Tatsu had clearly struck a nerve with his question. The power behind the siphon and what it had already done to the Weeping Forest—it scared her. Short, raspy breaths and the tremble in her fingers betrayed her fear.

"Try," Tatsu told her, with perhaps more force than strictly necessary.

"They have become more...complex," she said. "Less what plants feel like and more how animals feel. They are no longer a simple current of energy. The siphon has changed them by feeding them new life. I'm not sure if I would be able to influence them the way I can normal plants."

This would explain the Weeping Forest too, and its hunger for something living to slake its thirst with.

"What would happen to a person who got caught in the siphon?" Tatsu asked. "Would they be like the wolf we encountered?"

"I don't know if that would be possible." Leil frowned. "The human would know to leave and avoid the drain."

"But is it possible?"

She shook her head. "I don't know. I suppose that, yes, maybe it would be. I don't know what would happen to an individual after something like that."

They were silent for a long time, listening to the soft pops of Alesh's leatherworking needle against her pack.

"What happened to Akao today..." Tatsu started slowly. "What happens if we run into Zakio while we are in the castle?"

"We run." Leil pressed her lips together. "And we pray for a quick death."

Chapter Nine

TATSU'S NERVES WERE on high alert as the night of their raid approached. Outside the house, more voices floated through the air. The festival for the season changing and the beginning of summer was underway beneath the light of the starry sky. Akao appeared at the base of the stairs with a handful of musty, moth-eaten clothing, all made of linen the color of rusty nails.

"Servants' garb," he explained, and Tatsu was glad to discover that all of the belted tops had hoods. The extra shadows would hide their features from most wandering eyes.

He put his on over his own clothing, as did the women, and tied the fraying fabric belt around his waist. He didn't like being so far away from his weapons. There were no pockets to the loose pants; he wouldn't be able to reach his bow and arrows until they made it into the castle and could shed the disguises. He moved a few times to stretch out the fabric, seeing how far it would allow him to go.

Jittery and nervous, he pulled his cape-like tunic up enough to grab his knife, sheathed at his waist. With little effort, he cut through a bit of the pants at his midsection so he could reach his hand in and wrap his fingers around the hilt. It wasn't perfect and would take several seconds of fumbling, but he preferred the setup to having nothing. He strapped his bow and quiver of arrows on his back beneath the linen of the loose-flowing top, which meant getting to either of them quickly was a lost cause. The weapons on his back were awkward, but hopefully the folds of the fabric disguised the bulk of them.

Akao spent a few minutes tidying up their knotted belts and adjusting the hems of their sleeves before pronouncing them ready. His forehead remained furrowed, however, and Tatsu took little comfort in the expression. The bruises on Akao's face had darkened considerably during the last day and were almost the same color as the night sky.

"Keep your heads down," Akao said. "Servants are worth very little here. Walk with your eyes on the road and your shoulders hunched, and no one will give you a second glance."

Outside, the air was humming with electricity and filled with the smell of grilled meat. They walked slowly along the roads lined with swaying paper lanterns, hung up by long stretches of thin ropes tied around roof decorations. Tatsu tried to do as he was told and keep his head down, but he wanted to see at least something in Yuse. They'd observed little on their walk in.

The paths were filled with people, mostly walking in the opposite direction; they were clad in the same belted tops as Tatsu's party, only the festivalgoers wore fabrics with intricate patterns. The men sported wide-legged pants tied at their calves with strips of smooth leather. The women had clingy, tight-fitting leggings beneath their longer tunics. Even at the summer festival, all Runonians wore their trekking boots, and the clacking of the iron darts against the stone pathways mimicked a small stampede.

If this was the attire for the festival gathering, they wouldn't have to worry about any bystanders sneaking up on them. Still, Tatsu did his best to hunch over, trying to blend into his rust-colored servant's linen until he became simply part of the atmosphere.

After some time, as his legs cramped from carefully controlling his steps, they came across a thin river. It snaked between the wooden buildings, curving in a frenetic path. At the river's edge, large trees with low branches, plump with bundles of tiny leaves and five-petaled mountain flowers, hung over the water. It seemed late in the season to have such flowers, but there they were, the tree limbs full of them. Powered by the stolen life from the siphon, perhaps they never stopped blooming.

They walked beneath the trees and the lines of paper lanterns hung between branches, the flowers laughing as they passed.

Several bridges crossed the river, all curved arches of decorated wood with stoic animal guardians on the posts. Akao took them to the last one, sparse and plain, with paint so old most of it had peeled away from the wood in long strips. They approached a couple and a small family on their way across, but Akao had been right—none of them looked at their party with much interest at all. In fact, the little girl, clad in a linen shirt and matching pants painted with bright red floral patterns, moved to the opposite side of the bridge as they passed one another.

The roads on the other side of the river were quieter. There were passersby still moving toward the festival, but Tatsu's group had made it to the outskirts. The houses were dark and quiet, and as they wove between them, Tatsu could make out only the outlines of the wood-paned windows against the dark sideboards. The rhythmic clacking of metal against stone still echoed in the distance, but the sound was receding. The bulk of the festival had to be happening nearer the edge of town, where the fields promised more open space. Tatsu let himself breathe a bit, his shoulders starting to relax.

Akao led them to the end of the alley that let out into an open area. Past the small square, which bore the deep inset marks of high foot traffic and carts laden with goods, was the castle.

Unlike the wooden houses of the city, the castle had been built of stone—meticulously stacked and manicured stone, so smooth it resembled marble. The round tower base gave way to the courtyard behind it, and beyond that, another long wing of the palace, shadowy and confining. Hidden behind the larger walls, the garden was bursting with so much stolen life the branches and leaves hung heavy over the stones like fingers clamoring to escape the confines. Overhead, the closest tower blocked out the light of the moon, its darkened windows foreboding eyes watching them draw nearer and nearer.

The castle loomed impressively, but Akao took them around the side, where the building stretched out flat and low and looked less like a structure of imposing power and more like a tavern. Impossible tangles of vines on the far side crawled up the stones, and ornamental gargoyles perched on the roof's edge. Hidden behind bundles of creeping leaves, the door materialized into view at the last second, shrouded in darkness.

This, it seemed, held the servants' entrance, for Akao led them straight to it. He pushed at the clusters of vines, which reached out and curled gently around his wrists. When he rapped his knuckle against the door, it opened almost immediately.

The woman on the other side, dressed in the same rust-colored clothing, said something in Runonian Tatsu didn't understand. Akao gestured to the group and replied in the same vein. Tatsu's breath caught—if the woman took too close a look at them or suspected anything was off...

But her haggard face was impassive when she let them in, stepping aside so she could wait and close the door, seemingly unbothered by their appearance. Akao bowed to her and then began walking through the small room. Tatsu, not wanting to look out of place, copied his action, but perhaps he hadn't needed to. The woman's attention had already moved to the pile of linen laundry she was sorting into crudely woven, lopsided baskets.

They weren't alone until they reached the second, larger room. Akao closed the door behind Alesh's trailing form and pushed back his hood. There were beads of sweat on his forehead that he wiped at with the back of his hand, giving him away: he'd been nervous too.

"I'd tell you to keep your robes on for cover, but it won't do you much good," he said. "Most of your path lies in areas off-limits to the majority of the servants here. You'll attract just as much attention in the robes, and with them on, you won't have use of your weapons."

It felt good to shed the linens, Tatsu immediately more comfortable with his bow and knife in easy reach.

Akao crossed the room filled with buckets and wooden mops and a large number of cobwebs in the dark corners. By the time he reached the opposite side, their group was mostly ready. Alesh's dagger sheaths were settled on her hips, and Leil had rolled up her mage robe sleeves, exposing the gold bands on her wrists.

"You know the route?" Akao asked.

Alesh had spent a large portion of their time in the safe house memorizing the crinkled maps Leil had carried in her pack. "Yes," she replied, voice tense.

"Stay out of sight," Akao continued. "You need to avoid both the guards and anyone else you might see. If they alert Nota and Zakio to your presence, it's all over."

"We're ready," Leil told him, but perhaps it was only to get him to stop talking. Her mouth pinched anxiously at the corners, mirroring the furrowing skin of her forehead. The tension hanging heavy between them nearly stole Tatsu's breath away.

Akao opened the door and ushered them through.

They spilled into a dark corridor. Without any torches, Tatsu couldn't quite see where he put his feet, but a soft light glowed at the end of the hallway. They would have to follow the faint light cautiously and hope none of the servants had left anything littering the floor.

Alesh took the lead, creeping with little sound. Tatsu couldn't walk as lightly as her, and each squeak and soft brush made him wince, terrified a guard would hear the noise and find them. Yet, somehow, in an agonizingly slow fashion, they made it down the hallway without incident. The glimmer at the end came from a single torch mounted on the wall at the junction of the corridors.

Tatsu's insides were a knot of nerves and fear as they turned and headed toward the opposite end of the hallway, where a door emerged from the shadows. A wooden doorway, only barely visible in the dim, flickering light, recessed into the wall enough the surface looked like ink. Alesh got there first and knelt in front of it, pulling free several iron lockpicks from the hidden lining of her tunic.

Even the scraping of the pick in the keyhole was a crash of thunder to Tatsu's ears. The seconds might as well have been hours as they ticked by, and a single bead of sweat ran down the back of his neck.

When the door slid open, a staircase loomed on the other side.

"We can use a match for the first flight," Alesh whispered, and Leil produced one from her hanging velvet satchel. "After that, we approach the first posted guards."

Her eyes met Tatsu's, and he nodded. They would need to be very careful with Ral and the guards.

The group moved with care up the stairs. They, too, were stone and not wood, which kept the creaking to a minimum, but still afforded them little security. Tatsu's boots weren't designed to grip the stone as much as the traditional Runonian boots did, and he was afraid he would misstep and slide down with each stair. At the top of the first flight, Leil blew out the match, and they all had to take the steps one at a time. Tatsu kept his hand on the wall for balance, fingers sliding across the cold blocks.

When they crept into the soft light of the next floor, Alesh pulled a roll of coarse linen from her pack and a small vial. *Poison.*

She very carefully did not look at Tatsu as she let several drops of it soak through the material. With one hand, she motioned for them to stay hidden behind the corner, and with the other, she kept the damp rag held away from her body. She stepped silently to the corner, and then, after a few moments, disappeared around it.

Tatsu risked a glance at her. Near the middle of the hall, a single guard patrolled with his back to her, heading away as she snuck up behind him. The leather cushion of her boots absorbed most of the sound; her years of experience muffled the rest. She caught the guard before he reached the turn of the following corner and threw an arm around his shoulders, hand and linen covering his mouth.

It took him only a second to fall. She couldn't quite catch all of his weight, and the metal of his breastplate smacked against the tile flooring. The rest of his bulk she eased down after, but the noise might have already given them away. Even from his vantage point, Tatsu could see the unhappy purse of her lips.

She frantically waved them out from behind the corner.

"Hurry," she hissed and moved quickly down the hall, away from the guard. Tatsu sidestepped over the guard's body and hoped she'd merely put him to sleep. Thinking otherwise would make it too difficult to focus. It hadn't been the guard's fault he'd been stationed inside the castle, and he'd probably wished to be at the festival with the rest of the city.

The next hallway contained three doors that all looked the same to Tatsu, but Alesh seemed to know where she was going. She chose the middle door and repeated her earlier actions with the lock. This one took longer, and as the time crept by, Tatsu shoulders constricted tighter and tighter. Someone would notice the guard on the ground. Someone was going to find them, exposed and vulnerable in the corridor.

Somehow, blessedly, the lock snapped open.

Alesh pushed the door open and slipped inside, but even before Tatsu was through, the figures at the opposite end sprang into view.

"No," Leil whispered, her voice hitching. They had found a patrol in a place where they hadn't known it would be. They had mere moments before both guards turned toward them, but in that time, one of Tatsu's hands had already grabbed for his bow to ready it, the other halfway to his quiver.

Alesh sprang forward with her dagger outstretched, but she would never make it in time.

One of the guards shouted something in Runonian as he unsheathed his sword. The clack of metal hitting metal surrounded Tatsu's senses, reverberating through the hall as the soldiers began to move. Behind him, Ral whimpered in fear and confusion, and he pushed everything else out of his mind when he let his arrow fly.

It struck the guard on the left in the throat, and he dropped with a gurgle and a splash of red blood.

The kill bought them time when the second soldier paused to react, but before he could, Alesh was on him. Faster than Tatsu would have thought possible, she snaked around his figure and leapt up onto his back. Her dagger found the open space between his breastplate and his helm; he fell a few steps closer to them than the first guard had.

Everything was over in less than a minute, but the commotion would draw attention to them. Tatsu's hands were shaking so badly it took three tries to slide his bow into his harness.

"Let's go," Alesh said. She sounded only a bit out of breath as she cleaned the blood from her knife on the lower hem of her shirt. Leil and Ral surged forward to follow her, but Tatsu hung back, unable to tear his eyes away from the first guard, the one with the arrow still protruding from his throat. He knew he should get it and clean it to use later, but he couldn't move. He couldn't yank his gaze away.

He'd been hunting since he was ten using traps and bows and snares. He'd learned how to skin a hare before he'd learned how to read. He knew the feel of warm blood on his hands and the bitter taste of copper at the back of his throat, but he'd never known the sweeping, overpowering sensation of regret that tumbled over him.

This man was his first human kill.

A wave of emotion threatened to knock him backward as the figure of the guard began to blur the longer he stared, and at last he wrenched his eyes from it. The others were down the hall in front of him, paused and waiting. Tatsu dragged his arm across his eyes. It was enough. It would *have* to be enough. They had no more time to waste.

"I'm sorry," he gasped and stumbled away from the scene.

As soon as he reached the other three, Alesh turned and began to move again, but Ral's gaze followed him with open curiosity. Tatsu shook his head at her, painfully close to losing his composure once more. She leaned over and set her hand gently against his shoulder, her touch light and knowing, and when he glanced at her face, she nodded.

"Later," she whispered. It was the most aware thing she'd ever said to him, and that, more than anything else, pulled him out of his stupor.

He started after Alesh's sure-footed form, sucking in all the air his lungs could hold and keeping it there, waiting until his chest burned.

They reached another corner, and Alesh stopped short, nearly running into the stone wall in her hurry to cease her movement. She grabbed for Ral and slapped a hand across her mouth, the most forceful thing Tatsu had ever seen her do to her sister. Even in the dim torchlight, Alesh's dark eyes reflected terror.

He didn't dare ask what she'd seen in the other hallway. He pressed his body against the stone wall and breathed, slow and steady, afraid the pounding of his heart would give them all away.

A door closed and a lock slid back into place with a final *snick*, and then clacking footsteps moved away from their hiding spot—only one set of them. When he guessed they had made it halfway down the corridor, Tatsu risked looking around the corner.

A tall man with black hair tied back with a cord was walking toward a sharp corner in the corridor, his hands balled into confident fists at his side and his chin held high. Something buzzed at the back of Tatsu's awareness, and it shook him free of the wall. He pushed his face back against the stones and waited, trembling, until at the end of the hall the second door closing echoed.

Alesh let out a gasp as her body nearly collapsed to the floor in relief.

"That was him, wasn't it?" she asked, pressing the heel of her palms against her cheeks. "Zakio? He came out of the room we're heading for. He must have been checking on the siphon. Gods, that was close. We would have been found if it hadn't been for the guards."

Tatsu's throat closed up at the thought of the soldiers lying dead in the corridor behind them. As far as lucky breaks went, it was a gut-wrenchingly morbid one.

"He might come back," Leil said. Her voice, too, was shaking, even though she tried to school her face into something stronger. "We have to go now before he or his mother returns."

Alesh pushed herself back up from the wall and wiped her hands on her shirt. She checked around the corner a second time, clearly still rattled, and then waited for a pause before approaching the door Zakio had just come out of. She crouched down in front of the lock with her iron—Tatsu's every heartbeat pounding out another moment in which they could be found. There were bodies on the ground, and a trail of red betraying their path.

Somewhere up ahead, on his way out of the castle, walked a sadistic, powerful mage.

An angry snap sounded, and Alesh cursed softly, the iron in pieces in her hand.

"What—?" Leil started.

"Be quiet," Alesh hissed and slid a hand into her pack for another lockpick, this one thinner and more worn at the end.

Throat constricted, Tatsu nervously watched the shadows of the hall over his shoulder, cringing until the sound of the metal squeaking ceased. The door swung open with one final groan, and they were inside. He had hoped, stupidly, they'd found the end of it.

Instead, in front of them was a shimmering sphere of ice.

Chapter Ten

"WHAT IS THIS?" Alesh gasped. She stepped forward and almost tripped before stretching her hands out to touch it. Reflex, more than anything else, sent Tatsu lunging after her. They didn't know what the sphere was, other than it was magic and dangerous. He missed the back of her shirt, too late to stop her from pressing her hands against it.

His relief when nothing happened throbbed painfully.

"It's *cold*," Alesh said, her fingers gliding over the smooth surface. "It's solid ice."

Ral also seemed excited to touch it. She moved forward to push her palms against the surface and then laughed, delighted, moving around the curve of the barrier. Tatsu turned to Leil, veins still humming with nervous energy.

"Someone is going to find us," he said. "We need to get through this, and fast."

Leil's features hardened into a strange sort of frown. "Stand back." She held up a hand and with the other, lit a match with a quick strike against her leather belt. The flames jumped to her palm, hovering as if waiting to be commanded.

Alesh and Ral seemed reluctant but did what they were told and moved several paces back from the barrier. The fire between Leil's cupped hands grew larger and larger, whirling like a sea storm—she had to be feeding it more oxygen to increase it. The pull of the air was strong enough to capture Ral's loose hair and the feathers on Tatsu's arrows, tugging them all forward. When the eddy reached the size of a summer melon, Leil threw both arms forward, and the fire followed in a long channel.

Flames hit the ice with a loud, harsh squeal. Tatsu flung his arms up over his face when the heat of it bounced back at them, leaving him slightly breathless.

The icy wall remained standing when he lowered his hand.

"It's still there," Alesh said, mostly to herself. She turned on Leil, her face alight with anger. "You can't take it down? Have we come here for *nothing*?"

Leil ignored her. Sweat beaded beneath the scarf that covered the top of her forehead, and she didn't look up at any of them. When she raised her hands again, they were trembling slightly. She took several steps closer to the barrier. It appeared she was trying to manipulate the ice of the barrier itself, the strain on her face evident as she concentrated, *pulling*. When she yanked her arms back with a surprising amount of force, it seemed as though she expected the ice to follow, only nothing happened.

Her arms sank to her sides.

"No," Alesh said, and then again, with more force, "*no*. This can't—we can't get stuck here. We can't fail! We'll lose everything!"

"I...I can't," Leil told them.

Tatsu blinked back the hot sting behind his eyes. The weight of it settled around him all at once. They were going to fail. He was never going to be free. Without the siphon neutralized, they would go straight back into Aughwor Prison, and once the drain reached Chayd, it wouldn't matter where they were. Everything would be consumed and twisted, a mirror of the Weeping Forest.

Leil glanced at him, eyes narrowed and lips pursed.

To Tatsu's left, Ral was wringing her hands together. What would happen to her once both he and Alesh were arrested again? In the rare chance they could actually get back *out* of Yuse, they had nowhere left to go. They were still prisoners, and now, they had nothing to use as leverage.

Tatsu wasn't quite sure what he was doing when he started toward Ral, but he was determined not to go back to Dradela in chains. If they could get away, perhaps north, and Leil couldn't follow them—

Ral's eyes met his, and her hands stilled.

Then something within the ice sphere flashed, and Tatsu stopped in his tracks, staring at it. The warped and curved surface made it difficult to decipher anything. Then, flickering behind the translucent sheen, it seemed as if there could be something, or maybe he only felt it. Perhaps the movement stemmed from merely a trick of the light, but his bones reverberated with it, and a mumble shivered beneath his skin.

He moved forward to put his hand against the ice, and the barrier shattered around him.

Surely the sound shook the entire castle. In the roar, he could focus on nothing but the crash of the ice and the blinding light that accompanied it. He squeezed his eyes shut and threw his arm up to shield his face as the pieces of the barrier broke apart. They splintered and fractured until the wall was nothing more than dust settling on the stones of the floor. When the noise finally dissipated and the situation seemed safe enough to lower his arm, the ice had disappeared within the room, save for the thin powder dancing lightly around his boots.

Tatsu registered the rest of the room easily—several shelves, covered in bottles and glass vials, and in the middle, a high-backed wooden chair. Tatsu wasn't sure what he'd expected to find. A ball of energy, perhaps, or a large, enchanted gemstone, but definitely not this. The ice had concealed the true size of the room, and it was shockingly small to be housing something so important. Beside the chair were two small tables, each covered with several more bottles and a roll of linen.

Tatsu knew what he was going to see when he rounded the back of the chair, but the sight awaiting still struck him so hard he physically recoiled.

A young Runonian man sat slumped in the chair, unconscious and held up by a rope looped around his throat and the holes in the chair back.

"Gods," Alesh breathed, hands flying to her mouth. "I don't believe it."

The life siphon was a person.

As Tatsu leaned forward in horror, staring at the motionless figure, Alesh picked up one of the glass bottles on the closest small table.

"Tatsu," she said, low and urgent. It took some effort to tear his gaze away from the man in the chair, and when he finally did, she sniffed at the top of one of the vials and then raised the glass higher. "This is *itur*, from Joesar. This is—it's an incredibly potent poison. It renders the victim completely immobile. This is completely illegal."

She put it down and reached for another bottle. "And this is *umet*. This is all poison. It's all...there are so many black market toxins here, and I think they're using all of them together. I don't even recognize some of these. I don't know how he's even still *alive*."

He didn't look very alive. His hair, with ragged ends that fell halfway across his face, was completely white, as if all the color had been simply drained from it. His skin gleamed so pale Tatsu could partially see through it to the blue veins beneath. Stuck between his teeth was a piece of cloth, pulled around and tied behind his head. Tatsu started to reach for it and then stopped, realizing what it contained. Soaked with the noxious concoctions held in the nearby vials, if what Alesh said was true, the linen promised nothing but misery.

Tatsu stepped back, unable to completely tamp down his disgust.

"Tatsu," Alesh hissed. "These poisons are illegal everywhere. Why are they in the castle?"

He didn't have an answer for her. He paused, unable to get his mind to focus on the reality at hand. They had been so wrong. They had all been wrong.

Ral was hanging back, no longer appearing excited by the room. She seemed uneasy, glancing from side to side, and Leil—Leil was staring at the slumped, lifeless man with a stony resolve Tatsu had yet seen from her.

"Take him," she said, voice quiet.

"What?" Alesh started. "Are you kidding?"

But Leil's steady gaze never wavered. "He's the source of the siphon. We need to get him out of here."

"He's a *person!*" Alesh cried.

"Move," Leil ordered. She met Tatsu's eyes and didn't even blink. "They will find the dead guards. We've broken the barrier, and they'll know we're here. We have only minutes before we're all discovered."

She was right. Trying not to think too hard about it, Tatsu drew his knife out of its sheath and slid it beneath the cloth tied around the man's head and mouth. He took care not to touch the fabric with his bare hands but slid his knife through it with relative ease. The rope around the man's neck proved more difficult, but when Tatsu finished, nothing remained holding the man to the chair. His weight slumped forward, sliding almost to the floor before Tatsu could catch him.

"They will be upon us in a minute," Leil said. "Move. Quickly."

The young man was heavy but thin, with knobby joints and too-slender limbs. They must have been keeping him alive somehow, beneath all the poisons and toxins they put in his bloodstream, for he had to be alive to power the siphon. Tatsu groaned when he hoisted the man over one shoulder, the second heartbeat thudding there against his arm. He would have to escape the castle with the dead weight on his back.

As they ran into the main hallway, shouts sounded from around the corner and the haze of approaching torchlight bounced across the floor.

"They're here!" Alesh said, grabbing for Ral's hand. "We can't go back the way we came! Go to the left!"

Heavy footsteps of men wearing metal armor clattered in the hallway. Tatsu didn't dare look back to see how close they were, and the added weight of the man on his shoulder was already sending pangs down his spine. With Alesh in the lead, they raced down the hall and took the next corner. A harsh shout boomed, too close for comfort, and the added excitement of it caused Tatsu to take the turn too quickly, clipping the corner of the wall. Pain blossomed up through his elbow, but he clenched his teeth and kept going.

Runonian exclamations came from close by. Tatsu understood none of it until the cry in Common: "Thieves!"

"Which way?" Leil gasped, already out of breath.

"Left again," Alesh gritted out, but when she took the turn, she ran straight into a kneeling servant who was polishing the stones next to the wall. The two tumbled to the ground in a whirlwind of appendages, and the only way Tatsu could avoid joining the mess was to slide hard to the right. His boots squeaked angrily, and his knee twisted, but he did manage to keep himself upright. If he dropped the man thrown over his shoulder, he wasn't sure he'd be able to pick him back up.

"Go, go!" Leil cried. It took too much time for Alesh to scramble back to her feet, and the guards were gaining, dashing through the previous hallway. How would they find their way out? Tatsu's knee throbbed and his shoulders ached, and wherever they were heading, he just hoped it held the exit. Alesh was off and running again, but they'd lost precious time. The clanking of armor echoed too closely behind them.

The bewildered servant, still sprawled on the floor, yelled something at their retreating backs.

Another right turn, lungs burning. They managed to get down the subsequent staircase without falling, though Alesh almost ran into the wall again, and Ral let out a frightened little trill when they spun around the next corner at a breakneck pace. At the next junction, Alesh headed straight for the left-most door. She slammed into it with most of her weight, but instead of opening, her hands and shoulder smacked uselessly against it.

"Open!" she yelled, and Tatsu couldn't tell if it was a command or a question. All the breath left his lungs as the world stilled before it was obvious the door wasn't locked from the inside. Alesh got it open with just enough time for Tatsu to glance over his shoulder. The guards were there, turning the corner in pursuit. He had but a split second before one of them notched an arrow and fired. Tatsu threw himself to the left and the head of the arrow buried itself in the wood of the door panels.

"Split up!" he shouted to the other three, who were slipping out the doorway into the darkness of the city beyond. The guard was readying another arrow; a moment, no more, and Tatsu would have nowhere else to run. He spun and only just managed to keep the unconscious man's head from hitting the corner seam as Tatsu half lunged for the door.

He'd barely gotten through before the second arrow bounced off the stone wall behind him.

His eyes weren't ready for the sudden lack of light— the night black when he stumbled out of the castle. They were on the opposite side of the structure, but he didn't have the luxury of time to figure out where. He'd already lost sight of Leil and Ral ahead of him, and the stream of Alesh's hair was all that remained as she darted around the curved base of the nearest turret and disappeared.

Tatsu wouldn't be able to run for much longer. The bulk of the man on his shoulder was too much, and already, his arms were shaking with fatigue.

Instead of going forward, he went left, like a deer racing through the woods' invisible maze. If the guards expected them to make a clean break to the city, then he might have a chance to sneak past them by doubling back. Across the river, wooden buildings rose to meet the night sky, so he kept to the side of the castle and crept through the vines that curled into the dirt. A few reached to tug at his hair with soft laughter, but he didn't have the extra strength to shush them. As his eyes adjusted to the moonlight, he tried to steady and quiet his breathing as much as possible. He winced at the crunching beneath his boots, the result of so much additional weight.

The guards burst through the doorway in a cluster of shouts lost amidst the clamor of metal.

Tatsu pressed himself up against the side of the castle, squeezing his eyes shut and holding his last painful gulp of air. The guards split after a barked order, and, as he'd hoped, all three groups started for the river and the arched bridges leading beyond. He wouldn't have much time before more of them were called. The only reason they hadn't faced the entire royal battalion already was due to the combination of festival and catching them off-guard. Tatsu thought of the others. He hoped they'd have enough time to disappear, but getting out of Yuse was only the beginning.

They would have to return to Chayd with Runon's forces on their trail. Rushing through the Weeping Forest guaranteed a quick way to get them all killed, which meant they would need to take the pathways through the Turend Mountains.

When the guards' noisy footsteps had mostly faded away down the tapered city paths, Tatsu crept silently around the contour of the castle's smooth walls. Moving proved more difficult than he'd anticipated, keeping to the shadows without bashing the unconscious man's head against the stones, and the pain from his left shoulder throbbed all the way down his arm. The building he was hugging didn't meet back up with the high garden walls, but, instead, opened up into several smaller structures. Two steps toward them and the stench of manure assaulted his nose. These were the royal stables. His lungs screamed for air even as something quickened within him.

Someone smiled down on him. The smell of the horses would help to hide their own, at least for a little while, should the guards get dogs to track them. Tatsu moved to the well-worn wooden stables until his hand made contact with the siding, and he felt around until the door beneath his fingers swung forward.

Halfway through the stables, a figure emerged from between the stalls, outlined by the dim starlight streaming in from several long openings overhead.

"Ral," Tatsu gasped, and she turned to him.

"Tatsu, horses," she said, sounding happy. "Look."

Tatsu reached for her arm with his free hand. "Ral, *shh*. Come with me."

If she was there alone, then Alesh had somehow gone on without her in the frantic split. Alesh would never leave without her sister. Ral put them all in danger. Alesh would come to find her, even if it meant running straight back into the soldiers. Tatsu's lungs burned with exertion, but he moved Ral through the stables with quick, sure steps to the opposite side and a second set of doors.

Once outside, the sound of guards' voices and something high-pitched and piercing—like bowstrings far out of tune—reverberated through the night air. It took him too long to realize what the noise meant: the city alarm. They would have nothing to help them now. All the soldiers within Yuse, and the mages, would be summoned to track them down.

The sound shook him down to his bones trembling in his skin. He pulled Ral along after him toward one of the narrow streets leading to the houses at Yuse's city center.

As they made it onto the first road, Tatsu's twisted knee gave out. He collapsed against the side of the building—a storefront, dark within but still giving off the faint smell of drying herbs. Everything hurt. The throbbing in his knee matched the sharp pains running in his left shoulder, and he had to clamp his teeth together to muffle the moan swelling in his throat. There were footsteps somewhere nearby, an alley over, perhaps. *The guards.* He couldn't keep going. His fingers tightened around Ral's wrist in an unconscious apology. He wished he could have gotten her free. He wished he could save her, if no one else.

"Up," came the rasping, hoarse command from Tatsu's shoulder.

He jerked his chin up, more out of shock than compliance, and stared at the roofs. Their pitches were staggered in varying heights, overlapping against the sky, but on one of them, a figure was slinking noiselessly across the top beam.

The moon illuminated them, and it occurred to Tatsu how visible they were from the rooftops with nothing covering them. They stopped on the roof across from Tatsu. Their eyes met, and Tatsu's breath caught. The clanging of steel betrayed soldiers only seconds away from their position.

Alesh held his gaze and nodded, and the unspoken request—*take care of her*—hung in the air between them. In that moment, Tatsu couldn't tear his thoughts from her. The way her red blood had stained his fingers, the way her salty-slick bare skin had once felt beneath his own, the rough texture of her hair that had always made it so easy to plait... He tried to commit everything to memory.

He might never see her again, and all he could do was stare.

She stepped down hard on one of the roof tiles, sending it sliding and skittering down the slope until it crashed onto the street below.

The thudding of the armored steps immediately stopped, followed by several cries and shouts. Alesh ducked and took off in the opposite direction, across the slanted roofs, leading the soldiers away from them.

"Left," was the second order from the man slung over Tatsu's shoulder, his voice so rough Tatsu could barely decipher the word. Despite his overwhelming exhaustion, Tatsu stood, fingers still tight around Ral's wrist. Lost in Yuse's winding neighborhoods, he didn't know where to find the way out, but at least the streets were relatively empty. Alesh's obvious retreat had taken the majority of the guards toward the other end of the city, and the bulk of the festivalgoers were probably being kept outside while the soldiers searched. A wise tactic for cornering fugitives without having to deal with bystanders, but it also cleared out a path for their escape.

"Where are we going?" Tatsu asked through gritted teeth.

"The Shyreld," the man rasped, and then, as if those few words had been far too much, fell silent again. Tatsu kept them moving against the pain that flared up with every step. Ral remained quiet and didn't fight, but their progress was miniscule. In the distance, the exclamations of the guards sounded muffled and far, and Tatsu prayed Alesh had somehow gotten away.

She'd snuck her way out of more situations than he'd ever liked to think about, and now, he clung blindly to the desperate hope of it. Blind faith was all he had left. Everything else was too ragged and drained to focus on.

It might as well have been an eternity before they made it to the outskirts of the city. The sky above them would lighten soon with streaks of dawn, and they had to be far enough out by the time the sun rose to avoid being seen. They'd come to a part of the city with close-sitting, rickety shacks in varying states of disrepair, like the one they'd stayed in prior to their infiltration of the castle. Perhaps it would work in their favor to slip between the citizens as they returned from the festivities. The shacks situated nearest to the sloping mountainsides were the last vestiges of the capital before meandering pathways led up to the mine entrances nestled deep within. Going back over the Great Mountain Range would be impossible, but sliding along it over the useless, rocky hills was an option for getting away from the city, provided they avoided the small patches of cultivated land dotting the barer landscape.

But with each trudging step, Tatsu feared it would be his last. He could barely summon the energy to remember to breathe, and he let go of Ral's arm. The paths were more precarious than any they'd moved through yet and strewn with splintered old crates and food waste that stank of spoiled meat. It would have been difficult to move through it without making noise, even if he hadn't been at the end of his reserves.

Tatsu finally had to stop in front of the worst of the buildings. Pieces of the wood paneling were falling away completely to reveal a worn and dirty skeleton of notched, uneven beams beneath. Devoid of any signs of life, the structure had sunk inward, and the boards over the door were covered in a thick layer of dust long undisturbed.

"We have to stop," he said, and Ral didn't need any encouragement to go inside.

The house was deserted and full of cobwebs. Tatsu thought about apologizing for the stringy bits that caught in the man's face as he moved, but he simply didn't have enough energy. The stairs were creaky but stable enough to use, and on the top floor, he found a single large-size bed. Bowed in the middle, almost to the floor, the straw mattress sported a few thin moth-eaten blankets, but Tatsu had never been so happy to see a bed before. Relief hit him so hard he nearly dropped the man from his shoulder, just getting to the mattress before he did. The man's body bounced slightly on the straw and then settled, the mattress brushing so low it scraped the wooden floor. Tatsu froze when the room creaked low and long around them, but none of the floorboards splintered beneath their feet.

"Sleep now?" Ral asked, and Tatsu nodded, hardly hearing either her question or his own response to it.

"They might find us," he managed to get out, though he couldn't leave the building even if he wanted to—not now, not with so little left. He looked at the man strewn across the mattress exactly as he'd fallen and was surprised to find a pair of gleaming silver eyes open and looking up at him with obvious distrust.

"Don't give us away," Tatsu said. "Don't call them."

He got an unhappy half laugh in response, and the eyes never wavered in their gaze. "What do I have to go back to?"

"They'll track you."

"Only if I use magic," the man said, voice still like sandpaper.

"Don't use magic." Tatsu fell face-first onto one of the stale pillows and registered, in a fog, Ral climbing on the other side as well. He hoped she wouldn't run off if she woke. He wouldn't be able to stop her if she decided to leave.

The last thing he remembered before exhaustion claimed him was the stolen man's voice, words thick and strained, saying, "I can't."

Chapter Eleven

TATSU AWOKE WITH a start, blood pounding hard and sudden as the situation rushed back to him. He didn't know how long he'd slept, and he hadn't dreamt at all. For some reason, the absence of time felt worse than a nightmare would have. He couldn't immediately place where he was, even with straw poking through the fabric of his shirt. The shabby bed was warm with three bodies in it. Ral's rhythmic breathing lilted up at the end in a half-snore, and he turned over to find the third person already awake.

The man's eyes were open and staring at him, thinned at the corners beneath dark lashes.

"Sorry," Tatsu said, without really knowing why. There seemed to be little else he could say for the night before, and he still wasn't sure what they were going to do. He'd expected to leave with something he could hold in his hand or stash in his pack. And as his mind caught up with the reality, his heart sank. Alesh and Leil were gone, and he had no idea if they were still alive.

They had to get out of Runon.

The man didn't respond to his apology, and the hard distrust in his eyes didn't waver.

"It's almost night," Tatsu said after a quick glance out the shuttered windows. "It will be easier to sneak out in the gloom."

"Are you going to kill me?" the other man asked. He sounded better, as if the rest had helped his throat, but his voice still croaked, rusty with disuse.

Tatsu jerked in surprise. "I'm going to take you to Chayd. I'm not going to kill you."

Even if Alesh was...gone, Tatsu needed the bounty to be granted his freedom. If he was the only one left, he needed to take care of Ral. The siphon's true nature didn't matter. He still had to deliver the threat to the queen.

He received no response to his statement and wasn't sure if the silence meant that the man believed him or not. Either way, it didn't change the facts. Tatsu sat up, wincing as his sore muscles protested. It would be painful to use them as much as he needed to without another day or two of rest. He pressed his fingers against his calves and thighs, breathing through the dull throbs his actions produced. His knee, though still smarting, seemed to be a twist rather than a dislocation, and he was thankful for small favors.

"I assume you can't walk on your own," Tatsu said to the Runonian man.

"I'd like to see *you* try after that torture," came the growled reply. The man's fingers twitched, which Tatsu took as a good sign. If he could at least move those, the rest of his control would likely come back in time.

"You told me to go to the Shyreld," Tatsu said, changing the topic. "How do you know that's the best way out?"

The man's face darkened. "Because I know Runon."

"How?"

He received no answer, only a glare. Tatsu sighed, rolling his shoulders back and forth. They, too, ached fiercely, and if the man was still unable to walk, Tatsu was going to be carrying the weight again. He was not looking forward to pushing his body beyond its comfortable limits.

"Look, I'm not your enemy," Tatsu said. "I'm trying to get you out of here. Whatever was going on back there…"

The other man's fingers twitched again, but it seemed to be the extent of what he could move. "I don't want to talk about it."

"You don't have to. I'm trying to…help."

"Help," the man said, voice very flat.

Self-consciousness crept up and heated Tatsu's face. "Yes, help."

Quiet fell around them. Outside, someone was walking with an uneven, stumbling gait, approaching the house. A low murmur floated up, but then slowly moved away with the footsteps, and Tatsu's jaw unclenched.

"I'm Tatsu," he said, trying to ignore the gnawing feeling within. He didn't really blame the man for not trusting him. "Do you have a name?"

"It doesn't matter," the other man replied. "Not anymore."

Beyond the broken windowpane, the sky was still smeared with the reds of sunset, but the edges were darkening to purple and navy. On the opposite side of the bed, Ral sat up with a hand dragging across her face and hair tangled above her ear. She blinked, slowly, and looked at Tatsu before recognition seemed to dawn.

"Go soon?" she asked with a bit of a whine. "Hungry."

"We all need to eat something," Tatsu agreed, and then, looking at the third, motionless figure, added, "even you."

There was no answer. Tatsu would have thought the man asleep except for his still open eyes. Everything about his expression was guarded.

"Are you ready?" Tatsu asked. The only reply he got was a harsh, mirthless laugh.

THEY TRAVELED OUT of Yuse under the cover of darkness. Tatsu had never been to the Shyreld: the snowy stretch of undulating valleys and plateaus reaching up into mountain peaks. He knew where it was, however, so he kept them moving east toward the border, to where the hills of Runon met up with the higher, rockier mountains. Neither Runon nor Chayd could claim ownership of the Shyreld's coniferous-dotted ridges. This land of sparse vegetation and thin-air altitudes was under control of the nomadic clans that had always lived there. They traveled throughout the area with their families until the winter winds forced them together into the longest valley, half-protected from the freezing winds. For the most part, the clans kept to themselves, but occasionally traders ventured down into Dradela's markets with sleek furs and heavy pelts.

The man weighed heavily on his shoulder. Now that his consciousness had returned, Tatsu slung his length across his back rather than carrying him like a hunting prize. Tatsu's lower back ached within the hour, and the pressure on his knees flared up like hot flames through his hips.

The other man remained silent as they traveled. Tatsu wasn't sure if it was from embarrassment or ire, but either way, it kept their party quiet, and the silence was safer. Leaving Yuse and heading into the lands outside meant they'd lost the cover the buildings had provided, but they also had much less risk of running into anyone else. The singing foliage provided a bit of protection once they got past the rows of fields stretching out from Yuse's borders.

The landscape gradually changed. The trees—still impossibly green and filled completely with perfect, cookie-cutter leaves—continued to whisper above their heads. More than once, Tatsu had to duck down to avoid the spindly branches reaching for his hair. As they continued, the unblemished leaves were replaced with dark-colored needles and full, round cones. Grass faded away beneath their feet, replaced with more rock than dirt, and the spreading shadows stretched and spun with the rotation of the moon overhead. Little farming happened on the barren soil leading up to the tall peaks, and the only sign of human life was the well-worn pathway. The group walked along the deeply embedded cart ruts for a short while before branching off into a grove promising cover.

Tatsu knew they would have problems come daylight. They needed to rest, all of them, even with the slow and steady pace he'd been forced to adopt in order to keep his muscles from seizing. But they only had his single pack, with his single bedroll, and not nearly enough food for all of them to split. They used half of his remaining supplies during their small meal in the dead of night, when not even the insects were chirping.

He wasn't sure how far they made it the first night, but as the morning streaked over the mountaintops in front of them, he asked.

"We're still in Runon," the nameless man informed him. His arms dangled over Tatsu's shoulders, and were it not for the occasional twitch of fingers, Tatsu would have thought the limbs completely unresponsive.

"We need to stop soon," Tatsu said, "and find something else to eat."

He had only one cover to sleep beneath, but as he looked at the clear sky, it seemed they might not need it. Tatsu couldn't scent anything on the breeze alluding to more rain, and there were no billowy clouds, which often signaled a change in weather. He chose an open spot within a cluster of fir trees littered with pinecones but otherwise fine, and Ral helped him pick up the curved cones to clear the area. There were enough trees to conceal them, provided no one else shared their idea of sneaking through the woods.

"There's no way they aren't already on our trail," Tatsu said. It was actually the lack of guards behind them that worried him most. If he didn't know where they were, he couldn't prepare for anything, and the last thing they needed was to be surprised into a chase they couldn't possibly escape from.

The other man, however, seemed less worried. "Your friend led them in the opposite direction. They probably assumed we all went the same way, and she was simply the last one. It will be awhile before they figure out they were wrong."

"How do you know all this?" Tatsu inquired.

"I don't," the man said coolly. "But I can make a pretty good assumption about it."

The finality in his tone urged Tatsu to change the topic.

"And you're sure they can't track you if you don't use magic?"

The look he got in response appeared deeply annoyed. If nothing else, the man had figured out very quickly how to regain muscle control in his face.

"They're still going to find us eventually," Tatsu said after a long pause, waiting for his companion's reply that never came.

"Then I guess you have to hope we are far enough away by then," the man snapped.

The hairs on Tatsu's arms had been standing up since they'd snuck out of the dilapidated house in Yuse, but he couldn't pinpoint any direct threat. Besides the laughing tree cover, no nearby noises signaled any life. He spent some time with his senses focused outward, pushing through his exhaustion, but still came up empty. If anyone was following them, they were hiding too adeptly for him to detect.

He left Ral and the man alone, venturing off to track down sustenance, and ended up with a decent amount of snowberries on thin branches and a handful of edible leafy greens. He moved carefully around the singing plants, wishing to avoid any unpleasant run-ins with sentient trees. None of what he found would give them much lasting energy, but it was certainly better than nothing. He didn't dare make a fire for fear the smoke would give them away, so they ate everything raw. The berries were sticky and slightly bitter, and the pits stuck in his back teeth.

Ral looked happier, though she gestured at her boots while struggling to remove them. "Help? Too tight!"

Tatsu tugged the shoes free, and she wiggled her sock-covered toes in the air.

"Just don't step on any pine cones," he cautioned her.

"Ouch," she replied with a lopsided grin but stood up anyway. "Be careful!"

Something tugged within—a memory, maybe, or a fearful vision of the future without Alesh there to care for her. Ral had always been impetuous and brave. She was the only person Tatsu knew who still looked at the world in wide-eyed wonder.

Tatsu brushed his fear aside as he studied the loose hairs hanging down her back. Ral beamed back at him, still wiggling her toes.

When he sat back on his heels, he found the Runonian man watching him with narrowed eyes.

"You're from Chayd," the man said in his still-hoarse voice. "Why did you come to Runon?"

"Because the drain was going to hit Chayd." Tatsu figured the simplest answer was probably the easiest. "It was going to wipe out the entire kingdom and ruin most of what we rely on for food."

"You Chaydese," the man snarled. "You're so flighty as a people. Why don't you just run away, then, and save yourselves?"

"I'm not—" Tatsu stopped himself so quickly his teeth snapped together. The man raised one eyebrow and leveled Tatsu with a long look full of smug anticipation, and it took Tatsu another second to finish. "...flighty."

Oppressive silence hung heavy around them before the man said, "So I guess that makes you some kind of hero."

It sounded more like an insult than anything else.

"Then I suppose that makes *you* some kind of a weapon," Tatsu shot back, and to his surprise, the other man laughed. The distinctly unhappy sound rang with something hidden in its depths.

"You're right," he said. "That's what I am. A weapon. A *sacrifice*. They bled me dry for everything they could get out of me, and then they kept going, until there was nothing but an empty shell they had to refill just to keep alive."

The man's silver eyes were blazing with long-simmering rage, bubbling over the surface; his words, spat out like poison, were little hisses of loathing.

"Do you know what it's like?" he asked. "Do you have any idea what it is to be nothing more than a tool, something to use until it's no longer worth anything?"

Stunned, Tatsu didn't answer, and this seemed to amuse his companion further.

"So, hero, what do you make of your choice now?" he continued, a barbed taunt. "I knew you were coming—I could feel you, all of you. They took away almost everything I had, but they left a vague awareness out of cruel spite. I knew you were coming for me. And I let you take me."

"How did you know we weren't coming to kill you?"

The man's eyes were bright and hard when he replied, "I didn't."

WHEN HE SLEPT, Tatsu dreamt of his father. He pushed open the door of his cottage in the woods to find him cooking there like he used to before he got sick. It smelled gamey. A hare, perhaps, and with it, the air carried a faint bit of seasoning herbs. Tatsu wanted to cry from the comfort the familiar smell brought. It had been a long time since he'd felt relief so strong. He stepped forward, and his father turned to face him with a soft smile, the same smile Tatsu had always known, the one that crinkled at the edges and reached all the way up to his eyes.

"It's almost time," his father said.

Tatsu looked to the spit over the smoldering embers. "To eat?"

"I think everything turned out wrong," the dream-memory of his father said, sounding sad and casting his eyes to the dirt-strewn floor.

"It smells fine. Why are you worried about it?"

"Wake up," his father told him.

Tatsu opened his eyes to Ral sitting over him, bits of flyaway hair glowing bronze in the bright colors of the setting sun. "Wake up!" she repeated.

A ball of disappointment lodged behind Tatsu's sternum, aching in time with his heartbeat. Reality came crashing back: his father was gone, and they were in a precarious position. Tatsu pushed himself up on his elbows, and Ral sat back, a thoughtful expression on her face.

"Worried?" she asked.

Tatsu dragged a hand over his mouth, wishing he could do something to suppress the nervous clenching in his gut. "I'm always worried. I'm afraid there might be someone behind us."

"Bad man," Ral told him with a nod full of finality. "Bad man behind us."

Tatsu's thoughts whirled. "You're saying that the bad...that Zakio is behind us?"

"No," Ral answered, maddeningly unhelpful. She blinked owlishly at him and then smiled as she stood.

"Time to go," she announced, and the surrounding trees waved their branches back and forth, giggling as they swayed, the knots in their trunks seeming to rise in knowing smiles. Uneasy, Tatsu looked across the way to find their third-party member struggling to pull himself up, struggling with muscles that had been too long in disuse. His strain was evident by the sweat already beaded on his forehead, features pinched tight in frustrated pain.

"Shove off," he growled as Tatsu moved to try to help him. He even tried to swat but didn't have the strength or control to do it. Tatsu had to haul him by his underarms anyway.

"Need to take a piss," the man mumbled, angry.

Tatsu maneuvered him, half dragging and half walking, into the trees, and politely looked away, arms still looped around the man's chest, while the other fumbled for his belt. His fingers still didn't seem to respond as he might have hoped.

"Give me a break," the man replied to the awkward silence. "It's been years since I had to do this."

"Years?" Tatsu started and nearly dropped the extra weight. "That's impossible. How did they keep you alive?"

Finished, the other man was focusing on refastening the leather. "They fed me poison after poison to starve my magic. You had to have seen it all there."

"You can't live on poison, so that doesn't answer my question."

He got a sneer in response. "How do you think the siphon started? It was the magic's last desperate attempt to keep me alive. Oh, they gave me food and water until their gamble worked, but only ever enough to keep me from dying. The bare minimum. It's more than I could say about my dignity."

"But you said it's been years," Tatsu said. "How many?"

"Since the day I turned eighteen, so...three?"

Tatsu helped him back to the clearing where Ral was attempting to tie her boots.

"You'd have to be an incredibly powerful mage to be able to sustain yourself like that," Tatsu said, frowning as the other man tumbled to the ground in a somewhat undignified heap.

"I am," he replied with force and then appended, "I *was*, at least. I was the strongest mage Runon had ever seen."

"And humble," Tatsu added, raising his eyebrows.

Despite his current situation, unable to even walk on his own and still ragged, with long strands of drained-white hair in his eyes, the other man held his chin high. "I didn't *need* to be humble. I'd been trained my entire life to be the most powerful magic-user in the world. I was unparalleled."

But as Tatsu looked at him, he could see the cracks in the bravado, the seams torn apart by betrayal and unspeakable torture. The vulnerability exposed there made Tatsu uncomfortable, but he couldn't quite get himself to look away. Beneath the haughty attitude was a pair of very frightened, distrustful eyes, burning right through to Tatsu's soul.

"And now you're here," Tatsu said, quietly.

"Yeah," the man agreed, chin still lifted. "Life's *funny* that way, isn't it?"

Looking at his own situation, Tatsu couldn't think of a worse way to describe it.

Chapter Twelve

TATSU STOPPED THEM once outside a hunter's cottage to lift items that had been left out overnight. The newest member of their party had only a white tunic and loose-fitting linen pants. He was going to freeze before they even got to the Shyreld, so Tatsu pushed aside the pang of guilt. The iron-dotted trekking boots could be replaced easily in Yuse, and the fur-lined shirt helped to disguise the man's thinness. He thought about dropping a few coins on the doorstep but decided against it.

The Chaydese coppers would give them all away.

After the cottage, little life dotted the path. The lands near the border with the Shyreld became rockier as they followed the ghost of a path gradually taking them up into the slopes. It had been abandoned many years ago when the relationship between Runon and the rest of the world grew too uncertain to continue trading, but the trail remained intact enough to pick their way across. The elevation change, however, proved hard on Tatsu's knees; his thighs and lower back burned with every step as their pace slowed further and further.

They had to stop often to let Tatsu catch his breath. Frustration swelled within him, but with each turn, the path worked itself further up the mountains, and he knew they would not return to the smaller hills. Minutes of tortured walking stretched into never-ending hours guided by starlight, through ridges Tatsu thought would never end. Little by little, each peak came into view, and then there was another behind it, in an endless sea of stone.

Eventually, he stopped them again, and even filling his lungs with air was painful. He bent over as far as he could without the man on his shoulder falling forward and tried to steady himself. His legs were trembling from exertion, and although his burden didn't say anything about it, Tatsu knew the vibrations had to be shaking through him too.

"Tatsu okay?" Ral asked as he struggled to breathe deeply enough to satisfy his body's demands. "Breathe now?"

"No," Tatsu managed to grind out. One side of the mountain's stone face rose close enough for him to press his hand against, and having support seemed to loosen some of the tension. Still, remaining upright was a struggle.

With an arm looped around Tatsu's neck, the man's fingers flexed slowly, his fingernails scraping a bit against it.

"Put me down," he said, more of a demand than a suggestion.

"No," Tatsu repeated, not able to force any more words out.

"You're exhausted." A scowl was clear in his tone. "Put me down."

Tatsu so badly wanted to comply. He was almost convinced it was the best idea when the rock beneath his boots began to quake. It took all his control to keep from falling forward. He took a quick step to stabilize his balance, and then, when the tremor reversed, rocking him, he stumbled backward.

"What is this?" he gasped. "Earthquake?"

"Stop!" Ral cried out. She crouched on the ground, fixing most of her balancing problems. Tatsu couldn't do the same with the man on his back, so he braced himself with both hands against the nearest rock face as the mountains trembled for another long stretch before stilling completely again.

Tatsu waited before trusting the shaking was over. "Where did that come from?"

"Nota and Zakio," the man on his shoulder replied. His voice sounded different; the sneer had disappeared.

"That was *mages*?" Tatsu asked in disbelief.

"They're very angry. They must have figured out your friend led the soldiers the wrong way. By now, they've realized I could be anywhere."

Tatsu's heartbeat quickened again. "Was the earthquake a direct attack? Do they know you are here?"

"I don't think so," the other man replied. "I suspect this was just the furious rattling we happened to feel."

Somehow, that knowledge didn't make Tatsu feel much better. He took a hesitant step forward to test the path again, and high above their heads, he heard a deep, bone-rattling rumble. It reverberated through the stones in an overlapping chorus of echoes, rock thudding against rock. On impulse, he craned his head skyward.

"Tatsu," the man on his shoulder said, but Tatsu was so caught up in the clatter of noise above them he barely even registered the use of his name. "I think you might need to start running."

A violent crack boomed and then a monstrous roar as the rocks began to tumble down the slope toward them. Tatsu didn't need any further encouragement. He sprang forward with more energy than he thought he had left, knowing only how badly they needed to keep going along the path or risk being stranded within Runon's borders. His knees throbbed with each step, but he didn't dare breathe or pause. The rockslide was headed right down to the path they were now rushing to cross.

With Ral in front, they took the next corner only to find themselves skidding across a precarious cliffside. The old pathway stretched across the cliff with a sheer drop on the left and the thundering avalanche on the right. Ral managed to stay upright as she shot across it, but Tatsu wasn't as lucky. His bad knee twisted again as he tried to push his body too hard. Even with the fire in his blood, he couldn't remain standing as his leg gave away beneath him.

Tatsu cried out when he fell, but the crash of the rockslide swallowed the noise. His left shoulder hit first, and the stolen man flew off as they both tumbled and began to roll. Tatsu stopped himself by slamming both palms down against the path, but the other—

The force of the fall propelled him straight off the side of the path and the cliff, and he was helpless to stop the movement. A sharp cry sounded, and then there was only the roar of the avalanche again. The panic was enough to spur Tatsu into action. He threw his body across the path and ignored the sting of the ground and pebbles tearing into his forearms.

How he grabbed the man's hands before he fell completely down the rocks, he didn't know. But he clamped his fingers so tightly around the clammy wrist he was sure he was cutting off all the circulation to the man's fingers. His right shoulder slid out of place in an agonizing pop, and still, he hung on. The thundering rocks would be on them in moments, while below, the jagged stones promised a sure, messy death.

"Tatsu!" Ral shrieked behind him.

Fingers gripped his hand, tight and trembling. Looking down at the man, fear and desperate, terrified frustration were evident on his features. Tatsu ignored the pain shooting through his arms in order to count in his head one second, and then another, before he wrenched the Runonian back up onto the path with every ounce of strength he had remaining. He didn't manage to get him all the way, but Ral appeared beside him, and she dragged the man's legs up and over the side.

Every muscle in his body was screaming, but they couldn't remain there with the rocks still bearing down on them. Already, smaller ones were flying down from the incline—one narrowly missed Tatsu's cheek, and a second hit him squarely in the chest, almost knocking the wind from his lungs. He grappled for the man's useless body and, with Ral's help, dragged him away from the sheer cliff and back to the safer zone between stone.

A second later, and the rockslide crashed down across the pathway where they had been only seconds before and continued down the cliff.

Tatsu collapsed and took one heaving, burning breath before he vomited. His head was ringing, and his stomach clenched again, emptying its meager contents onto the ground. Numb, he pushed himself away from the mess and slid down the rock. He gasped in whatever air he could, though his vision blurred.

Across from his position, the Runonian was doing the same thing. Their gazes locked, tears shimmering on the other man's face.

"You should have let me die," he rasped, though it lacked heart.

"Maybe," Tatsu replied.

"Safe now," Ral said and knelt beside Tatsu. "No more rocks."

Tatsu reached out to grab Ral's hand, squeezing it tightly. "Thank you."

She just gave him another enigmatic smile and slowly pulled her hand away. They stayed there for a long time, struggling to find the energy to keep going, even long after the dust from the rockslide had dissipated.

AFTER THAT, THEY made slow progress to the border between Runon and the Shyreld. The mountains to their left grew taller, until they nearly touched the stars in the sky, and the sides of the peaks were dotted, and then coated, with a layer of white snow. The air grew cold and biting, Ral's cheeks stained a permanent red.

They had to take frequent breaks as they progressed, and Tatsu's body was nearing the breaking point. Even with the quick naps he took each time they stopped, it was impossible to continue the way they were. As dawn arrived again, the man slung across Tatsu's shoulders said, "We're almost to the border now."

Relief didn't seem to help the pain in Tatsu's joints. "We need to rest. It will be daylight soon."

He set the man down on the ground. The pain in his shoulders flared up again as soon as the weight was off, worse without the pressure, and it pounded in time with his heart until the edges of his vision went red.

"Ral, I need you to stay here, okay?" he said, trying to keep himself steady. "I need you to watch over him."

She nodded, expression serious, and settled down next to the immobile man.

"Where are you going?" he asked, sounding very tired.

"To find us a place to rest," Tatsu told him. Everything felt different here, and the feeling had started well before the rockslide. He couldn't get a read on the mountains. The sparse vegetation growing along the sides the path was little more than reedy weeds, and while he thought he should be glad to no longer hear the unnatural singing of the trees, the silence summoned worse fear. Somehow, he'd actually grown accustomed to the tree's voices.

His body was in so much misery it took several tries to even reach out and note the things around him. He closed his eyes and tried to settle his senses. There wasn't much within the stone, but traders had once used the road to sell their goods.

It took him about twenty minutes to find the cave in the mountainside, half-hidden behind several boulders. He didn't think anything remained inside, because the season was well past both hibernation and cub-bearing, but he checked anyway, and found it long since deserted by whatever had used it. Bits of molted fur littered the ground, and he left them there, hoping the scent would scare off any smaller animals wishing to join them.

When he returned to the others, he found the Runonian struggling up on his elbows again—and failing—and Ral sitting patiently with her arms looped around her knees.

"Come on," he said and hauled the man up onto his back, promising himself it was only a short while longer. "I've found us a place to stay."

Ral seemed happy when they got to the cave.

"Bears!" she said and grabbed a bit at Tatsu's arm with too-sharp nails. "Babies?"

"Not anymore," he told her, "but maybe in the past, yes."

He shifted the man down on the ground, and then he pulled out his pack. He didn't have much that would burn, but he always kept a bit of kindling with him. It was an old rule his father had made when he was young: be prepared for anything. He tugged out several handfuls of wood shavings and half an old book. The pages and chips would give them something, at least.

Once Tatsu had the fire going and had checked to make sure it wouldn't jump outside the small circle of rocks he'd made, he pulled out the remainder of their food supplies. He sectioned out a bit of what they had, though they probably needed all of it to regain their strength. His stomach was growling too much for the handful of dried jerky strips to satiate it.

"You're resourceful," the man said when Tatsu handed him his share of the rations.

Tatsu glanced up but couldn't get anything from his expression. "It comes in handy."

"I bet it does," the man replied, maddeningly neutral.

They ate the rest in silence. When they were finished, Tatsu stoked the fire and decided to leave it going. Hopefully, it would scare off any other beast wanting to use their new cave, and the paper wouldn't burn for long.

He'd nearly fallen asleep when he was roused by a commotion across the circle of embers. He leapt up, senses singing on alert, until he realized it was just the Runonian. He'd slapped a palm against the side of the cave, and the action echoed through the rock. He was half off the ground, held up by a single trembling elbow, his body shaking with exertion. Though he smacked the wall again, the wobble in his body wasn't entirely from strain. He was crying, shoulders shaking with sobs.

Tatsu moved across to him, but as soon as his hands hit the man's back, they were violently shrugged off. "Go away!" he rasped, emotion choking him.

He tried to get himself up again, but it was a lost cause. His arm gave out, and he fell to the ground, face first, tears mingling with the dirt and streaking on the underside of his chin.

Tatsu tried again, and this time, his assistance wasn't rejected.

"You shouldn't be so hard on yourself," he said softly and got an angry gasp of a laugh in response.

"This is degrading. Look at what I've become. The most powerful mage in Runon—and now I'm an invalid. *Useless.*"

Slowly, Tatsu eased him up so he was sitting with his back against the cavern wall.

"Your muscles should come back, but you have to be patient," Tatsu told him. "Look at what we went through. Your body is exhausted, and your mind is too. Pushing yourself is only going to hurt your body further."

The man's head was back against the rock, chin high, his silver eyes fluttering closed. He laughed again, hoarse and angry. "I'm not sure I really care anymore."

"Then you're letting them win," Tatsu said and frowned.

"Haven't they already?"

Tatsu's eyes were heavy and threatening to close, but he shifted so he was kneeling in front of the other, who was staring up at the ceiling with obvious surrender. "I can't speak for you, but I can't imagine you'd want the people who did this to you to feel like they won. I know it's..." He stopped, contemplating. "It's actually hard to keep going like this without knowing your name."

"Yudai," the man said. He sounded lost, his throat full of emotion. "My name is Yudai."

Tatsu could only stare. Sitting in front of him was a man devoid of strength, hair white with trauma and the siphon's aftermath. His posture slumped and defeated; his face, with its high-defined cheekbones and slender nose, slack with grief. A hair-raising shock, like lightning, seemed to run through the man's veins, but maybe Tatsu was imagining that. Maybe he was projecting something onto the forlorn figure because he knew the name. He'd heard it before, because they all had—whispers remaining even after the kingdom had pushed away the rest of the world.

The name of the king's only son.

"Gods," Tatsu breathed into his hands. "You're the prince of Runon."

"Don't," Yudai snapped, eyes hard. "Don't you dare look at me with pity."

Tatsu shook his head. "I'm not."

He was telling the truth. He felt no pity when he looked at the man now glaring at him, Yudai's foolish pride still boiling despite everything. There was something primal in the way Yudai pushed back against help and sympathy, something that reminded Tatsu of wounded predators in the woods. He was cornered and limping but still dangerous. He had been carved from sharp teeth and hard claws designed for fighting.

"Stop it." The paleness of his complexion made the color on his cheeks stand out all the more.

"Sorry," Tatsu said automatically and tore his eyes away. "It doesn't change anything."

"It should," Yudai replied. "I'm a prince. I'm *royalty*."

It was biting and acerbic and entirely bravado, and the snub made Tatsu's chest swell with something he couldn't name. Silence stretched between them, rife with fear. Yudai had left himself vulnerable. When Tatsu looked back at him again, only dread glimmered, reflected in Yudai's eyes. What a harrowing kind of terror to be entirely at someone else's mercy when you didn't even have the strength to try to get away.

"Well, I suppose you'll be rather useless at hunting and cooking, then," Tatsu said, keeping his voice light. He thought perhaps he should be wary of this man who had the power to sentence them all to a quick death for their crimes, but he couldn't muster it. His heart went out to the half-broken figure in front of him, who had lost everything. Tatsu took it all in, letting it bottle up inside him. He didn't fear this prince.

Undisguised gratitude flooded Yudai's features but was schooled quickly into indifference. "I wouldn't know a thing about any of that, naturally."

"Royalty is a bit hopeless," Tatsu commented.

Yudai snorted. "Well, we have many better things to be doing."

"Like sleeping, I hope," Tatsu said, rising to his feet. "We have another long night waiting for us if we're going to get moving across the Shyreld, and we all need our rest."

He held out a hand to assist Yudai in scooting away from the wall and resuming his horizontal position on the floor, and fingers in his lingered just a second too long. *Thank you*, the gesture seemed to say, and then Yudai's hand retreated.

"Tonight..." he started.

"I'll wake everyone when the sun goes down," Tatsu said.

Yudai's mouth pinched at the corners, but he was clearly struggling against sleep the same as Tatsu. His body, free of the toxins and poisons and control mechanisms he'd been under, needed just as much rest to right itself and fix the damage as Tatsu and Ral did to keep moving.

Tatsu slowly lowered his body to the ground, and as he did, he glanced over at Ral's curled form. Her eyes were open and gazing back at him. She gave him a slow, closemouthed smile and closed her eyes again to nuzzle her face into the crook of her arm, as if she hadn't been awake at all.

"You—" Yudai began from across the embers.

Tatsu, still staring at Ral's figure, cut him off. "Good night, Your Highness."

Chapter Thirteen

WHEN THEY STARTED up again, it didn't take long for the mountain pathway to deposit them in a wooded area that, according to Yudai, shouldered up to the border of the Shyreld itself. The resurgence of cheerily singing trees was jarring, but Tatsu's body was so tired he found himself paying little attention to it as it fell away at the back of his awareness.

The trees offered a positive change as well. Tatsu left the other two alone for a short time to go hunting and returned with a large-eared hare. It was gamey and tough, and he had to start a fire to cook it, which opened up the possibility of being seen. But the renewed burst of energy from fresh food seemed to help all of them, and Tatsu had been in desperate need of the rest.

By the middle of the night, the snow Tatsu had seen for days on the mountain peaks found its way down to their path. He stopped the group again, when the sky was at its darkest, not wholly trusting that the light from the makeshift torch he'd lit wouldn't give them away. The boots they'd snagged for Yudai hadn't come with socks, and in the continuing temperature drop, they needed to do something about it.

Tatsu had several strips of hard leather for fixing snapped belts, and straps, and a roll of linen fabric. It would have to do.

"Stay still," he instructed Yudai, who was fussing and pushing himself up into a seated position. He managed that, though his legs were slow to respond. "We'll wrap your feet with these and put the shoes back on. They were a little big anyway."

When it became obvious Yudai couldn't quite get the boots off by himself, Tatsu was rewarded with a low, frustrated growl.

"I told you to pace yourself." Tatsu frowned and leaned in to help. "After what you went through..."

"What I went through." Yudai laughed. "Do you know what they called the chair they chained me to? They called it my 'throne.' It was a joke to them."

"That's..." Tatsu started and then quieted, sitting back. His veins froze with a harsh and angry burst of renewed loathing.

Yudai leaned forward with a manic look in his eyes. "Do you know the first thing they took away? My voice. But they left my awareness enough so I would register the pain. They laughed every time I tried to scream without sound. They starved my body for months, *years*, before they figured out the formula they needed. Before the toxins and my magic together were pushed to the breaking point, and then...that was it."

"How did they keep the siphon outside of Runon?" Tatsu was horrified and curious despite himself.

"They controlled my magic through the poison. They could manipulate my magic just like any other life energy once they changed enough of its chemistry. They're powerful, but they were afraid of me."

"Why?"

Yudai's too-pale features darkened. "I was stronger than them. But that's not why they needed me gone. I'm the king's son. There's magic in the royal bloodline now."

"You mean..." Tatsu said slowly, trying to put the pieces together. "...they didn't want royalty to have magic?"

"Why would they? Mages are rarely born nobles. They're born common, like most people. It's only because of their magic that they're given their high status and wealth, and only because the crown needs the services they provide. But if the king has that power himself..."

Tatsu sat back on his heels. "They aren't needed. The demand for their magic is gone."

"And they go back to being *nothing*."

Tatsu thought about the golden cuffs Leil wore beneath her dark robe. All the riches in the world wouldn't mean much if you were at the beck and call of the crown. He didn't want to feel anything for mages capable of such cruelty, but an inkling of sympathy throbbed beneath his ribs.

"You said you were better than them," Tatsu ventured, uneasy.

Yudai laughed again, rougher this time. "I was. That's the irony, isn't it? I'm free, but I still can't use it. I can't use my own magic because of what they've done to me. They've locked me out. They've broken me."

His face twisted further as he added, "But I can still feel it there, at the sides of my consciousness. They always did leave that part alone. I know it's still there."

Tatsu stared at the leather of his boot, where the material had worn shiny from use.

"The mage with us earlier, she called you *soelm*." Tatsu raised his gaze back up. "That's the Chaydese word for mages like you."

Yudai smiled, and even in the dim light of the torch, the rage was clear in it.

"There is no word for mages like me," he hissed and then fell mute, stewing in his memories. Tatsu let him be.

How the man was moving *any* of his body after so long was a mystery, but from a magic that responded to starvation with a life drain, perhaps anything was possible. The idea of a force so powerful it refused to let its host die terrified him—in the hands of the wrong person, such power could destroy the world. Tatsu thought of Zakio and the aftereffects of his rage on Akao's face back in Yuse and had to push back the resulting fear.

Tatsu busied his hands with unrolling the linen and preparing the leather strips in an attempt to focus his thoughts elsewhere. Ral, who had observed their exchange with a neutral expression, moved forward and gestured that she wanted to help.

"Okay." Tatsu handed over the supplies. "Put the leather strips on the bottom of his feet, like the sole of a boot, and then we'll wrap the linen around it to hold them in place. It'll help keep his toes warm when we hit the mountains."

When Ral approached Yudai and reached for his leg, he flinched away.

"Not scary," she told him with a gentle hand on his knee. "Not scary."

Yudai allowed her to take his leg. He studied her, eyes guarded, as she carefully followed Tatsu's instructions and began to wrap the linen around both his toes and the leather. There was something in the way his eyes tracked her movements, a wariness tinted with something else—respect, maybe, or appreciation. Yudai let her finish, and as she started on his other foot, Tatsu leaned over to check her work. It was done well. The linens were wrapped with smooth lines, not too tightly.

"Finished," Ral sang, sitting back. She looked proud as she crossed her arms over her chest.

"It's good," Tatsu told her.

Even Yudai looked pleased, or at least softer than he had before. He had enough strength to pull the boots on over the layers of linen and lace them back up. Tatsu waited as he finished, afraid to break the atmosphere, and yet...

"I have to ask," he said. "The king, your father, he let this—"

And just like that, the moment was shattered. Yudai's face closed off like a steel gate had swung shut, eyes growing hard and distant even as his mouth curled up.

"I don't want to talk about my father," he said, his voice dangerously low.

"I have to know why he—"

"I said, *I don't want to talk about my father.*"

Yudai claimed not to have access to his magic, but Tatsu didn't know that for sure. And rage shimmered as an undercurrent, fury barely held beneath the surface. For perhaps the first time, Tatsu understood how powerful this man was, even *with* blocks put up to keep his abilities denied. It was in the air, the calm before the storm—the moment of no return. The air crackled with subdued sparks, waiting to explode.

The hair on the back of Tatsu's neck stood at attention, somewhat out of sync with the shivers running down his spine.

"Okay," he whispered. "We won't."

Yudai didn't say anything else, and Tatsu hesitated before reaching to pull the other man up and swing him onto his back. The copper taste in the back of his throat had dissipated, but he wasn't willing to bet on the clouds having passed yet.

The prince remained silent as they struck up their journey again.

YUDAI HAD REGAINED choppy control of his legs by the time they reached the long slope signaling the end of Runon's territory and the beginning of the Shyreld. Tatsu's shoulders rejoiced without the added weight, but Yudai's insistence on trying to walk on his own slowed their pace further. Tatsu had to put an arm around his back to shoulder half the weight so the three of them could continue with any speed.

Ral's unclear warning and the lingering tension in the air kept urging him to move quicker. Tatsu sympathized with Yudai's desire to function more on his own, but there was a limit to how much he would go along with.

He voiced this thought aloud and received an annoyed glare in response.

"I'll walk through my own kingdom, even if I need your help," Yudai said through clenched teeth, face strained with exertion.

Ral moved to his other side, trying to help, and only succeeded in grabbing hold of his upper arm. Still, Yudai didn't shrug her fingers off.

Moving up the incline was slow going. On both sides, the mountains rose into the sky, the white of the snow-covered peaks getting lost in the gray of the low-hanging clouds. Halfway up the slope, the trees had stopped singing, but Tatsu didn't notice right away. By the time he did, he guessed it'd been an hour, at least, since the gentle whispers of pine needles had skirted their path. There were a few trees in the area, but their foliage was sparse. With so little nearby to gather information from, Tatsu fumbled blindly in the silence, ignoring his nerves in favor of continuing. His body twisted uncomfortably to one side in order to keep Yudai more or less upright.

At the top of the hill, Ral stopped suddenly and dropped her hold on Yudai's arm.

"Ral?" Tatsu asked, craning his head over his shoulder to look back at her. "What is it?"

The color of her face was unnaturally ashy, a mottled brown. She tightened her hands into fists at her sides, staring ahead of them, beyond Tatsu and Yudai's position. Tatsu turned to follow her gaze, and when he did—

He wished he hadn't.

The spindly coniferous trees that had dotted the snowy landscape were no more; in their place, gnarled and twisted trunks of black bark bent to the ground. The Weeping Forest, when drained, had been a mass of putrid decay-mangled life. The Shyreld had fewer trees to display the horror, yet, somehow, the absence of the foliage made it seem even worse. The Shyreld was a desert of life, and the only thing left behind was the tortured, crying remains.

"*Gods.*" Yudai fell out of Tatsu's grasp, knees hitting the snow. His fingers curled and grasped at nothing, helpless, as the keening cry of a wounded animal forced itself out of his throat.

It hurt Tatsu to look at, but deep down, he'd been expecting it. They'd already made their way through one of the siphon's victims, and it made sense for the drain to have extended in both directions. But for Yudai, who hadn't seen the earlier carnage, how much worse must it have felt? The torn edges of the Shyreld had to have gleamed red on his hands.

One of the nearest trees gave out a mournful groan as its branches twisted toward them, reaching as far as the blackened bark would allow. The scraps of leaves were not the festering webbing of the Weeping Forest, but congealed globs of pine needles that looked to have melted around the cones. As the tree extended its branches, one of the masses fell into the snow, where it sank and nearly disappeared entirely from view.

"Yudai," Tatsu began, and was immediately interrupted by the other man's sob of rage.

"No," Yudai moaned. "No, *no—*"

Behind Yudai's kneeling figure, Ral burst into tears. She took a wild step forward and threw her arms around Yudai from behind, burying her face in the shirt on his shoulder as she cried. It startled Tatsu; she'd been so blissful and calm when they were in the Weeping Forest. Watching Yudai rail at the world made the Shyreld feel so very different.

They were no longer just looking at the aftermath of destructive, all-encompassing power. Instead, they were standing on the battlefield of Yudai's own guilt.

How did it feel for Yudai, knowing he'd been the cause of it? His feet were rooted where he stood. Tatsu wasn't sure what to say or do. Nothing would be enough.

Yudai buried his face in his hands, smearing bits of snow across his forehead and hair with trembling hands. "I can't—I came here as a child. I knew this area—"

"Not you," Ral said, shaking her head against his shoulder blades. "Not you."

"I knew, but I didn't *know.*" He sounded wrecked, voice so warped it was almost unintelligible. "I could feel it when it happened, but I couldn't *see* it."

Ral's distressed noises were enough to spur Tatsu into action, at least. All of his muscles unfroze at the same time. He moved forward to mirror Yudai's position in the snow, reaching forward to grab the other man's hands and pull them away from his tear-streaked face.

"Don't you dare beat yourself up over this," he hissed, surprised by the emotion in his voice. "This wasn't you. This was never you."

"You don't know me." Yudai's eyes were wide and desperate as if searching for the pardon he couldn't grant himself. Tatsu's response caught in his throat and stayed there, threatening to choke him. He could see Yudai's self-image hanging in his haunted expression—a monster made of an unquenchable magical appetite.

And then the snow began to melt in a circle around Yudai's stooped body.

A warning rang in Tatsu's ears. Yudai had said something back in the half-collapsed house, in a time that seemed so long ago, hours lost and strewn across the jagged peaks.

They can only track me if I use magic.

"Stop it," Tatsu said and squeezed Yudai's fingers hard. The wind was heating up, too fast, too much, in a wild whirl of magic bottled up for far, far too long. Whatever was going on inside Yudai promised to draw the attention of two furious mages so powerful they could shake the very mountains bordering their homeland, and all of that collared energy was preparing to erupt around them. He didn't know which threat was worse: bringing the enemy to their doorstep or being devoured whole by the man he was trying to steal away.

Yudai replied with a half-swallowed cry. "I don't know how."

The snow hissed into nothingness as the temperature grew. Ral squeaked in alarm and righted herself a bit, hands still clasped on Yudai's shoulders.

"Hot!" she exclaimed. "Wait, hot!"

The heat penetrated every part of his body. From the feel of the wind whipping around his face, the only possible ending to the escalation was an explosion. Tatsu leaned in, jerking Yudai's arms forward. "Yudai! Control it!"

"I can't—" Yudai started and yelped when Tatsu gave his arms another firm tug. Their eyes met and held. Yudai took a deep, shuddering breath without tearing his gaze away. "I'm *trying.*"

"Look at me," Tatsu demanded. "Yudai, you can control this."

There were too many emotions on Yudai's face to name. Under Tatsu's gaze, he bit down on his bottom lip and all his features hardened in concentration. The heat swelled, flaring up, and then, like a candle being blown out, it dissipated in a single burst of wind.

The sudden coolness stung, intense and biting.

Tatsu's breath came out in a half-laugh, half-gasp of triumph. The smile on Yudai's face echoed the same emotion, torn between elation and surprise, and for a second, Tatsu felt invincible. They both started laughing hard enough to shake their knees against the bare ground beneath them. The onslaught of relief took Tatsu's breath away. It took too much time for Tatsu to drop Yudai's fingers, and his hands felt empty after.

"Great!" Ral lunged forward to hug Yudai over his shoulders once more, laughing. "Yudai, good, good!"

Yudai tapped her hands in a way that seemed fond and fumbled his way to his feet on legs that still shook under his control. Remnants of tears were frozen against his skin, but his expression had smoothed itself out. Ral continued giggling as she helped Yudai up. Her feet danced a bit in the half-melted remains of the snow and the dark rocks poking their way through.

Despite the immense relief, a nagging seed of fear remained. Yudai hadn't been able to get control over any part of that display of magic other than finally turning it off. Would what had just happened be enough magic to grab the attention of Nota and Zakio? If it hadn't, they could continue their climb through the mountains. But if it had…

His throat closed off as he gazed at them both. Maybe the twinge in his senses was nothing. Maybe it hadn't been big or long enough to catch the mages' gaze. But he wouldn't wager anything against an enemy who was powerful enough to use a person as fuel for their own perverse desires. If he was right, and they *did* arrive, Yudai probably wouldn't be able to muster up that magic energy again.

If he was right, there was nothing they could do once the enemy was upon them.

UNLIKE THE WEEPING Forest, the Shyreld's drained trees were easy to avoid. Giving them a wide berth didn't entirely stop them from grabbing, though, and each time Tatsu saw one of them reach with a low, somber wail, his blood ran cold. He knew what the punishment for getting too close to them would be. Just thinking about the bone crunch that had signaled the end of Brund's life sent shivers up his spine. But there was something grotesquely captivating about the mutilated branches and twisted bark. Something in him wanted to go near and see them. The trees were like the sirens in one of his father's old books, luring sailors away from the safety of their ships in the Oldal Sea.

He was afraid to ask the others if they felt it too; tiptoeing around Yudai seemed the right decision at the Shyreld junction of their journey, and he doubted Ral would give him much of an answer. For a while, it seemed like the alluring trees and the increasing growl in his stomach were their only problems.

That was, until the storm began.

The wind started up in bursts, giving them still pauses between which they could catch their breath, only to snatch the air away again with another icy wave. The cold had a bite so sharp it went straight through Tatsu's shirt and pants, chilling him to the bone. During the time when the wind calmed, the trees' whispered pleas echoed in his ears just like the roar of the wind had: *come near, come closer, save us.*

Even throwing his hands up over his ears didn't block out their appeals.

They kept moving, but they were in a race against time. Ral's nose was red-tipped and Tatsu's fingers were stiff with pain. As the wind picked up with more urgency, the murmuring disappeared. The snow began when they reached the second of the rocky white slopes leading into the higher mountain paths. Big, fat flakes danced down from the clouds at first but turned quickly into a continuous wall, catching in Tatsu's eyes and gathering on the incline. Within an hour, conditions had deteriorated to the point where Tatsu could no longer see more than a hand span in front of his face.

For Yudai, the push was even harder. He was already struggling to fight his legs into submission, and the extra push against him with the snowstorm seemed to be too much. He faltered several times before he fell, his lower legs getting lost in the already accumulated precipitation.

Yudai was shaking in snow already beginning to harden into crust by the time Tatsu reached him.

"We can't keep going in this!" Yudai shouted as both Tatsu and Ral helped him back onto his feet, up and over the wind-blown snow hills.

"We have to find a place to stop," Tatsu replied. He couldn't yell loud enough to keep the wind from stealing his words, but both Yudai and Ral seemed to understand. To continue, Tatsu supported most of Yudai's weight as the man's strength failed completely. Dragging both of them through the snowdrifts was painstakingly slow, and Tatsu's shirt soaked through within minutes. The wet fabric froze even as it clung to his skin; he was sure his skin had iced over, and there was nothing to do about it.

Somehow, they all managed to keep going, but Tatsu had to clench his teeth to keep them from chattering. By the time he'd maneuvered them around a small grove of mangled trees and found a crevice in the mountainside large enough to shield them from the worst of the wind, he could no longer feel the tips of his fingers. The crevice had a dusting of snow already blown within but was relatively untouched thanks to the high rock cover jutting out dark above it.

He deposited Yudai on the ground inside the alcove, trying to ignore both Yudai's gasp of pain and his own aching joints.

"There's not enough dry wood to start a fire," Tatsu said, even as he was trying to slow his rapid heartbeat.

Focusing on the words summoned blackness at the sides of his vision, all his attention on the cold. "I can try with what's left of our kindling, but everything here has been drained—"

Ral raced past Tatsu, back into the raging storm, past their sheltered corner.

"Ral!" Tatsu shouted. It took him too long to register her flight, and even longer to try to get his body moving again. By the time he managed to flounder out after her with jerky limbs, she had disappeared, a ghost fading without so much as a word.

His heart dropped like a lead weight.

"Ral!" Tatsu tried again. Fear took hold, tightening everything inside him until he could barely find breath. His mind went black, and his vision red—flashes of her face from his memories distracted him to the point where he had to put his hands up to shield his eyes and focus his vision. He strained to identify her outline in the snow, but he couldn't see a thing. "Ral! No! Come back!"

But she was gone, and she'd left nothing behind.

He screamed her name again and started off after her, digging through the snow in a frenzied whirlwind of motion. But then, a second later, Yudai's weight smacked him hard from behind and knocked them both to the ground.

"Stop!" Tatsu shouted, trying to fight the other man off. He threw his hands back, twisting his arm nearly out of its socket, and still couldn't quite reach. "I have to get her! I have to go after her!"

"It's suicide!" Yudai yelled.

It didn't even matter that he was right, and that Tatsu could feel the truth of the words in his freezing limbs. He sucked in a breath that burned the entire way down into his lungs. Snow clung to his eyelashes and his nose. For a second, his mind went blank with guilt. The storm had reached its peak. But she was out there in it, and she hadn't come back.

"Ral!" he screamed into the void.

When she failed to reappear after a few moments of Tatsu flailing against Yudai, his stomach turned over on itself. He wanted to be sick, though there was too little in him to actually complete the action. He dry heaved slightly as he struggled against the rock and snow. She was gone, lost in the overwhelming whiteness.

He knew this, but his body wouldn't stop fighting. He wasn't sure he'd ever be able to stop fighting. He'd promised to keep her safe. Alesh had *trusted* him to keep Ral safe. But she'd run off, and he couldn't go after her without accepting his own death.

If he died, the whole mission would have been for nothing. Yudai would never survive on his own in his weakened state, and Nota and Zakio would come for him.

Chayd would still fall victim to the life siphon.

"No," Tatsu moaned, but his strength had fled. It had all been stolen by the wind and the snow, from carrying Yudai over several rocky hills, and from Ral running away into the searing brightness of the storm. He had nothing left. "No, no—"

"You won't make it," Yudai's voice said, very near Tatsu's ear. "You'll never make it."

Tatsu heaved a sob that brought searing bile up his throat. "She left. She's gone."

"You couldn't have stopped her." His voice, full of sympathy, made Tatsu feel even worse.

"She's gone," Tatsu repeated and let his face fall forward into the snow. He wanted to lose his breath entirely and let his consciousness drift away on the wind. But Yudai had other plans, and he smacked Tatsu roughly on the back of his head. The impact was enough to startle him out of his misery, and he crawled backward into the secluded crevice on instinct more than anything else.

His shaking back hit the rocks, the tears leaking from his eyes a blinding burn of heat against his chilled skin. "She's gone, she's gone—"

"I'm sorry." Yudai's voice was pained. "I'm sorry."

He said it, again and again, over and over, but all Tatsu could think was that everyone he'd ever cared about was dead.

Chapter Fourteen

TATSU TRIED TO build a fire using the leftover kindling in his pack, but his hands were shaking, and he couldn't get the spark to take to the shavings. It took what felt like hours to finally get the flame going, and even then, it was more smoke than fire. When he inquired about the possibility of Yudai using his dormant magic to increase the warmth, he received a tight-lipped grimace in response and took it as a negative. The only option was to make do with the smoking embers as best they could, even when they filled the small crevice with cloying clouds of soot.

Tatsu had a pair of leather gloves he normally used when working in the woods. They shared them, back and forth, for long enough periods of time that their fingers could unfreeze. The rest of the time they spent as close to the small fire pit as possible. Taking the gloves off to hand them to Yudai caused Tatsu's fingers to ache fiercely, and he spent his time without the gloves, slowly clenching and uncurling them, trying to keep his circulation quick.

His lungs hurt. Grief and regret tasted like blood, coppery and sharp, in the back of his mouth. He tried not to think about Ral out in the snowstorm, wandering lost and cold, but he couldn't seem to push the thoughts away. Every time he closed his eyes, he saw her disappearing into the blinding white. Wishing everything would just disappear, he sat back against the stone wall with his hands pressed tightly against his face.

"Tell me about her," Yudai said quietly.

Tatsu tried to bite back years of memories. "She was the sister of an…old friend. I know it didn't seem like it, but she was smart. She just knew things."

He shifted his back against the cold rocks. They were poking into his ribs, through the still-damp fabric of his shirt, and somehow, the jolts of pain were helping to keep him grounded. The ache of his empty stomach seemed very far away.

"We didn't mean to bring her with us," he continued. "But she was alone, and somehow she'd gotten herself through the woods to where we were. I don't know how. She seemed to be able to do things like that. The other mage, the one who went with us to Yuse, she said Ral felt strange."

"She did," Yudai confirmed, but his face scrunched in thought. "I can't quite put my finger on what it was, though."

"She loved flowers," Tatsu whispered. "Ever since I first met her, she'd always loved flowers. She was always happy, like sunshine. And she was brave. She was never afraid to explore the world beyond her house. Her curiosity overrode all of that. She wanted to see and experience everything."

Yudai put a sympathetic hand on Tatsu's shoulder. It felt only marginally better to have the weight there.

Tatsu shook his head, burying his face in his hands again. "I failed her. I promised to take care of her, and I failed."

"Who did you promise?"

"Alesh. Her sister." Tatsu squeezed his eyes shut. Thinking of Alesh brought on a wave of renewed despair, and his bones ached. "She was with us in Yuse. She protected us from the guards and drew them off, and now I don't know if she's...alive."

A long silence hung between them. Out past the rocks, the wind howled as it blew in gusts across the mountainside. Tatsu's toes were freezing, but curling them up inside his boots seemed to help. Yudai, huddled nearby, was leaning in, in an effort to conserve body warmth. The press of his thigh against Tatsu's was part comfort and part heat, and welcome either way.

"This friend, Alesh," Yudai started, slowly. "You loved her."

"I—yes." His neck spasmed. "A long time ago."

A slow intake of breath, and Yudai asked, "What happened?"

"Their parents died when they were young. And Alesh had to take care of Ral. It was hard for her, and she didn't have any money. The only options she had were illegal, and I...couldn't accept it."

Tatsu let his head fall to his knees. "It took a while for it to get bad. It started small—a small job here and there around the city. But then she joined up with one of the smuggling gangs for more constant work, and someone got hurt. An old friend. I couldn't accept what she was doing and what she was becoming, and that was the end of it."

He slowly extended and flexed his hands, out of reflex more than anything else—his body stiff and unyielding, not wanting to respond to his commands. Detached and floating, he regarded himself from above, suspended in a gray haze of grief.

It seemed Yudai wasn't sure what to say. In truth, Tatsu wasn't sure there *was* anything to say, only painful seconds to keep breathing through, over and over again.

"Tell me about your life," Tatsu whispered, with the heels of his palms pushed hard against his eyes.

Yudai barked out a laugh. "*What* life?"

"Your life before the siphon. Just...tell me about something else. Something better."

"What is there to tell?" Yudai asked, voice hoarse. "The privileged prince got what was coming to him when the mages in his father's court used him as their magical trump card."

Tatsu shook his head. "There has to be something good."

"It was all good. That's why it's so terrible."

"Just..." Tatsu's voice broke. He wiped at his face with the back of his hands but only half succeeded in brushing away the errant tears. "Just tell me something."

He could only see Yudai out of the corner of his eye, the image blurring, but Yudai's face softened. Perhaps because Tatsu was simply that pitiable. Truthfully, Tatsu didn't really care. He desperately needed something else to focus on.

"When I was fifteen, my father held a ball in celebration," Yudai began. "And I was furious. All the entire event was meant to do was show off that I was growing older, and that my station made me a lucky catch. My father wanted to draw out the nobles and let them begin squabbling with one another over which daughter would be lucky enough to marry me."

"I-I'm s-sorry." The intensity of the genuine feeling left Tatsu a bit rattled. At fifteen, he'd been living in his woods and keeping out of sight, wishing he could fade away completely from the citizens living in Dradela. At fifteen, his father had died, but at least Tatsu had been free to live life as he wanted to.

Yudai sighed. "It was every bit as terrible as I imagined it would be. And back then, that was the worst thing I could think of. Marrying some noble's daughter because her father was greedy for power. But the food was good, and my father is an excellent judge of imported wine."

He trailed off, and when Tatsu looked over at him between splayed fingers, Yudai smiled. It wasn't sardonic or rueful, but a real smile. One corner quirked up higher than the other as it slowly spread across his face. It was easy to see why the noble daughters would have been clamoring just as hard as their fathers for the princess's crown. The dying embers painted his face with orange, and even still, there was something intoxicating about the expression when it blossomed across Yudai's features. Even in the confines of the mountain cave, it warmed the air through.

"I snuck onto the roof halfway through with a bottle of spirits and my steward," Yudai continued. "And I made the clouds dance."

Tatsu was surprised by the small laugh that made its way out of his throat, floating upward. "And it wasn't such a bad night after all."

"No," Yudai said, but his smile faded. His face took on a hooded shadow, as if he'd just reminded himself of the abilities he no longer had access to. When he turned away, the darkness concealed too much to make his features out. "No, it wasn't."

"Did you...you said you lost control of your magic. But that they kept you aware."

"Yeah," Yudai replied, and his voice was thick with emotion.

Tatsu breathed out, twice, ignoring the burn in his lungs. "And you were just...stuck. In that chair."

"Not completely." Yudai's gaze was focused somewhere else, farther than the rocks and the blizzard outside. "After a while, I figured out how to move my finger. Just one, my index finger. It was the only control I ever managed to take back."

"One finger?"

Yudai laughed. "Once I figured it out, I would move it every time I felt my father come in. I wanted him to see it. I wanted him to know I was aware of him being there. I think it bothered him. He stopped coming by the end."

They were both quiet for a long time. Tatsu listened to the howl of the wind and waited for it to rip through his body as well, but it never did. They remained safely tucked into their alcove as the storm raged around them. Yudai handed the gloves back to Tatsu and even the leather felt like ice. His insides had frozen over just like the half-dead branches outside.

"Do you think she's..." Tatsu started but choked on the words left unsaid.

"Don't." Yudai's voice, too, was warped.

Tatsu squeezed his eyes shut against the renewed onslaught of tears. "She was so good. She was such a good person."

He didn't have the strength to say the rest, but from the way Yudai shifted against him, Tatsu thought the other man understood. He'd lost one of the few purely good people he knew, and now, only the two of them remained, miserable and shivering in the cave.

"How do you keep going when you've lost everything?" Tatsu whispered.

Yudai shook his head. "I don't know. If you figure it out, let me know. I don't have anything left either."

The reality sobered him. Tatsu blew on the skin of his wrists, exposed by the gloves, and asked, "Do you think Zakio and Nota will follow us here?"

Yudai didn't answer, but the bleakness in his gaze was all the answer Tatsu needed.

THEY STAYED UNTIL the wind ceased screeching through the rocks. Tatsu fell in and out of a fitful sleep, haunted by nightmares that were more memory than fabrication. His body woke each time he became too cold, or whenever Yudai's shaking jostled him into awareness again. The fire, barely hanging on, eventually devoured all the kindling Tatsu had left and extinguished itself in one last puff of smoke. Tatsu kept passing the gloves between Yudai and himself, though he wasn't sure how much it was actually helping.

The last bit of sleep he got was a longer chunk of time than the rest. He woke to a calm-like quiet, with Yudai's face pressed against his shoulder and limbs tangled up in his own. Body heat had been enough to finally lull them both into a decent rest. Tatsu slowly pulled himself free, wincing as he unlocked his knees and wrists, which ached in protest.

They both roused enough to stumble out of the crevice into a world covered in heaps of wet, white snow. It clung to the sides of the mountains where it had accumulated, and the trees—silent, now—were encumbered with so much of it they bent down in full arches toward the ground. At any other time, Tatsu might have thought the scene beautiful.

Instead, the frozen landscape caused his stomach to churn.

"We have to find Ral."

"We will," Yudai told him.

But Tatsu could tell it was only said for his benefit. There were no footsteps in the snow after all the accumulation. There was no way to know where Ral had run off to. And even if they did find her, the odds were just as high they'd find a frozen corpse instead of Ral's tired smile. As Tatsu took a hesitant step onto the snowbanks, his boot sank until the snow was against his knees. With his next step, his hope sank as far as his foot had.

"She...she can't have gone far." Tatsu was trying to console himself, and he knew it, but he had to focus. If he were back in his woods tracking a creature, he'd plot out the most likely path. He was too emotional to really be able to sense anything else.

Closing his eyes, he stopped moving and took two deep breaths. He imagined he'd returned to his forest with the smell of trees and damp dirt surrounding him. He let his thoughts settle inward and took note of his body, the coolness of his skin and the pain in his limbs. Then, he stretched outward with all of his awareness as he would if he were hunting.

But the Shyreld held much less. Back home, the trees blocked out most of the sunlight with their thick trunks and foliage. In these wintry mountain peaks, heavy snow dampened the whispering of the gnarled trees. Soft snippets of moaning called out to him, and he let it sweep past his focus. He pushed through it until it barely registered at all.

Tatsu concentrated harder. The air in his lungs escaped in a low whistle as he simply *felt*. So little life pulsed around them that his efforts rang barren, and the rest of the sweep throbbed aching and fierce. Tatsu rolled both shoulders back as he tried to find the scent of anything living. He imagined it carried in on the cold breeze that bit at his cheeks, but the truth was he couldn't sense anything. The sharp sting of loss jolted him out of his brief serenity.

"The snow was coming down too much for her to make good time," Tatsu said with a heavy heart. He opened his eyes once more and the shock of the white made his eyes sting. "She wouldn't have gone backward, so the only way to go is up. It's the same way we'd be going to get back to Chayd."

He sounded much more certain than he was. In truth, his hope was ebbing away onto the frozen snow piles, and he didn't have enough energy to pull it back. He could feel nothing out on the ice-topped path, and he hadn't any idea where Ral would've gone.

"The tribes live up along the mountain paths," Yudai volunteered, but he still seemed wary. "At least they did before...what happened."

"Then let's get moving."

Tatsu's stomach growled angrily, but he ignored it too. He'd gone longer with less before, and Ral was more important. The only way to get his body going was to push all thoughts aside of Ral caught in one of the large snowbanks, trapped by the storm and covered, unable to get out. If he thought about it too much, he'd fall apart. He kept his eyes firmly on the route in front of them and his hands on the leather straps of his pack, just to clench them tight and give him something to set his mind on.

Yudai, it seemed, had other plans.

"Tatsu," he warned, and Tatsu knew what he was going to say. He couldn't hear it—he couldn't stand for the words to be said out loud. Giving sound to them would be giving them life, and he couldn't bear it.

"Save your strength for walking through the snow," he said, harsher than he intended.

Yudai bit his lip and didn't try to broach the subject again.

Moving was slow. Yudai had already had problems getting his gait back, and the storm hadn't helped matters. But Tatsu wouldn't be able to carry the other man and get them over the Shyreld, not as drained as his body already was, so he had to let Yudai figure out the mechanics on his own. As Yudai fumbled with getting his too-large boots free of the deeper piles, Tatsu used the extra time to scan the area.

The sides of the mountains sloped steeply as they continued up toward the clouds, and the few trees around the base were a stark contrast of black against the snow. Only bits of them were visible, lost amongst the sea of white, and whatever brush might have existed, scraggly around the trunks, was completely buried.

Tatsu kept them clear of the trees, but as they moved, the voices grew louder again. They whispered in his ear and begged him to move closer. He wondered how they stayed alive in the nutrient-deficient soil made up mostly of pebbles and clay, and a constant blanketing barrage of snow.

Come close, come close, we need you.

"If we don't find one of the camps before nightfall—" Yudai started.

"We will," Tatsu replied.

A sigh came from behind him. "And if you're wrong?"

"Then we both die. And we'll share Ral's fate."

After a few hours, Tatsu tried to slide back and help Yudai but was rebuffed. Yudai shook Tatsu's arm free of his shoulder with a sour look on his face. There were beads of sweat visible on his forehead, beneath the tendrils of white hair.

"I *can* do this," he mumbled, though it seemed mostly aimed at himself. "I don't need your help."

Tatsu let it go without comment. If Yudai's stubborn pride kept him on his feet after exhaustion, it was a welcome aid. Perhaps Tatsu should be more worried about the other man using up all his energy, but Ral was simply more important. Each step he took over the dunes of snow seemed to beat out her name in time with his heart.

The nearby trees began to shake free from the white piles and reach for them with long, thin branches. The energy the trees carried spurred them into action.

At one large junction, where the trail widened into a broad, mostly flat mini-clearing, Tatsu stopped to stare at the trees.

"What is it?" Yudai asked. He was out of breath and leaned forward with his hands on his knees to redistribute his weight, but even that action wasn't quite stable. Tatsu kept his eyes on the gnarled branches as an uneasy feeling crept up his spine and settled at the top.

"What if she didn't know to avoid them?" he said, voice soft. "What if she went too close?"

It took Yudai a while to make the connection. "But then we'd see her there with them. All the snow would be disturbed from it, right?"

Yudai hadn't seen what happened in the Weeping Forest. As much as he tried to put it out of his mind,

Tatsu's thoughts raced back to Brund's untimely death at the tree's desperate desires. The last thing Tatsu wanted was to have to explain what had happened. If not for his own sanity, then for Yudai's—it would weigh even heavier on his conscience if he knew.

Tatsu struggled with how to voice his fears without giving too much away and alerting Yudai to it. "It's...possible that it would be obvious. But the storm was long, and they could have..."

"What, killed her?" Yudai scoffed. "How?"

Tatsu grimaced. "They need living energy," he said, skating around the truth.

"They're *trees*. And they were half-dead already. There's nothing left to them but bark anyway."

Tatsu just shook his head. Yudai might have been right. The trees in the Shyreld lacked the rotting webs of the Weeping Forest. Without that, it might be impossible for these bare remnants to devour anything living. He didn't want to chance it, but he let himself entertain the possibility.

Either way, it was best not to dwell on possibilities. Tatsu got his legs moving again, but resuming the trek across the snow at least helped him to focus on something else.

A long time later, the huffing from the other man grew louder over Tatsu's shoulder.

"Thank you," Yudai said. The words came out so quietly Tatsu almost didn't hear them over the crunch of his boots against the thin layer of ice beginning to form on the snowbanks.

"For what?" Tatsu asked.

"For not telling me whatever it is you were afraid of back there with the trees."

Exhaustion helped keep annoyance from flaring up at being such an open book. Tatsu wasn't used to having people around him for so long. There hadn't been any need in the woods, and, now, he'd lost his ability to keep his emotions contained. His defenses had dwindled. It was terrifying, mixed up in all the other fear erratically pumping through his veins and his bone-weariness outweighed everything.

"You don't need to worry yourself sick over anything else," Tatsu admitted.

Yudai didn't answer for a very long while. His breathing remained labored, and Tatsu had to admire him for refusing to ask for help when he was clearly struggling.

"I should," Yudai said, "but thank you anyway. You're not such a bad guy, I guess."

"You thought I was?"

Yudai barked out a harsh laugh. "You came uninvited into my kingdom, sneaked into my castle, and stole the prince right out from underneath the mages' noses. I just assumed you were going to kill me to stop everything."

"I told you I wasn't going to kill you."

"That doesn't necessarily mean I believed you," Yudai replied with an unreadable expression on his face. His features, still strained, seemed to have rearranged themselves into practiced indifference again. "That kind of person doesn't exactly invite trust."

"I'm taking you to Chayd." Tatsu was pretty sure he'd said the exact same thing before. "They'll protect you there and keep you safe."

"Why?" Yudai's voice was quiet. "You really ought to just kill me. You'd be keeping the world a lot safer than if you let me live."

Tatsu frowned at the snow beneath his boots. "I'm not in the habit of killing innocents."

"You don't know me."

"Look, there are a lot of terrible people in this world, but I don't think you're one of them."

He stopped and turned to look at the man behind him.

"Easy," Yudai replied with a smile bordering on fearful. "I don't think thieves are supposed to be this compassionate."

Tatsu huffed a small laugh. "I wasn't the thief. I was just the guide."

"I don't know." Yudai shook his head, and the drained strands of his unruly hair seemed to blend in with the white behind him. "You might have stolen more than you realize."

After a long pause, Tatsu turned back to the path.

"I know you're tired, but we have to keep going. We have to find Ral before the sun goes down."

He ordered his body to keep on high alert for signs of life as they started up again, but he couldn't seem to ignore how his heart had jumped up into his throat, hammering out its traitorous rhythm against his ears.

AS THE SUN sank lower in the sky, so too did Tatsu's hopes.

His muscles shook with exertion, and he imagined how much worse it had to be for Yudai's still-clumsy control. With his chances of finding Ral alive slipping further and further away as the sunlight faded, his feet dragged. His determination to find her had been like a candle burning in his chest to keep him moving, and with it extinguished, nothing remained.

He stopped when they reached another plateau of snow and ice flanked by jagged mountains, unable to push himself to continue. His fingers ached with the cold. Stiff and frozen, none of his limbs wanted to obey his commands. The exposed bits of his skin burned in a dangerous warning sign, but he could do little to heed its call. He was too hungry and weak to keep going much longer.

The regret he'd been running from seemed to catch up with him all at once in an overpowering wave threatening to bring him to his knees.

"Ral," he tried to call, but it came out more like a whimper.

It hurt to breathe; the cold threatened to freeze him from the inside out.

"Tatsu," Yudai said. "Tatsu, look."

Tatsu was slow to comply with the order. When he did, squinting his eyes to make out the bare, white-covered area at the base of the next peak, he realized the dark splashes weren't just outstretched bands of rock. The shapes were organic, man-made. They were signs of *life*.

"Gods," Tatsu whispered. "It's a settlement."

"It's one of the nomadic tribes," Yudai said, but Tatsu was already moving. His legs seemed to lope forward of their own accord, heedless of the snow blocking his way. Strength he hadn't felt in hours suddenly surged like fire through his veins, propelling him with speed he no longer thought himself capable of. He nearly slipped once when hitting a thicker cover of snow, but even that barely slowed him down.

As he drew closer to the shapes, which revealed themselves to be tents stretched across standing poles, a telltale plume of smoke billowed up outside one of them.

The gray of it nearly blended into the rocky backdrop, but the outline lingered, curling and twisting.

A fire.

It took too long for Tatsu to reach it. He feared his lungs would burst when he finally slid across another bit of compacted ice and tumbled toward the burning logs. The heat rippling out from the circle of stones and wood hurt when it hit his face, momentarily stunning him.

The figure seated next to the fire jumped up in surprise, hair swinging from side to side behind her shoulders.

"Ral!" Tatsu exclaimed and couldn't stop himself. Icy fingers forgotten, he lunged forward to gather her in his arms, squeezing so tightly she let out a little squeak. "Ral, *gods*, you're okay, you're okay—"

"Tatsu!" she cried out, sounding happy. She hugged him back, hands clenching at his shirt and pack.

Tatsu drew back a bit, to clasp her face between his hands and check her for injuries. She looked fine, and she was beaming at him.

"Ral, I'm so happy, I'm so—I thought you were lost. I thought you were gone," he babbled. He couldn't help it. The relief that swelled up inside him was intoxicating. He came close to choking on the palpable happiness.

Ral cocked her head to one side, eyebrows rising. "Tatsu, sad face?"

"Yes." Tatsu laughed, giddy. He pulled her in again, relishing the warmth of her figure as he embraced her once more. "I was sad, I was so scared for you, but you're okay."

Yudai's much slower steps sounded behind him, finally reaching their position.

"Yudai too?" Ral asked.

"Yes, Yudai too," Tatsu replied. "We were so afraid for you. You disappeared in the snow."

Tatsu turned, Ral still held close to his chest, and was surprised to find Yudai's eyes were fixated on something else across the fire.

"Yudai, she's fine, she's—" He cut off abruptly when it became clear the other man's gaze wasn't wavering. In his expression was something between disgust and terror, and it made Tatsu's blood run cold. The good feelings vanished in a wave of trembling apprehension.

He turned to follow the line of sight. After a few seconds of letting his eyes adjust, he made out a figure on the other side of the rising gray smoke, seated low to the ground and partially hidden in the fire's deep shadows. With an awful sense of foreboding, Tatsu took several steps to the right to get a better look.

The figure was a woman—or at least, what was left of her. She might have been old, or she might have been young; Tatsu couldn't tell. Her skin, stretched tight and taut across her bones, made her look like a skeleton painted with deep brown berries. So tough and leathery it looked badly burnt, her skin seemed to be the only thing keeping the jumble of her body together. There was barely anything left to her. Even her clothes hung off her sharp angles, much too large to be of any use when the entirety of her body had wasted away. Her hair was nothing more than several white wisps fluttering around the back of her head and her shoulders.

She sat on a chair with her fingers curled tightly around the arms, and Tatsu wasn't sure if she'd be able to get out of it.

"So, life-stealer," she said, her voice the rasp of crackling parchment, "we finally meet."

Chapter Fifteen

IT TOOK A moment for Tatsu to realize what had happened, and then the onslaught of horror threatened to pinch the air from his lungs. It seemed to take Yudai the same amount of time; the other man stumbled to his right and threw up in the snow.

Listening to Yudai miserably choke up bile, Tatsu couldn't tear his eyes away from the woman in front of them. Impossible to tell if her eyes were open or not, the shadows were nothing more than slits in the ruined skin of her face.

"No," Yudai moaned, pressing his hands against his eyes as if he were hoping to block out the sight entirely. "No, no—"

"I knew you would come," the woman told them. "It is one of the gifts of my tribe. But it has waned of late, and I am not much longer for this world."

"How," Tatsu asked, a question that wasn't really a question. "How...you were here when the siphon hit? Why didn't you leave?"

The woman sighed, and it sounded like air rattling through wooden panes. Tatsu worried that if she moved at all, the thin, stretched layer of skin would no longer hold. "We are the Oldirr. This is our home. Leaving a place that has been our land for centuries is no easy task."

"But you could have saved yourself." Tatsu was desperate for something he knew remained out of reach, and that was the worst of it. "You might have gotten away before—"

"It was too late, child," the woman said. "Once it began, we were bound to its power here. We were helpless when it fed on our life and bled our tribe dry. This was our fate. The world has grown around us, but we have not changed enough with it. Now, the magic we revere is used as a weapon between kings, and we were doomed to be caught between them."

Yudai heaved a sob into his hands. He hadn't stood back up. Looking at his slumped body, Tatsu wasn't sure he'd be able to move. "I'm sorry, I'm so sorry."

"I don't understand," Tatsu said. "I don't...you should have left."

"There is a story of my people, of the Oldirr," the woman started. "It is the tale of the mountain hawk that made its home in the rock face. Even when the rocks fell, the raptor would not leave. It was bound to its home just as we are. This land is all we have. Where could we have gone that would welcome us?"

Tatsu opened his mouth to answer her and realized he had no answer. The nomadic tribes followed the old ways, ways that Chayd had long since grown distrustful of. Decades of fighting with Joesar had pushed his home kingdom inward, like Runon, until it no longer looked at its neighbors without seeing threats. The old ways meant alchemy and bloodshed, too close to the Joesarians. No one would have welcomed the tribe.

He stared at the weathered face of the woman and couldn't seem to fully sate all his rage, though he didn't know where it was aimed.

"You saved her," he said and involuntarily pulled Ral a bit closer again. He was loath to let go for fear she would disappear again. "You saved her in the storm?"

"I did nothing," the woman told him. "I merely gave her a place to stay."

It didn't answer the question of how Ral had made it through the blizzard. Had the woman somehow given Ral a path to follow between mountain crevices? Was her voice a beacon Ral had sure-footedly followed? Unsettled, Tatsu stepped back a bit. Against his side, Ral's fingers curled up in his shirt. She seemed unaffected by the woman's drained body, but aware of the tension that had settled heavy around them. Her shoulders curled in a bit on themselves, as though making herself small enough to disappear.

"Rise, life-stealer," the woman commanded.

"I—I can't," Yudai admitted, voice thick and warbled.

"You must." Her tone held command in it. She must have been the elder of the Oldirr. She must have been in a position of power. Drained of life and left half-dead, hanging between the balance, she still spoke with all the confidence of someone used to making demands. "You have no other option."

Yudai did stand, but his body visibly rebelled against it. He managed to get his weight onto his feet and looked at the woman across from him, and on his cheeks, flickering flames reflected on the tears.

"My people used to be nearly 600 strong," the woman told him. "We have been here for centuries. I know these mountains like I knew my own children, right down to their mercurial mood swings. Now, I am all that is left. The siphon has consumed our tribe whole."

"I didn't mean for this to happen," Yudai whispered, trembling.

"It does not matter," the woman told him, not unkindly, "for it happened all the same."

Yudai's features pinched tighter. "I have to do something to help."

"You cannot. I will die."

It felt like a physical blow, though Tatsu knew somewhere deep within him there could be no other outcome. She was a charred, brittle ember barely sparking against the cold mountain air. Whatever kept her clinging to life had been nearly extinguished. Her fingers, still tightly wrapped around the arms of the chair, had not moved an inch since they arrived.

Yudai might as well have taken a knife to his belly. He half collapsed, sagging forward with a ragged moan of despair. "No—"

"You cannot reverse this, life-stealer. What is done will remain as it is."

"Then why am I here?" Yudai cried.

"Because the gods have willed it so," she told him.

Yudai hissed something angrily in Runonian, and Tatsu hoped it was a curse. For what seemed like an eternity after that, all that could be heard were Yudai's hitching sobs. Tatsu grabbed a bit at Ral's arm, and she sniffed in sympathy as she gazed over the fire. The Oldirr woman sucked in a long but shallow breath, and something seemed to ease within her. The atmosphere around the camp lifted, enough so that the chill of the wind no longer bit at Tatsu's face.

"I have waited for you to come. My purpose is finally complete," she said.

This snapped Yudai out of his misery. His head shot up, eyes hard. "No. You can't die. We'll find a way to save you, to reverse this—"

"You must stop this from happening again," the woman said, and it took Tatsu several seconds before he realized she had moved. Her head, perched atop a neck so thin and stretched it didn't look like it could support the weight any longer, had twisted to look at *him*. The slits of her eyes, orbs sunken into the pockets of her skull, seemed focused on him across the smoke.

"I—" Tatsu began and couldn't finish. He felt strangely and suddenly vulnerable. "I'm just a guide..."

"My people have a saying," the woman told him. "'He who shapes the ground, so shapes the world.' Your hands are black with dirt, but you hesitate to sow the seed."

At a loss, Tatsu's free hand balled into a fist at his side. "I don't understand what you're telling me to do."

"When the time comes, you will," was the response. When she spoke again, her attention had shifted.

"Come here, child," she said. Ral's warmth moved away from Tatsu's body as she stepped around the fire pit. She knelt at the feet of the woman, unfazed by her mummified body.

"The old ways favor you," the woman told her. "Around my neck is the symbol of my people, etched into stone. Take it."

Obediently, Ral stood. It took her a little while to get the necklace free from the wisps of hair and over the stretched skin of the woman's head. The necklace looked heavy—rounded stones carved through and strung across a rope-like chain.

"So pretty," she murmured. Looking at it, she seemed entranced. She cradled it in her palms as a precious treasure and gently slid one fingertip across the largest stone in the middle.

"You can see the future," Tatsu said. "You have to tell us what's going to happen! You have to give us advice so we'll know what to do."

The woman sighed again, and it seemed weaker. She couldn't be dying already. They'd only just arrived. "You already know what to do."

"No, I don't—how could I?" Tatsu tried, desperate, but his thoughts had already grown dark.

"Night is not kind to strangers in the mountains," she told them. "Sleep in one of the tents. You must leave at sunrise."

Yudai sputtered out something of a laugh. "We can't just sleep now that we've been here—"

"Sleep, life-stealer," she told him.

"My name," he said with a shaky inhale, "is *Yudai*."

The woman smiled, the tight skin of her face stretching—smooth across her chin and wrinkled at the corners of her mouth—until it seemed it would burst open. "I know. But you had to remember that yourself."

At a loss, Tatsu looked to Yudai, who seemed just as aghast. Ral, however, patted the Oldirr woman's knees in a strange gesture of closeness and stood. She held the gifted necklace to her chest, smiling at Tatsu.

"Tired now," she said. "Sleep?"

Tatsu could only shake his head. The woman had given him nothing but riddles he was too exhausted to possibly puzzle through. The painful ache of his near-frozen fingers had returned despite the warmth of the fire. "I—yes. I think that's the only thing we can do."

He moved toward the woman, to try to help her from the chair and into one of the sleeping tents, but she refused him.

"I do not sleep," she said, "but you, blood-bridger, do."

"What did you call me?" he asked, stung. He took a step back as his lungs tightened in discomfort.

"When the time comes, remember who you are. You walk with one foot on each side, afraid to choose. But choose you must."

Tatsu shook his head. "I don't...that's not who I am."

"And you know who you are?"

Tatsu struggled to breathe in the oppressive air enough to satisfy the ache within. Something terrifying thundered on the edge of his perception, threatening to overtake him. Staring at the shell of the woman before him, he couldn't settle his racing thoughts.

"What *are* you?" he asked instead, as if throwing her own words back at her.

"The difference between us," she replied, "is that I've always known the answer."

He could think of nothing else to say.

They were all exhausted, but their bodies had more pressing needs to attend to first. There were baskets of preserved salted meat the woman pointed them to near the pit, and jugs full of cold mountain water. They ate in silence around the fire pit, and when their bellies were full and their limbs had regained the lost warmth, Tatsu followed Ral to the farthest of the tents. They were made from animal hide, well stitched and thick, cured with oils to keep them soft and pliable enough to slip over the wooden poles. The inside warmth wasn't significant, but furs lined the ground in small heaps. Ral slipped between them with no hesitation and a contented sigh, but Tatsu couldn't push away thoughts of the men and women who used to own them. Those people were dead now, and this was their only legacy.

He paused long enough for Yudai to make his way inside as well. The other man wouldn't meet Tatsu's eyes and refused to speak. He just curled up in one of the piles of fur with his back to them both, his head held in his hands.

There were so many things to decipher. The more they discovered, the less Tatsu understood. His mind hadn't completely cleared the terror he'd been using as fuel after Ral disappeared, and he was still worried about one of the mages tracking them from Runon. His thoughts were still racing, but his body was too exhausted to keep it up. His eyelids began to droop before he got his pack off and his boots removed. The furs were warm and soft, and against all of his wishes, he drifted off immediately.

In sleep, at least, he could escape from their problems.

HE WOKE TO the Oldirr woman's anxious shouting.

"Get up, get up!" she exclaimed, immediately throwing Tatsu's body into shock and panic. He bolted from the furs, falling over himself to get his boots on. It had been too long since he'd woken to such urgency, and his body was ill prepared to deal with it. He fell while working the second boot back over his toes, but Yudai and Ral were both out of the tent already.

Tatsu expected a blizzard or an avalanche, but everything was as it had been the night before. In the morning light, the empty shells of other tents looked much like the one they'd slept in. Assembled around the fire pit, they tapered off near the delicate joining of two large sheets of rock. The few near the front had only furs in them, but near the back, Tatsu thought he could see much larger objects within the array of pitched leather. A second glance through squinted eyes, and the edges came into focus: bodies.

The tents were full of bodies.

He had to tear his gaze away, stomach heaving in a painful threat. He managed to steady himself by staring at the snow, but the image was already burned into his brain. It would haunt him every time he tried to sleep.

The elder woman was still in her seat around the fire pit, and it didn't look like she had moved. Tatsu wasn't even sure how she was managing to amplify her voice with such a decayed windpipe.

"You must go," she insisted as they hurried to her position near the smoking embers. "He is coming. He is coming for you."

"Who?" Tatsu demanded. "Zakio?"

But all the blood had drained from Yudai's face, paling his skin further. "Gods. He found us."

"Did he track us? From the magic Yudai used back at the border of the Shyreld?" Tatsu asked and was ignored.

"How close?" Yudai asked, a command more than a question. The despair from the previous night had disappeared, replaced with the cold facade of a man raised to be king. With his shoulders squared and his chin high, he looked every bit a warrior prince from the old tales. "How much time do we have?"

"You must go now," the Oldirr woman said. "And even then, you cannot outrun him."

"No," Yudai agreed grimly, "but we can try."

The sun had not yet completely risen. Above the towering peaks, the sky was pinking with the dawn. The snow clinging to the tops of the peaks had a rosy hue that seemed out of place with their harsh reality, and all the shadows stretched out beyond the crags looked warm. The settlement itself wasn't close to many of the mutilated trees, but one sat near the incline of the rocks, waving its branches in visible agitation.

Even the half-dead trees were reacting to the mage on their tail.

"Yudai," he said again, trying to force himself calmer, "what can we do?"

"Nothing." Yudai's face was hard set, a mirror of the mountains behind them. "He's come for me. We knew he would come for me."

"He's come for *us*," Tatsu reminded him.

Ral grabbed hold of the old woman's frighteningly thin arm. "Come too! Come, come!"

"Go, child," the woman told her. "Do not forget what you have seen here."

"We have to keep heading to Chayd," Tatsu said. "They might not have mages as powerful there, but they *will* protect you. I promise."

Yudai's mouth melted into a thin line. "I don't—"

"Go!" the Oldirr woman exclaimed. "You must go!"

"Yudai! Chayd!" Tatsu said. "It's the only way!"

With a growl that Tatsu couldn't entirely read, Yudai wrenched himself away from the dying fire and the dying woman. The set of his shoulders gave away his unhappiness; princes were not pleased at having their decisions made for them. "Then take us to Chayd!"

Tatsu started off, continuing on the path through the mountains, but stopped when Ral had not followed. "Ral!"

"Goodbye." Ral reached out and touched the Oldirr woman's hands one last time. "Fly, hawk."

Then she took after Tatsu, and the party started up again.

From the mountain peaks, the way to Chayd was muddled. He had only a vague notion of the path they needed to take and the direction they needed to go. From their place between the slopes, he couldn't see out to the land beyond, but he was pretty sure the old trader's route would loop around and down, eventually depositing them within Chayd's territory. The passage was still full of snow that had frozen overnight into something far more dangerous, making it impossible to get them through as quickly as needed.

Before Runon, Leil had said the *soelm* were mages powerful enough to control people. A *soelm* mage was tracking them in the treacherous mountain pass, and all of the drained trees were wailing in terror.

They ran.

They ran until they could not run any more. Tatsu kept their pace frantic until the sun was overhead in the sky. They slid down the icy slopes and climbed back up the next incline on their hands and knees, leaving fingers red and puffy from cold. They ran until Yudai nearly collapsed, unable to continue, and Tatsu and Ral had to each take one of his arms to keep going.

Tatsu thought his heart was burning up, but still, they kept moving.

He didn't know where they were, but as they reached yet another summit, a break appeared in the clouds. Below, a long stretch of green trees fanned out near the bank of a thin, snaking river. Green meant the drain hadn't reached it. He feverishly hoped it signaled the Chaydese border.

"Keep going," he said, gasping for breath, though he was saying it more for himself than for Ral and Yudai.

Yudai was unable to keep up with their steps, his feet dragging. He had to be freezing, but he bit down hard on his lip and let nothing slip out. Ral kept mewing in discomfort, her face pinched and beads of perspiration matting her hair to her forehead.

Their pace dragged. As they made their way down the trail switchbacks, Tatsu heard something behind them. He didn't recognize it right away, with all of their clumsy thudding, but after a while, he couldn't ignore it—a wind much too warm and the steady plodding of hooves against packed snow.

"Yudai," Tatsu started, the rest of the words dying in this throat. Whatever they would have been, he never got the chance to continue.

Zakio found them first.

The mage raced through the passage they'd just cleared on a silver horse that moved like lightning. All around the racing horse, the snow and ice hissed as it burned away and ceased to be, evaporating into the air. Tatsu could feel it, the magic working its way through, and it smelled of scorched bark after a tree burned. He had only enough sense to throw them all to one side before the mage and his horse came crashing through, barely avoiding their being run down.

It might have been an easier way to go out. Zakio's mount reared up with its front legs stamping at the air and then turned. The horse was clearly exhausted, judging from the sheen of sweat on its haunches. It snorted, black mane flying in either direction, as its rider pulled sharply on the reins and loomed over their position flung into the snow.

They had been so close. The trees below burned in Tatsu's mind, taunting him.

"Well, well," Zakio said, and laughed. "Our little runaway mage. I'm amazed you got this far, to be honest. You were never one for outdoor skills."

"I'll kill you," Yudai spat. His body was alight with long-suppressed rage. "I'll tear you to pieces for what you did to me."

Zakio dismounted. As he drew closer, Tatsu got a better look at him. His heavily modified mage robes bore little resemblance to the ones Tatsu had seen in Chayd; the dark velvet alternated with leather, cleaner and closer in cut. More like embroidered armor than anything else, the fabric rippled as Zakio approached with the swagger of someone used to getting his way. His black hair was pulled back with a small tie, and his features were long, chin pointed.

Tatsu remembered the swagger from when they'd nearly run into Zakio in the castle. The enemy stopped a few steps away from them, his mouth twisting into a smug grin.

"I really don't think you will. I really don't think that you can."

When Yudai didn't respond, Zakio laughed again.

"Isn't that right, little prince?" he asked. "I knew it when I felt that uncontrolled display at the edge of Runon's lands. You can't control your magic. You can't even use it. You would have been to Joesar by now if you could, yet here you are, quivering in front of me like the spoiled brat you really are."

Zakio took a step forward and leaned in.

"It's been awhile since I was here," he said, "but I still know the way. You were never going to be able to outrun me on these trails."

A bubble had lodged in Tatsu's throat, swelling against the sides.

"What's the matter, Yudai?" Zakio asked. "That tongue of yours is never so silent...at least, it wasn't until we found a way to still it completely."

"You're a monster," Tatsu hissed. He surprised himself, and, by the look on Zakio's face, he wasn't the only one. Zakio regarded Tatsu before a slow, wide smile broke over his face. The expression turned Tatsu's blood cold. He wanted to reach for his bow, for the familiarity of the wood in his hands, but fear froze him in place.

"And you," Zakio said, and his grin widened. "I've been dying to meet you. Oh, we have so much to talk about. I was planning on dealing with you after taking care of our prince, but if you insist on going first…"

"No," Yudai said. "Don't you dare. Don't you *dare* touch them."

Zakio let his head fall a bit to one side. "I'm hurt you think so little of us to assume we don't want you back. We miss you, little prince. We miss all the wonderful energy you bring."

Yudai launched himself at Zakio, but all Zakio did was step aside and chuckle as Yudai ended sprawled out in the snow. Then Zakio let both hands fall to his sides, stretching out his fingers, and Tatsu could *feel* it. The magic began to coil in his palms and weave outward. Bits of snow rose in the air on either side of his body, lifted by an invisible force. Ral's hands went to her mouth, eyes wide with fear at the sight of it.

"I'm here to take you back to Runon," Zakio said, "but Mother won't mind if I have some fun with you first. She knows how much I like playing."

The air crackled with electricity, and in Tatsu's skin, pinpricks of lightning skipped across his arms and cheeks. Leil had told him about magic and its limitations, but now there were rocks at the side of the path and ice that had frozen into sharp spires jutting from the overhangs. They all began to rumble and shake as Zakio's magic built up like a tidal wave.

Tatsu grabbed for his bow and notched an arrow, letting it fly. But a large stone flew up from the ground and hovered there in front of Zakio, blocking him like a shield. The mage was able to use his magic to protect himself *and* control the rocks hovering in front of him at the same time. *Soelm.*

His help was useless, but still, Tatsu readied another arrow.

"Yudai!" he yelled.

With a growl, Zakio threw his hands forward, and the spikes of ice went with them, skimming across the windblown snow hills toward Yudai's kneeling form.

"No!" Yudai cried, throwing his head down to cover it with his arms.

And then his magic *roared* to life around him.

Chapter Sixteen

THE MAGIC FLARED up around them, buzzing through the air and simmering beneath Tatsu's skin. He thought that he realized it before Yudai did and started forward in a stupid attempt to warn the other man. But then Yudai lifted his head and the magic began to whirl, and, by the gleam of triumph in Yudai's eyes, it was intentional.

"You—" The surprise was audible in Zakio's tone as the spikes of ice hit what seemed to be a dome of energy around Yudai's body, and then dropped uselessly to the snow. Zakio staggered back a step as Yudai stood.

"You weren't hiding that all this time." Zakio put his hands up in the air, as if he were preparing for something. "I would have felt it if you had been controlling it. The poison—"

"Clearly had some unintended consequences," Yudai finished for him, voice cold.

Zakio's lip curled in an ugly sneer. "But you're still weak and barely keeping it in check. I can feel how tenuous your control is. That magic of yours certainly is resourceful, isn't it?"

"Don't you dare talk about me," Yudai hissed.

"It's reacting," Zakio continued, ignoring Yudai completely. The disdain was gone from his face, and instead, Zakio moved toward Yudai with unabashed curiosity. "It's reacting in *fear* to me. That's why it exploded like that. This is amazing, honestly. To see power so pure it's almost sentient—"

At that moment, Yudai pushed his magic outward and caught Zakio completely off guard. The energy spread out like ribbons from his fingers and picked up the first layer of snow that had pooled along the curving path. It gathered the flakes and bits of ice and spun them into a circle, faster than Tatsu thought possible, before launching all of it in a rush of freezing air. There was so much force behind it Tatsu winced when it made contact with Zakio's chest. The amount of speed it picked up in mere seconds was more akin to a cataclysmic storm wind than a push of magical energy. It stung Tatsu's cheeks, paces away from the blow, and, too late, he tried to raise his arm to protect both himself and Ral kneeling beside him.

Tatsu had thought it would knock Zakio completely off-balance, but he was wrong. The mage had managed to patch together a crude shield made of several sharp-cut rocks collected from the mountainside. It blocked the brunt of the icy wind, but Yudai was faster.

Before the initial blast of snow and ice had even dissipated, he was already readying a second blow. His fingers spun together and grabbed at bits of nothing, and then the air began to spin. Faster and faster, until it was moving in blurs of white, the miniature storm emitting heat against Tatsu's face.

Leil had told him that mages couldn't make what wasn't already there. But Yudai was *creating* fire, using the air as a makeshift spindle.

Yudai let the fire go with a cry of pent-up rage, years and years of frustration and loathing worked into a single, guttural exclamation. The fire exploded from between the palms of his hands—a stream of searing heat so intense the snow below it fizzled into vapor—and a line of melting mush surged directly toward Zakio and his cobbled stone shield.

Tatsu threw himself to the side, grabbing Ral on the way down.

Only a brush of the flames hit Zakio before he flung his arms wide and gathered snow around his body to soften the blast. As the snow absorbed the fire, Zakio rolled to the side somewhat awkwardly and landed badly on one knee. Puffs of fire on his shirt hissed and turned to steam when they made contact with the snow on the ground, and he seemed not to notice. Yudai ceased his projectile fire, and Zakio leapt up to use the opening it created. Congealing the snow he'd been holding up as the shield, he launched it across the space between them.

The barrage of magic whipped back and forth in front of them, faster than Tatsu had ever seen anything move before. His eyes seemed a second behind; by the time he caught up with what was happening, one of the mages was already a step ahead. It seemed impossible—and dangerous.

He tightened his arm around Ral's shoulders, but she seemed entranced by the display.

"Tatsu," she whispered, and one thin finger pointed out at the fighting. "Watch magic."

The only word Tatsu could summon in his mind was *incredible*. A split-second look away, and the mages had shifted their positions, bearing down on one another. Between Yudai's hands, small rocks whirled, and in front of Zakio a semicircle of ice rose rapidly. With every attack, there was a parry, but worry clouded Tatsu's thoughts. Yudai's strength was only a fraction of what he needed. If he didn't have enough control over the magic he'd just found inside himself again, he would lose.

Tatsu had a feeling losing this battle meant losing a great deal more.

Zakio let loose the ice in a rush so strong shaved shreds pushed against Tatsu's face. They weren't much more than slivers, but the sting of the cold forced his eyes shut, shoulders clenching in pain. Only a moment later, when he reopened his eyes, Zakio was soaring through the air with his hands stretched out in front of him.

It was clear he was aiming for Yudai, only Zakio stopped halfway through the air. With a sharp cry, Yudai sent Zakio's body backward with a crack against the mountainside wall. Fragments of the stone rained onto the snow at the base, but Zakio's body held firm where it was. Yudai crossed the space with big, purposeful steps before the other mage could respond, one hand outstretched with clawed fingers.

Even Tatsu could tell that the wave of snow directed at Yudai was weak. From his position against the rocks, Zakio's features twisted in frustration and pain. Yudai merely smacked the flung snow down with one arm, and it dissipated.

"Son of a bitch," Zakio spat, still unable to wrench himself free of Yudai's magical hold.

"That's exactly what I was going to say to you," Yudai replied, his cheeks pink, forehead streaked with rivulets of perspiration, face contorted in rage. He had the upper hand, but he wasn't going to be able to hold it much longer. His body, weak and drained, had fallen too far out of practice. Against the white and gray backdrop, his fingers trembled as they reached out to hold Zakio in place. He was stretched beyond his limits.

In an instant, Tatsu could see that Zakio knew it too.

Zakio threw both hands forward in an explosion of sparks, rocks screeching against other stones until the air filled with electricity and the crackling from the magnitude of it. Yudai's body was tossed back like a ragdoll. He folded into the snow, nearly disappearing into the whiteness, and Zakio staggered away from the mountainside with a palpable air of triumph.

When Yudai finally pulled himself up, one hand wiped at his face and smeared bits of the snow across his cheeks. He started to get another attack ready, one that Tatsu could feel in the air as he had the fire, but Zakio was too quick. He gestured up to the sky with a flick of his wrist, and Yudai's body complied with the order.

Around Zakio's boots, the snow began to simmer, evaporating into tendrils of rising steam.

"I'm a little disappointed," he said, his hand still in the air as he kept Yudai's body hovering above the ground. "I thought that magic would put up more of a fight. The famed mage heir. My, how your father gloated about you."

Yudai's glower could have cut the very stones of the mountainside. Behind his back, his hands were bent stiffly and unnaturally, his fingers clenched into furious fists.

"It's strange, isn't it?" Zakio asked. "How your father was so proud of your magic, but never really of you. Do you think he actually cared about you? Or were you just power for him?"

Yudai's eyebrows twisted in emotion. Zakio began moving forward slowly, leaving a trail of melting snow behind him. The space they'd been using as their fighting ground looked like the aftermath of an avalanche that had struck on a late spring day. Patches of white ended suddenly with circles of brown, and the piles of snow were so uneven they looked like mountains themselves.

"Mother told me to bring you back alive," Zakio continued, and his voice dropped low. "But I think it makes much more sense to kill you now and tell her that it was the only way to save myself."

"You know what she'll do then." Yudai laughed harshly. "With me gone, she'll finally convince my father to marry her and produce another magical heir. She won't need you anymore. She'll have everything she ever wanted by herself."

His words seemed to strike a chord in Zakio. The man's features twisted as the air began to tremble and buzz with suppressed energy.

Ral whimpered, pressing a hand to her mouth. "Tatsu, no."

"Yudai," Tatsu breathed. Fortunately, Zakio seemed to think of them as mere annoyances, something to be dealt with later. He didn't so much as glance in their direction as the entire clearing began to shake with his fury. Something about the feeling rang a bit off, a song in discord— Zakio was losing control.

And then, all of a sudden, Tatsu could *feel* it: Yudai's magic. It was as though the entirety of it had materialized out of nothing until the magic was the only thing Tatsu was aware of. Zakio realized it too, but too late, because he'd slipped away from his hold on his own energy. Zakio shouted a wordless exclamation of surprise and reached out with a hand to manipulate Yudai's body further as the trembling air began to spiral about them in a lopsided cyclone. One of Yudai's arms was wrenched away from his body and twisted, but instead of fighting it, Yudai let his entire body rotate with the motion. He spun around using Zakio's own force until he was righted again, and that was when the blast of magic, pure energy and control, erupted from him.

In a fit of desperation, Tatsu shielded himself and Ral from it, though determined to keep his eyes open to see what happened. With tears streaming down his cheeks from the sheer might, he forced his gaze to stay on the two.

Zakio's body slammed into the mountain wall once, with a sickening crack, and then whipped to the side away from the rocks before plummeting to the ground. The patchwork of melting snow did him no favors. The shock and thud of his body hitting the dirt reverberated all the way through Tatsu's bones.

Not even a second later, Yudai was upon him. In an instant, Zakio's own knife was in Yudai's fingers, wrenched free of the sheath with such force the leather split completely down one side. Yudai held it against Zakio's throat and leaned in, seething with contempt.

"Make your last words good ones," he demanded, voice hoarse and raw. "You *used* me. You carved everything good out from me and used it as a *weapon*."

"Yes." Zakio laughed. "How lucky we were to have a king cold enough to sacrifice his own son."

"I should cut your tongue out before I kill you," Yudai threatened, leaning closer.

Zakio just laughed again, spitting blood that beaded red on his lips and chin, and then twisted his neck to look at Tatsu instead. "Don't let him kill me."

"What?" Tatsu asked. "Why should I help *you*?"

"Because we have the same mother," Zakio said.

It took a minute for the words to sink in, and then Tatsu's body took over, and he was rising to his feet and lunging forward. The spiral of magic that had just disappeared seemed to have moved to his mind, jumbling all his thoughts until he could focus on none of them. They all screamed through his brain until only one managed to get past his lips: "Yudai, *wait!*"

Yudai's face pinched in displeasure, but Zakio kept laughing.

"You're lying!" Tatsu gasped, his chest tight, too tight, as though all the air in the world was simply gone. "It's not true. How would you—?"

"We knew who you were as soon as Yudai disappeared from the castle," Zakio said. "I've known about you my whole life. But you...you were born without magic. You were weak. And if there's one thing my mother can't stand, it's weakness."

"No," Tatsu replied. "No, I would have—my father would have told me."

Another harsh laugh from Zakio's throat, and blood bubbled up at the corner of his mouth. "Told you what, *Chaydese*? That you were worthless? That you were useless? Our mother wanted nothing to do with you once she learned the truth. She had no use for you or your expendable father."

Tatsu would have sworn the mountains had fallen on top of him. He tried to wish the words away but couldn't. He stumbled back with his hands over his face, wishing his fingers would block out everything. His brain was desperate to reject what Zakio was telling him, but the hammering of his heart told him the truth. Swelling in his throat, it threatened to choke him. With every aching beat, his body *knew* the words were true.

His mother was High Mage Nota of Runon. And she'd willingly deserted him.

Tatsu doubled over, stomach seizing.

"Enough," Yudai hissed and slashed the knife clean across Zakio's throat. Tatsu couldn't quite get himself to look at the angry red splatter on the dirt and snow for more than a second before bile rose bitterly in the back of his throat. The contents of his stomach ended up another spray of color against the white.

Yudai rose and turned to face Tatsu. The rage fled from his features, replaced with something softer. "You didn't know?"

"How could I have known?" Tatsu cried out.

"You broke the barrier. The magical barrier, at the castle, when you freed me. I knew it then. The magic at work there was coded to Nota's blood. Only those who carry her blood could have gotten through that."

All Tatsu could do in response was moan.

A soft hand on his shoulder signaled Ral by his side, but she said nothing, and Tatsu was glad. Betrayal burned hot through his skin, engulfing his senses. His father had never told him and had purposely kept all information regarding magic from him. Had it been deliberate? Knowing that his father wished him to be in the dark about his own heritage caused Tatsu's blood to boil with rage. It nearly overflowed until the shame set in—shame that his mother was someone evil enough to use another human being as a free source of magic energy. Shame that his mother was draining the lands around Runon and turning them into nightmares.

Shame that his mother looked at him as an infant and thought him useless.

Tatsu's knees buckled, and he went down hard, though he barely registered the cold of the snow between his fingers.

He was startled from his own misery when Yudai cried out, aghast. Tatsu turned to find him staring down at his hands.

"It's gone," Yudai said like a question, as if he couldn't believe it himself. "It's gone, my magic—I can't feel it anymore. It's disappeared again."

He spun, enraged, and threw himself on Zakio's bloodied body.

"It's gone!" he screamed. His fist made solid contact with Zakio's face, and then again. The awful smack of it rang through the pass. "It's gone, it's gone, you *bastard—*!"

Tatsu leapt to his feet without thinking. He grabbed for Yudai's shoulders to haul him back and away, and even then, Yudai's fists kept swinging. He kicked and grabbed at Tatsu's arms, but his body was tired and spent, and Tatsu won.

"Stop it!" Tatsu demanded. "Stop it! He's still my brother!"

"And he's *dead*," Yudai replied with a hiss. "They've ruined me!"

Finally, Tatsu let him go, and Yudai fell to his knees with an angry glare. He didn't move to make any further attack on Zakio's corpse, though, so Tatsu let him be. His emotions flooded one atop another, unable to be reconciled, until they were so heavy he could barely keep standing. Each breath was a battle to keep in, and even worse to push back out.

He stared at Zakio's lifeless body, trying to catalogue everything: the curve of his nose, the line of his cheeks. He tried to find parts of himself mirrored there, but everything was red. He knelt by the body and couldn't seem to move.

His father had refused to tell him anything. He'd grown up never knowing anything about his mother. Suddenly, that ignorance seemed very dangerous.

"Not you," Ral said, patting his shoulder. Tatsu was sure the gesture was meant to be compassionate, but it only served to propel him closer to embarrassing sobs. "Not you, Tatsu."

"We have to go," Yudai told him. He sparked with anger at his magic falling out of his reach once more, but he seemed to have settled down somewhat. Still, Tatsu thought he read something like loathing shimmering behind his gaze.

Tatsu turned back to Zakio's still figure, sucking in painful lungfuls of air. *Brother.*

"Tatsu!" Yudai snapped.

It barely registered, but Tatsu still lifted his gaze to look at him.

"We have to go," Yudai repeated with more force. He stopped a few paces from Tatsu and leaned in. "She's going to come after us. She's going to kill us all. You were right; it's safer in Chayd."

"Right," Tatsu whispered. "Safer."

"Tatsu, stand up," Yudai ordered.

Ral's hand on his shoulder did feel like comfort, right at that moment. Tatsu was glad for it. He managed to stand up, though shaky on his feet. The mountains seemed much colder than they had been, and past them, the world no longer appeared in focus. With the shift, none of the edges lined up. Everything blurred and blended together, as though someone had run their hand across a wet painting and smeared all the shapes.

Tatsu ran his hands over his face, but it didn't do much to help.

"Zakio's horse," Yudai said. Tatsu had forgotten all about the beast, which had disappeared down the trail when the magic battle started. "We might as well take it."

"Yeah," Tatsu replied weakly. He found the stallion stamping at the ground around the next curve in the downward sloping pass. The mount's reins had tangled around a jagged gash in the stones and kept it from going further. Spooked but unharmed, the animal snorted as Tatsu ran his hand over its muzzle to soothe them both. When he led it back to where Yudai and Ral were waiting, he avoided looking at the dead man in the snow.

"Yudai, you ride first," Tatsu said. "We need to move fast."

It was probably a testament to how drained Yudai was that he agreed without an argument and swung a leg up onto the saddle with practiced ease. Ral shifted in to wrap her arm around the horse's neck and run her fingers through its black mane. She kept up with the animal's rhythmic gait as Yudai urged it forward.

Tatsu gave one last, lingering glance at Zakio's body. When he turned to continue down the mountain with the others, it felt as if *his* blood had been spilt across the snow instead. Perhaps it was his soul they were leaving there, amidst the ice and rock.

Chapter Seventeen

IT TOOK DAYS to get out of the mountains.

The days blurred together, leaving Tatsu perpetually light-headed. For some hours, they were skating down atop loose pebbles and trying to keep their balance. And at other times, they found the path relatively solid and easy to climb. They took turns riding on Zakio's horse, which didn't do much to aid their pace, but did help with their exhaustion. Fortunately, Yudai had gotten back full control of his appendages between Runon and the Shyreld. He no longer seemed to be struggling with each step to get his legs to comply, and his progress sped the party up tremendously. As they made their way toward the Chayd border, the peaks gradually began to flatten and slope, losing the high elevation that allowed spires of rock to disappear in the misty clouds.

Finding caves became harder as the mountains faded into large hills. They slept when they could, in the crevices they could find, and climbed when they couldn't find shelter, using the light of the moon as their guide. In the dark of the nights, sometimes the only sound was the rhythmic clopping of the horse's hooves against the ground. Yudai was quiet, but then again, Tatsu was too. Whenever his mind wandered, it went back to Zakio's body. Every time he closed his eyes, he imagined what his past would have been like had he been aware of his parentage. He obsessed over the idea of the family he'd never known, even though none of his imaginings would have been real. He fixated on it, so focused that he tripped several times on the pathway's loose pebbles.

When he slept, he saw Zakio's face, along with the guard he'd killed in the Yuse castle hall. His dreams left him rattled and off-kilter. While awake, he was skittish in a world filled with a strange haze.

Somehow, all of it had settled into a familiar ache by the time they reached the flatter grasslands that streaked away from the mountain base. The pulsing in Tatsu's blood hadn't eased, but he'd grown accustomed to it—a hard stone settled between his lungs, pressing against his sternum.

Chaydese land afforded them no welcome. As they neared Dradela, the grass faded into sparse patches, punctuated by uneven holes of slightly orange soil. Already, the warmth of summer floated on the breeze. Too many days in the mountain pass had left him unprepared for the onslaught of the tropical heat.

"We're in Chayd," he said, and even to his own ears, his voice sounded lifeless.

Yudai, walking beside him, remained silent. He stared off into the distance, toward the coast of the Oldal Sea and the hub of Chayd's settlements.

"Do you think we're in danger still?" Tatsu asked.

Yudai made a noncommittal noise that answered nothing.

"Can you use your magic?"

This got Yudai's attention. His features twisted into a scowl as he said, "No. I can feel it there, but I can't access it. I'm blocked from my own power."

He turned to face Tatsu, and his expression didn't change.

"And before you ask," he continued, "no. I don't know how to get around the block."

Tatsu hadn't been preparing to ask but kept that information to himself. Too much in his head vied for his immediate attention. He looked quickly at Ral sitting atop the horse, and she seemed happier than either of them. Being back home seemed to be a much more pleasing situation to her than it did to Tatsu.

Getting closer to Dradela caused his skin to buzz in anticipation, and nothing about the sensation was particularly pleasant.

As they started to move away from the mountains, they encountered one of the wide, clear rivers that ran across the southern half of Chayd's lands. It would cost them valuable time, but it was too tempting to pass up. They took turns stripping off their clothes and washing their skin clean in the pleasantly cool water.

Tatsu kept them moving after that. Without the rocky hills, they would no longer have the possibility of a stone cave shelter. It took the better part of an afternoon for them to reach one of the small farming settlements decorating the land past the capital's city limits. The beginnings of Dradela's castle spires loomed in the distance, but it was too far to reach without a rest. The outpost offered their only relief.

He approached the village with care. Fields extended past the small circle of wood and sandstone buildings, full of green leaves and illuminated by the setting summer sun. They walked beside lines of trees thick with fronds and budding with small, coin-sized dates. In other fields, heavy bunches of still-green grapes hung from wooden trellises. Farming communities were poor, but Tatsu was banking on compassion to needy neighbors.

It wasn't until he caught sight of a woman, hair braided up in a tight bun, that he realized he had overlooked a glaring problem. When she saw them, she straightened from the small plants she was tending. Her initial expression was of surprise, and then, as they drew nearer, of worry. The bottom of her dress caught on long leaves as she took several quick steps back, but she seemed not to notice.

"*Lyek,*" Tatsu said, hoping the old Chaydese word for peace would soften her. He held his palms up toward her to show he was unarmed. But her eyes flitted between them at a frantic pace, and Tatsu could guess what she was seeing: a mob. Between Yudai's shockingly white hair and obviously Runonian features and Ral's unbraided hair floating behind her like a tattered curtain, Tatsu, himself, was scarcely helping the sight. They were already unwanted.

"Get back," the woman said and scrambled up higher onto the small mound of dirt behind the field's rows. Her feet carried her in the direction of the buildings. "We don't want any trouble."

"We're not here to cause any," Tatsu told her. "Please, we just need a place to stay—"

"*Dreyth,*" the woman hissed at Yudai, and Tatsu's heart sank.

He kept his hands up, though his body was already trembling. "No, he's not a monster. I know it looks bad, but we aren't here to hurt you, I promise."

"Monster?" Yudai exclaimed, incredulous, leaning forward against the horse's slick neck. The woman took the moment of distraction to turn and flee toward the safety of the structures. The cloud of dust she kicked up behind her stung Tatsu's eyes before it resettled on the ground.

He wiped at his face, aware he was only worsening the problem by smearing sweat and dust across his skin. "She didn't mean it. People here are...well, things are difficult in the outskirts."

"She *did* mean it," Yudai snapped, bristling, "and that's the point, isn't it? I'm an outsider."

"So am I." Tatsu sighed, giving his face one more pass with his fingers.

Yudai laughed. "The difference is that I'm dangerous."

Tatsu wanted to argue that, only he never got the chance. The woman had found others in the village, and a handful of them were approaching. Several carried weapons—though only one was a real sword—and others had mere farming tools, rusted and weathered from use. It was the type of crowd meant to scare off bandits and thieves, and any hope Tatsu might have still had was lost.

"Travelers," one of the men said, stopping several paces in front of Tatsu's group. He was a big man, with black hair tied back behind his ears and a scraggly beard that hadn't been trimmed evenly. "Best be moving on."

"We don't mean any harm." Tatsu kept his hands up; the men might be little more than farmers, but he was willing to bet the desire to protect their village would easily overpower his ragtag trio. "We're just looking for a place to stay."

His statement invited an audible reaction from the crowd, clearly negative by the tone. Tatsu expected an immediate rebuff, but the big man in front was silent. His eyes roved over Yudai and his scowl, and then Ral and her vacant smile, taking in everything, right down to the layers of grime covering the hems of their clothing. Tatsu's opinion of him rose.

He motioned Tatsu forward and stepped off to the side from the rest of the people.

Wary, Tatsu followed him.

"The woman," the man said, voice low, when they had slid far enough away, "she's not right in the head, is she?"

Tatsu stamped his fury down. He knew it would do him no good to lose his temper, no matter how much he wanted to. "No."

The man nodded and murmured, "Is she dangerous?"

"What?" Tatsu cried out. "No! No. She's just...she's innocent."

"Then it wouldn't be right to turn you away," the Chaydese man said. Close up, Tatsu could see all the wrinkles in his brown skin. There were spots of darker color from years working in the sun, and a notch in his left ear, as if his head had come too close to an axe and emerged the loser. He smelled like sweat mingled with dirt and fermenting fruit left on the vine too long.

The scent, strangely, offered comfort; the earthy tones reminded Tatsu of his father.

"I've got a barn that's empty right now," the man told him. "There's enough hay to sleep in, and a roof over your head. Your mount can stay there with you. It might not smell the best, but..."

"We'll take it," Tatsu said in a rush, afraid their good luck would fade if he hesitated. "Thank you."

"Just get the Runonian out of our village by sunrise tomorrow," the villager said.

When Tatsu looked back at the other two, his mind was a discord of competing emotions. "All right," he agreed.

THE HAY IN the loaned barn loft tickled his back and poked through the linen of his shirt, but the location was infinitely more comfortable than the bareness of cold stone. Out of the mountains, the air was much warmer. Normally, Tatsu would have been irritated by the early heat and mugginess, but after so much time spent in the snow, it felt wonderful. They dozed off quickly, lulled to sleep by the snuffles and snorts of Zakio's horse echoing inside the wooden structure.

Tatsu woke suddenly sometime during the night. Cracks from split boards in the roof allowed slivers of moonlight onto the unevenly stacked bales. He blinked once and then again, trying to focus in the darkness, before he realized there was a figure kneeling over him.

Shock propelled him up. His throat seized until he recognized the free-flowing tendrils of hair.

"Ral?" he whispered. In his dream-addled state, he'd automatically assumed the figure was Nota, come to avenge her son in a crackling fury. Ral's hand flew to his mouth to cover it, though it landed awkwardly and ended up pressing against only one side of his lips.

"Tatsu, choose." Her voice was low but impassioned. "Choose!"

"What?" Tatsu asked, after her fingers slid free of his mouth. "Choose what?"

Ral leaned forward and something cold and hard smacked into his shoulder. He didn't immediately recognize the pendant the Oldirr woman had gifted her. It still hung around her neck but had fallen free from her shirt and was swinging from side to side like a pendulum. Despite the warm air, the pendant was cool.

"Please!" Ral insisted. "Choose!"

Tatsu shook his head. "Ral, I don't understand. Choose what? What are you trying to say?"

"Tatsu," Ral said again, her voice a groan of frustration.

"I don't understand," Tatsu repeated. "I'm sorry, but I don't."

From the cracks in the ceiling, bits of starlight were filtering brighter into the barn, lining up, jagged and irregular, across the hay-strewn floor. They twinkled in and out of existence as clouds passed overhead, pitching the barn into near complete darkness every few seconds.

Ral sighed. He could just make out that she was shaking her head from the glowing outline of her form against the shadowy backdrop, and then she leaned in further. Instead of reaching for his mouth again, her palm slid across his eyes to close them.

"Don't think," she whispered, and he found himself nodding off again against his own will. The last thing he remembered her whispering was a single word, over and over: "*Feel.*"

THE NEXT TIME Tatsu woke, morning sun had begun to fill the barn. It was very warm already, and his clothing clung to his skin. Worried they were already past the time the village had asked them to leave, he sat up to find Yudai and Ral already awake with a small basket sitting in front of them.

"The farmer brought out some food," Yudai explained, passing a hard roll to Tatsu. "He didn't seem particularly happy about it. He probably just didn't want us bothering anyone else in the village again."

The bread was made from coarsely ground starch and at least two days old, but after so long surviving on dried and salted staples, it still tasted delicious. Chewing through the rock-like exterior took quite a bit of effort, and they sat in silence as they ate. Halfway through the roll, Tatsu remembered the strange events of the previous night.

"Ral, what did you mean last night? When we were awake?"

She cocked her head at him, a crumb of her bread stuck to the corner of her lip. "Awake?"

"No, you said things to me. And I didn't understand what you meant."

"Breakfast?" Ral asked and held out the remainder of her roll to him.

"What are you talking about?" Yudai asked, frowning. "I don't remember either of you being awake and speaking to each other last night."

Feeling foolish, Tatsu waved Ral's offered gift back. "No, I'm fine. Sorry. I must have been dreaming or something."

But the strange feeling lingered. He was sure he hadn't been asleep during that time, and it had seemed all too real to have been something his mind conjured up. Ral gave him nothing with her blank expression, and Yudai just shrugged it off.

The villager's threat hung heavy over their heads, and as soon as they were finished eating the stale bread, they set off again. Dawn was an hour or two over the plains of Chayd, and the wispy tuffs of long grass looked yellow in the remnants of the sunrise still streaking pink across the sky. It was good to see foliage that neither attacked them nor sang to them, a reminder, at least, of how they'd managed to stop Yudai's drain before it got to Chayd's border. Tatsu let Ral ride the horse so he could stretch his legs. Walking through the stubby trees with their branches splayed like fingers eased a bit of the pressure in his mind. In Chayd, everything was as it should have been.

They walked until midday and stopped to rest. If they kept on at the same pace, Tatsu wagered they would reach Dradela by late afternoon the following day.

He said as much to his companions as he rubbed the horse's muzzle briefly.

"If we're lucky," he added, "the weather will be good enough for us to sleep outside tonight without much trouble."

"If we're lucky," Yudai repeated, face somber.

As Ral took off her shoes and wiggled her toes in the air, Tatsu moved to Yudai's side. "Are you still worried about what happened back in the village?"

"I'd be a fool not to. I'm the enemy here. How are people going to welcome the prince of their aggressor? Particularly in their capital city?"

"The queen will protect you. It's in her best interest to keep you safe and out of Runon. The minute you go back..."

"Yeah," Yudai agreed, but his tone was grim. "I know what my future is in Runon."

Silence permeated the space between them.

"Maybe you don't have to stay in Chayd," Tatsu started slowly. "Maybe you can go elsewhere. Across the mountains to Joesar, perhaps."

Yudai laughed. "The people of Joesar are sentimental and naïve. They cling to their old beliefs and practices while the rest of the world laughs at them."

"Chayd has been fighting with Joesar for decades. I don't think Chayd is laughing."

"Yes, and while both their gazes were turned away, Runon took advantage of it. The Joesarians are fools. They still believe the old gods will protect them because they fail to see the truth."

Tatsu's throat was dry when he asked, "And what is the truth?"

"That *we* are the gods here," Yudai said, leaning closer. "And we care nothing for prayers."

Tatsu stared at the ground beneath his boots. A few tendrils of weeds poked up between small stones, reaching up and around the rocks to get to the sun. Even weeds were flexible enough to stay alive. Tatsu thought about Zakio again, his body up in the mountains and his blood on the snow. A fresh wave of anger rose up in his throat and burned, but he tried to ignore it. It clouded his mind too much and made it hard to stretch out his focus to the world around them.

Later, after evening had fallen, the air was warm enough that sleeping outside was far from the worst thing they could do. They were short on bedrolls still, so Tatsu offered his roll to Ral and let her set it up on the ground while he knotted the horse's reins around a nearby tree branch.

Settling down beneath several blissfully motionless trees, Tatsu stared up at the sky. It was too cloudy to see the moon or stars, but they were there. He laced his fingers behind his head. The previous night's dream of Ral remained in his thoughts, and he tried to push it away, dismissing it as shock and exhaustion propelling his mind into bizarre realities and nothing more.

"What does it feel like not being able to use your magic?" Tatsu wasn't sure if Yudai had fallen asleep or not. He waited a long time before the other man moved. Brush crunched beneath his weight.

"Like I'm only half of myself," Yudai whispered in response.

Tatsu's temples throbbed. "I know how you feel."

RAIN FELL IN fat drops as they arrived in Dradela, the warm sort of rain that lingered in the air and made everything heavy. The humidity was worse within the city, even in the outskirts where the traders had set up. Tatsu tied off the horse for the last time out near Dradela's farms and gave the creature a fond pat on the neck before they continued on, drawing closer to the city. A good horse was always in high demand, and the animal wouldn't remain in solitude long before someone decided to claim it. If the horse was lucky, the new owner would be more compassionate than Zakio.

Too many smells mixed together—spices and incense, baked meat pies and carved fruit slices on small sticks—making it claustrophobic to walk between the stalls. Weaving between the tented trading stands without being caught by one of the more overzealous assistants took practiced skill, and Tatsu was too weary to do it well. Twice, they were stopped and offered heavily discounted wares, and extracting themselves from the transaction took far too much time.

As they made their way past the city walls, Tatsu remembered the last time he'd done the same walk. He had iron around his wrists and guards flanking him on either side. The memory would have been worse if Ral hadn't been walking next to him this time. He didn't bother to keep his face down as they made their way—they were already too much of a spectacle to go unnoticed, and exhaustion kept his mind elsewhere. The truth was he was too tired to worry about drawing attention.

The only thing saving them from further scrutiny was that people were staying inside during the afternoon rain. They wove through the merchant district, its muddy streets already spotted with puddles of standing water. Paneled roofs channeled water down and into the street through holes in the eaves, but all this did was splatter bits of it off the piled boxes and barrels sitting by the storefronts. By the time they made it to the noble estates, all three of them were soaked.

Guards found them within the noble district with its high garden walls made of glistening sandstone. Tatsu should have seen it coming. Few cared about scruffy-looking outsiders in the trader stalls, but the estates were a different story.

"We're headed to the palace," Tatsu told the guards, heading them off. "We need an audience with the queen."

The shorter guard laughed. "The queen does not meet with commoners and thieves. Go back to Iah where you all belong."

But the other guard was staring at Tatsu intently, his face a mask of concentration. His gaze shifted slowly to take in Yudai's sopping white strands, and then his mouth pursed. Between Yudai's telltale silver eyes and the bedraggled state of their clothes, they were unique enough to warrant a pause.

"Wait," the second guard said, holding a hand out to stop the first from turning and leaving. "The smaller one is Runonian. The queen will want to see them. He's telling the truth."

For once, looking unlike the Chaydese gave Tatsu an advantage. Both guards were paying attention. A small crowd gathered to watch, the nobles dressed in their finery standing in doorways to avoid the rain. The last thing Tatsu wanted was to explain Yudai with an audience. A quick glance over his shoulder showed him the other man's high-held chin but wary, guarded expression.

The first guard sniffed in annoyance. "Fine, but if we get scolded for bringing street trash into the palace, it's on your head."

The guards led them the rest of the way, and Tatsu was glad for it. He wasn't entirely sure he'd remember the twists and turns to get to the palace gates. The last time, he'd been too distracted to commit them all to memory. And, all the noble estates looked the same, except the school with its wide-open windows and the apothecary with its swinging sign out front. But the rest were a blur of white sandstone.

The rain came down harder as they walked, and by the time they reached the great stone pillars in front of the palace, Tatsu's hair was sticking to his face in wet clumps. He felt wildly out of place as the guards led them into the palace.

His boots left muddy footprints in the entryway, but then again, so did the guards'. How many times throughout the years had palace servants had to scrub the shimmering floor stones free of footprints? Their footsteps echoed through the vaulted ceilings, and Tatsu hunched his shoulders unconsciously, wishing the sound away. The clattering was too loud for a space decorated with painted vases and wall-wide frescos. To the left, two brown-clad servants looked up in curiosity as the guards stopped them outside the double wooden doors leading into the receiving room.

"We will announce you to the queen," the second guard said. "If she wishes to speak with you, then you will be summoned within. Wait here and don't touch anything."

There was little chance to do so, anyway, as a pair of doormen remained in the room with them, and both were wearing swords on their leather uniform belts. Between the servants and the doormen, Tatsu felt that all the eyes in the room were focused squarely on him. He looked to Yudai to keep his mind off of it, but he was pacing through the foyer while taking stock of all the tapestries on the walls.

"Is it like being home?" Tatsu asked.

Yudai frowned, running a finger over the shoulder-height molding separating the painted wall from the stones beneath it. "No. It's much more...colorful than our castle. It feels much different."

"I'm sure you'll have ample time to explore it. I mean, I assume they'll keep you here, just because it's the safest place."

"There is no safe place for me," Yudai said and frowned. He looked up at the images painted bright across the mounted sandstone—the historical invasion of the mainland, the naval forces adrift on angry blue waves, and the settlement of the sandy shores. The frown stayed on his features even as he slowly moved beneath the pictures and studied them.

Behind Tatsu, Ral was also admiring the huge, walled scenes. She stood beneath one closest to the door that showed a Chaydese man wearing traditional royal dress, riding on a magnificent horse and holding a sword in each hand. Through the hall, soldiers and women in colorful sashes processed, and beyond, the bright burning orb of the sun beamed in bright yellow. Ral seemed entranced by the painting, and when Tatsu approached her, she lifted a finger to point up at it.

"Riding," she said. "Many riding. And pretty dresses."

"It *is* pretty, isn't it?" Tatsu agreed. "It's the story of King Leuket and his journey across the mountains. He founded the kingdom of Chayd, thousands of years ago. They say in the legend that he was both a king *and* a mage, but many people believe it's not true."

His father, at least, had never believed that part of the tale and always made sure to tell Tatsu when reading it. *King Leuket's Triumph* had been one of the few books his father kept in the cottage when Tatsu was growing up. It wasn't one of the books Tatsu had learned to read from, and the story had taken him quite a while to get through on his own.

Ral turned to him, face wiped clean of her usual mirth. "Tatsu believe?"

"Believe what?" he asked. "You mean about King Leuket? There's no proof he had magic. And even if he did, it certainly ended with him. No one else born from the royal line has had it."

"Tatsu, choose," Ral said.

His not-dream from their journey to Dradela came rushing back. Tatsu took a step away, muscles clenching in apprehension. "What? Ral?"

"Happy!" she announced, and the expression was gone. Her mouth split into a wide smile. "Alesh!"

"A-Alesh?" Tatsu stammered just as, behind him, footsteps and an audible gasp reverberated through the vaults above them. He spun, scarcely daring to hope—but there she was, racing across the stone floor with her braids streaming out behind her.

"Ral!" Alesh cried, and within moments, she had wrapped Ral up in a tight embrace. The two of them spun a bit across the floor, a whirl of color and emotion, before stopping. Alesh's face was streaked with tears. She choked on her words at first, mouth opening and closing several times without anything emerging. Then she stepped back, her hands on Ral's shoulders, and looked her sister over as if inspecting her for injuries.

"I can't believe you're okay," Alesh said and looked like she was going to burst into tears again. Alesh glanced at Tatsu, and her features remained warm. "I can't believe you're *both* okay!"

"What are you doing here?" Tatsu asked.

Alesh shook her head and brushed away the last bits of errant tears from her cheeks. "They kept me here to wait until they found you. Without the siphon, the whole thing was unfinished, and they didn't know what to do with me. They didn't necessarily want to put me back in Aughwor, but they couldn't just let me go either, I guess."

"So they kept you prisoner," Yudai said, breaking his silence. "A fancy prisoner in a palace, but still under lock and key."

"You're awake." Alesh stepped away from Ral, toward the door, putting space between herself and Yudai. "That's lucky."

Yudai's eyebrow rose and disappeared beneath tendrils of white hair. "Lucky? For you, it seems."

Tatsu stiffened when Yudai turned to him.

"You didn't tell me about a deal," he said. "From what it sounds like, there's a lot you kept to yourself. This whole time, you told me you were only taking me back to Chayd for my own protection."

"It's not what you think," Tatsu started, hands unconsciously rising in a defensive gesture. "We had to get you in order to be let free. But I swear, it's not the reason I brought you here. It's safer, I promise—"

"Safer?" Yudai echoed, incredulous. "Tatsu, this was a plea deal, and I was your *bargaining chip*!"

"But no one knew what you were!" Tatsu cried.

The big double doors of the receiving hall opened then, and the two guards from earlier strode out in their gleaming gold-plated armor.

"The queen will see you now," the first one said and, after eyeing Alesh standing in the back with one hand on Ral's wrist, added, "all of you."

Tatsu followed the soldiers inside, drawing his shoulders in to take up the least space possible. The queen's hall was exactly as he remembered it, only more oppressive with all the shadows. Behind the throne stood the mages, though it was too hard to tell from their hoods casting shadows on their faces if Leil was among them. The court advisors, lined up on either side of the dais, appeared less conflicted than Tatsu remembered them being before. And in the middle, the queen sat regally on her throne with the indigo ribbons threaded through her coiled black braids.

"Welcome back, Tatsu," she announced.

"Your grace," he murmured and gave her a jerky half bow.

Her dark eyes swept to Yudai, who was glaring in her direction, shoulders bunched and angry. "And I see you are not alone. Prince Yudai, welcome to the kingdom of Chayd. I'm afraid you might find our hospitality somewhat lacking from what you might expect as a *royal guest*."

A myriad of emotions flickered across Yudai's face. It showed everything all at once, and then, in a single second as realization dawned, his expression solidified to only one: rage. Yudai whirled on Tatsu with fury etched into every feature, his hands clenched into fists, shaking.

"You sold me ou—" was all he got out before the guard behind him leapt forward.

The soldier had a white handkerchief in his armored hand and pressed the linen against Yudai's mouth, his other arm looping around the mage's shoulders. There was only a second, maybe two, before Yudai's eyes rolled back in his head and his body slouched forward. The guard's arm abruptly pulled away, leaving Yudai's body to slump to the ground in a heap of muddied white cloth and drained-white hair.

"What are you doing?" Tatsu exclaimed and tried to jump forward to help Yudai, but two of the court nobles moved in front of him and blocked his path. He turned to the queen, who had risen from her throne and was gliding closer in a flurry of brightly colored sashes. "What have you done?"

"He is far too dangerous to be left as he is." The queen's features were stony as she gazed on Yudai's collapsed body with disinterest. "And Runon would see us all burn for the theft. They will not stop until they have him back."

"He's a person!" Tatsu cried.

The queen's gaze flickered to Tatsu and didn't change in the slightest. "There is much to reclaim from the failed negotiations. The retrieval of the siphon has saved Chayd from a battle with unimaginable loss of life and given us hope to stand our ground against Runon's demands. You see, then, that this was the best option. Chayd would have lost the direct assaults or been devoured in the siphon's rage. In doing this, we have avoided both of those tragedies."

Tatsu's mind raced, alight with frantic energy as he pieced together the last thing Yudai had been trying to say to him. He stared at Yudai's unmoving body with growing despair.

"You knew," he said, heart sinking. "You knew the whole time that the drain was a person. You knew all along it was him."

It hurt just to say it. Watery bile bubbled up like fire to the back of his tongue and tasted like copper, and then the crushing horror threatened to knock him clean off his feet. "And you knew about me."

The queen didn't answer, and she didn't need to. Tatsu knew it down to his bones.

"You sent me because you needed me to open Nota's barrier," he whispered. He pressed his hands against his forehead, but it did nothing to slow the agony. "You knew it had to be me. That's why you didn't send anyone before us. That's why you didn't just send your soldiers."

Then he whipped his head to Alesh, still standing with an arm curled protectively around Ral's shoulders.

"You said Runon was keeping him unconscious with black-market toxins from Joesar," he said in a rush, unable to stop everything from spilling past his lips. "All those bottles, you checked them when we were in the castle."

Alesh's eyes flitted nervously to the queen's impassive face and then back again. "Yes."

"And when the guard showed up during your smuggling job, you were carrying bottles of something," he continued. "You told me you could hear the glass clinking."

"Tatsu," Alesh said, voice hoarse, "don't say something you'll regret."

But it was far too late for that. Tatsu knew why Alesh had been caught, and it wasn't because she and her group were smuggling. The crown wanted what she'd been bringing in.

"You set this whole thing up just to get me here." Tatsu whirled, spitting, hands clenched into fists as he faced the queen once more. A line of mages behind her throne and a company of armored guards standing tense at either side of him, and it was all he could do not to launch himself at her. "Two birds with one stone, right? You did all of this because you needed me. You needed my *blood*. You *used* me!"

"It is time you take your leave of the palace." Commanding, the queen descended the small staircase from the throne to the rest of the chamber, the skin of her face shimmering like bronze. "You have fulfilled your end of the bargain, and thus I grant you the reward of your life. When Chayd rises to the glory we are rightly owed, see that you use the freedom well."

"No!" Tatsu yelled as the two guards from earlier approached from both sides and grabbed his arms. Their fingers were tight about him, and the metal of their wrist gauntlets dug into his flesh. "You can't use Yudai like Runon did!"

The queen raised a hand in the air. "I offer this reward to you only once, so remember this— You will not be granted a second chance."

"You can't do this!" Tatsu tried to kick at the ground but managed nothing. The guards hauled him back, away from the throne and the queen's dais, away from the mages in their imposing semicircle and the advisors whispering to one another behind their hands. "He's not a thing; you can't use him like this! You'll destroy the whole world!"

"Go back to your woods, *feas*," the queen commanded. "And find that you stay there."

Behind him, Alesh and Ral were being pushed out as well. Tatsu peered through the bodies and the gleam of polished armor at Yudai's body on the stone floor, a heap of stark white against the jeweled tones of the room.

"Yudai," he gasped, but the guards were stronger. They shoved him roughly through the entryway, and then the doors shut resolutely behind him.

Chapter Eighteen

TATSU TRIED BANGING on the doors several times, his palms smacking hard against the sanded wood, but they didn't reopen. When it was clear he would not be readmitted to the receiving hall, he spun on his heels. The guards were just as impassive as ever.

"Let me in!" he cried. "You have to let me back in! I have to get him out!"

They ignored him, staring past him as if he wasn't there. They stood motionless by the opposite doors with eyes focused on the wall above the door itself.

Furious, Tatsu whirled halfway around to face Alesh and Ral.

"We have to get him out." He felt short of breath, as if he'd just sprinted through the forest on a hunt. He pressed a hand to his chest to try to ease the sensation, fingertips pushing against his sternum, and it didn't slow the frantic waves of his thoughts. "We can't let her keep him like this."

Ral cocked her head without a word.

"Tatsu, please," Alesh tried. "Slow down. What was that you said in there? About the queen needing your blood?"

"My mother." Tatsu turned to the door and slammed his hands against it several times, hard enough to rattle the wood against the frame.

"Your mother?" Alesh asked. "How do you know about your mother all of a sudden?"

As he continued to bang his palms against the door, he answered, "My mother is a mage in Runon. She's the one who tortured Yudai. We have to get him out!"

"I don't understand," Alesh said. "I don't... Tatsu, what's going *on*?"

"She's going to use him!" Tatsu exclaimed, and nothing helped the iron vise gripping his lungs. "She's going to put him back on those poisons and keep him half-dead so she can use his power against Runon!"

"Tatsu, no," Ral said.

Alesh shook her head. "There's nothing you can do, Tatsu."

"I brought him here!" He sank, crouching on his heels, and pressed his hands against his face to try to stop the onslaught of regret. He'd been the one to deliver Yudai straight into another hell. The torture might as well have been dealt by his own hands. The fingers against his face weren't even his anymore—they were Nota's, tying Yudai to the chair, and Zakio's, forcing the toxins against his lips.

"That was your job," Alesh reminded him. "It was the mission, remember? The way we got our freedom back?"

Quiet but frowning, Ral reached for Alesh's hand.

"How can you say that?" Tatsu demanded. He rose and ignored the way his knees groaned in response. The bile in his throat had soured from guilt to anger, and it was far easier to deal with the stinging fury in his veins. "How can you just leave him here, knowing what's going to happen to him?"

"We have to!" Alesh told him. In the shocked silence, her eyes searched his face for something he didn't seem to possess. "What do you think will happen if you try to do something stupid? What will the queen do to you if you go against her?"

Tatsu stared at the doors, willing them open.

"She'll kill you." Alesh grabbed at Tatsu's arm, catching his sleeve, and her fingers trailed across the material. "The only reason we can leave right now is because you *did it*. You stopped the siphon, and you saved Chayd. That was what we were supposed to do. It doesn't matter how it happened."

"What do you think Yudai's siphon will do to the rest of the world when the queen uses it?" Tatsu stared down at Alesh's fingers bunched in his shirt. "The rest of the world will *die*, Alesh."

When he looked up again, her lips had flattened as she studied him.

"We're free because we made a bargain. And we won."

"I can't let her use him like this," Tatsu said.

Alesh laughed, devoid of mirth. "You don't know anything about him."

"He's a person," Tatsu hissed. "You said so yourself when we found him in Runon. He took a step closer to her and was pleased, somewhat, when she didn't flinch away. "And even if you don't care about that, she's going to put so many poisons in his system that it should kill him just to use his magic to destroy everything outside of Chayd."

"We're people too, Tatsu!" Alesh flung her arms wide, staring at him. "We're free to go. You're willing to abandon us for him? After how long we've known each other? We have our lives back."

"At the expense of his?" Tatsu snapped. "That's hardly fair."

Alesh glowered at him. "Life isn't fair."

"Don't give me that," Tatsu said, his voice a low growl. "I've always been there for you—"

"Have you?" Alesh interrupted him with another laugh. "Really? Because from where I'm at, it seems like you gave up pretty quickly when you didn't like my choices."

Tatsu's throat threatened to close completely. "Help me."

"I can't. I *won't*. I have to be here, to take care..."

She cut off abruptly, scowling, reaching out to take Ral's hand in her own, her gaze on the marbled stone beneath their boots.

"I have to take care of Ral." The anger was gone from her tone. "I'm not going back to Aughwor."

"Alesh." Tatsu reached for her, missing. "Don't do this. I need you. I *need* you to help me."

"I'm sorry, Tatsu." When she finally did meet his gaze, sympathy glimmered in her eyes. A dozen other emotions swirled there, but none of them agreed with him. "There's nothing you can do now. Everything else will get you killed, and you know it."

"Don't—" The space between them stretched and tore, impossible to cross again. Tatsu's thoughts churned with resentment he only barely kept smothered; he clenched and unclenched his fingers, refusing to look away first. Alesh held his gaze for minutes that felt like hours, and then, finally, she dropped her head.

"You're free, Tatsu," she said quietly. "Go home."

Tatsu squeezed his eyes closed, and in an instant, the image of Yudai's body on the receiving hall floor flashed unbidden. When he opened his eyes again, Alesh was already walking toward the exit, toward the great pillared statues, their eyes watching her turn her back on him when he needed her the most. She pulled Ral along with her, but after a few steps, Ral stopped and spun, pulling her hand free from Alesh's grasp.

She rushed to stand in front of Tatsu and pressed her fingers against his sternum.

"Choose," she breathed, eyes wide. "Choose, Tatsu."

Ral gave his chest one final push, right over his heart, and then she flashed him a sad sort of smile before returning to Alesh's side.

Tatsu watched them both go, leaving him alone with the palace guards. It was a long time before he followed, his stomach twisted into angry knots.

RETURNING TO HIS once-beloved cottage felt strange.

Even the air had changed into something heavy. The trees outside were just as they had always been, and despite Tatsu's long absence, nothing in the cabin had changed, save for the cobwebs gathering at the ceiling corners. But inside, the air was no longer welcoming, and Tatsu sat for a long time trying to figure out what had changed. He'd lived his whole life in the small room, and suddenly he felt as if he didn't belong.

Everything in the cottage reminded him of his father. The memory of the two of them carving out a life there was no longer the blessing it had once been. Emotions churned in his gut, and all he wanted was to be rid of them. He thought of his father's reluctance to go into Dradela and how much easier their life in the woods had been. He thought of his father's tight-lipped silences when the nights grew long and dark and the magic carved absences in all their conversations.

His whole life he'd believed his father shielded him from the cruelties of other people, but the truth was his father had only ever been protecting himself.

Tatsu grabbed wildly at the first thing he could find—an old leather bag he no longer used—and flung it as hard as he could against the opposite wall. It wasn't nearly heavy enough to make a solid impact. He grabbed for something else, and his fingers found one of his heavy plates.

That, at least, created an impressive crash when it hit the wallboards and cracked into several pieces.

"You lied to me." Tatsu seethed at the memory of his father and the nothingness the man had left behind. "You lied to me!"

Another plate followed the first, and it quickened his blood to watch the pieces of clay clatter to the floor. The impacts against the wall sent clouds of wood particles and dust into the air, and they lit up in the late evening sunlight streaming through the western window.

His mother was out there. His mother was in Runon. His mother was *alive*.

With a furious exclamation, Tatsu picked up the cast iron pot and flung it after the two plates.

That jolt shook the entire cottage. It rocked all the way up his bones and rattled his teeth, and all he could think was how he wished he had enough to bring the whole house down around him. The house his father had built with his own two hands because hiding proved easier than dealing with the questions of Tatsu's origins, tucked away in a forest of no use to most Chaydese.

"You stuck me here my whole life," he whispered, hands balling into tight fists. "You told me it was for my own good. You let me be the outcast because it was easier for you to run from the past. And you let me believe all the rest of my family was dead!"

He hadn't realized until he stopped speaking that he'd been shouting by the end, and his throat grew hoarse and rough.

There was nothing else to throw, but the throb of rage pulsed too deep inside him. Tatsu whirled on the rickety table and flung everything off the top of it. His leatherworking punch and awl went flying toward the fire pit, and the small bundle of furs that had been lying on the table scattered across the floor. Then he kicked the table at the weak, uneven leg, splintering the wood. The entire table went down a second later.

By the time the second cloud of dust had settled, his eyes were stinging with hot tears. He pressed the heels of his palms against his face, but nothing could stop them. As all his energy fled, he collapsed on the floor, unable to discern whom he was angrier at: his father or himself.

It was a very long time before he pulled himself up and staggered to the bed, but he spent a sleepless night staring up at the ceiling. As the sun rose, he blearily mimicked it and set out into the woods. The traps had been left out for far too long, and his catches had been picked clean by scavengers. Even cleaning and resetting them didn't summon anything within. He couldn't get his focus to settle on the wires and claws his fingers curled into place. It was impossible to forget the image of Yudai, lying on the floor, unable to escape being used again. And Tatsu had left him there.

Lungs burning and head aching, his temples throbbed with each heartbeat.

With his traps yielding nothing usable, few options remained open to him. He gathered what edible bits he could and stewed the starchy roots into a paste, his stomach growling in dissatisfaction when he went to bed.

The next day, he looked at the mess he'd created in the cottage and ignored it. The dried bloodstain remained on his front stoop, and he left that as well. Without his bow, he made his way to the opposite end of the forest and walked the shadowy paths in silence. He stretched out with his senses, wishing that the old hum of his woods would soothe all the tattered parts of his memories.

Tatsu returned to his cottage that night empty-handed.

Nearly everything in the house had once belonged to his father. The bits and pieces they'd collected over the years gathered dust on the rickety wooden shelves by the bedframe. There was only a small pile of books and ledgers, but Tatsu moved to it, seized by the idea he might discover a hint behind his father's actions there. As he rifled through the aged, bound leather, he found nothing. All he had were stories, trading reports, and journals about the woods themselves. His father had left no trace of his secrets behind, and Tatsu hated him for it.

As soon as he rose the next morning, before dawn had broken, it became clear he wouldn't be able to put off a trip into Dradela to restock his wares. The idea of returning to the city soured his mouth, even as he was readying his pack to leave, but as much as he hated to make the five-hour journey, it seemed better than sitting around in his father's retreat.

Tatsu arrived in Dradela just as the sun found its highest point in the sky.

The city's vivid colors mocked him as he approached. His limbs pounded with dull apprehension, though he kept to the traders at the outer bounds with their brightly colored awnings. Amongst the travelers, at least, he could always seem to blend in. He had a small stash of coins and several cleaned furs he'd been saving, and it would be enough to get him bags of smoked, salted meat and a sack of imported grain.

The last trader he approached hailed from the small kingdom of Rad-em, positioned between Chayd and Joesar along the Oldal Sea. She was very pleased with the light color of the hare pelt Tatsu bartered.

"It will make an excellent lining," she told him in Common, her gnarled hands sliding over the fur. "Runon's closed off, but Chayd and Joesar stopped fighting, which opened up the mountain passes. There's good foraging to be had on those peaks, and we'll need heavier clothes to pass through."

She carefully rolled the pelt and slipped it into a worn wooden box.

"Are you leaving for the mountains soon?" Tatsu asked.

"After the queen's proclamation," the woman replied, and Tatsu almost dropped the bag of grain on his foot.

"What proclamation? When?"

The Rad-em woman shrugged. "I've no guess as to what it concerns, but the guards have been spreading word all through town. The fourteenth day of Samaru at midday. It will draw quite a crowd, so I'm planning to stay and catch the last of the customers."

"That's only two days from now," Tatsu said.

"Come back if you need anything else before then," the woman told him with a wide, crinkling smile.

In his haste to leave, Tatsu ended up stumbling over his own boots, nearly falling. There was nothing else the announcement could be about—it had to be Yudai. The queen was going to unveil Chayd's newest acquisition in a grotesque celebration while the rest of the world lay trembling in fear.

She was going to parade the mage through the streets like a prized warhorse.

"Thank you," Tatsu mumbled, already turning away from the woman with his goods. The sack slung over his shoulder swung heavily, but not as heavy as his heart, a tumor pulsing angrily.

He didn't remember the long return to his cottage. He just found himself there after the sun had set and the night insects had begun to sing, staring at the cold, charred remains of his attempted meal.

HIS FEET TOOK him to the woods' edge the next day. He couldn't help it. When he finally stopped, he found himself at the same cliffside he had once been on with Ral, on a day that felt like a lifetime ago. The decayed brown line, still there, had moved closer to the trees. The divide hadn't quite reached the outstretched roots, and that, at least, Tatsu was glad for. While the siphon had stopped its advance, the spindly brown husks left behind remained as they had been.

Tatsu knelt by the start of them to peer closer. He knew better than to touch the withered grass stalks, but he couldn't quite stop himself from reaching for them. The buzzing wrongness beneath his skin had returned, and it served only as a reminder of everything he'd experienced. The mountain peaks beyond the cliffside were still covered in mangled trees, bent and hunched over on themselves, and when Tatsu closed his eyes and focused, the whispers from them carried on the breeze.

His mind flashed to Zakio's ashen face in the snow.

And then, there was something else: Leil's voice as they sat beneath the curved dome of the branch-covered barrier she'd created.

As Tatsu stared out at the dead trees on the mountains, his breath caught. The queen was going to use Yudai as revenge. She was going to unveil him to the crowds in Dradela, to a celebration, to people cheering that Chayd would finally come out the victor. But Yudai said it had taken years to get the formula right. He said they'd only managed to manipulate his magic once they changed the very nature of it through toxins and chemicals, lacing his blood and bone with poison.

Chayd had no *soelm* mages.

Tatsu's fingers curled into the still-living green just a step away from the siphon's drain line, and his hands came up with clumps of dirt and broken blades of grass. He stared at it as he let the mud and green bits tumble to the ground.

Chayd had no mages strong enough to control Yudai's magic. The drain would be a wild, feral force, and they were going to unleash it on the rest of the world without any way to keep it in check.

Tatsu sucked in a deep breath. He thought of Yudai and his temperamental moods and sharp tongue, and tried to ignore the flash of betrayal he'd seen in Yudai's eyes in the queen's receiving hall. The memory of it stung, and Yudai's absence was a hole aching in him. Tatsu missed him, missed the barbed insults and threatened pride, the way Yudai's smile grew on the right side before the left, off-kilter.

Tatsu turned from the siphon's aftermath and fled back into the woods.

He ran through the trees to his cottage, not bothering to stop and check his snares or to gather anything from the berry bushes he passed. His lungs were burning by the time he threw open the front door, but somehow, he hardly noticed it.

The cottage lay quiet and still. Tatsu stared at the remnants of his father's life strewn about in various stages of disarray.

"You were a coward," he whispered to his memories. "And you taught me to be a coward with you."

The anger in him was replaced with something else—something like iron. He'd spent too long living the life of someone who hadn't had the strength to live his own. His father had molded Tatsu into what he wanted because it had been easier, but his father was gone.

Tatsu grabbed his leather traveling pack, dumped the contents on the floor, and set about repacking it.

Setting aside his full quiver and bow first, he gathered his hunting and skinning knives. The dried meat he stuffed into the smaller pouches before tying them off with thick cord. When the essentials were packed, he looked at the mess he'd left. Half his cooking wares were still on the floor where they'd fallen, and most of them in pieces. He didn't bother to pick any of it up.

He grabbed his hooded tunic and slipped it on despite the summer heat. His skin prickled beneath the wool, but he pushed the discomfort to the back of his mind. After sliding his bow and quiver across one shoulder and slinging his pack the opposite way, his gaze paused on his father's old boots, sitting against the wall and covered in dust.

A split second later, he grabbed them too and shoved them into his pack.

A strange, bitter taste lingered on his tongue when he walked out the front door. The birds in the trees were trilling their afternoon song, and it should have helped to calm him. He stared at the door, shut behind him, trying to memorize everything about the cottage. The image of it was shrouded in pain, but still, it had been his home. It had been the only home he'd ever known.

Tatsu pursed his lips and bid it a silent farewell. Then, straightening his shoulders to bolster his own resolve, he started out through the forest.

He wouldn't get to Dradela before nightfall, but it didn't matter. There was only one thing that did anymore.

Chapter Nineteen

HE FINALLY MADE it back to Dradela under a dark sky streaked with stars. Tatsu knew of a few inns that made most of their coin housing the relatively constant supply of traders, and they didn't look twice at him or the copper bits he gave in exchange for the room. The inn was worn and shabby but comfortable enough, and, in truth, Tatsu didn't care much. He skipped the evening meal and retired right to his bed.

With his hands in his lap, he sat for a long time on the worn blanket, staring out the window to the darkness of the city beyond his room, not feeling much of anything. Was he supposed to be nervous? His mind numb, Tatsu rolled over and closed his eyes against the stale-smelling pillow.

The next morning, he gave only a curt nod to the innkeeper as he left. Already, the news of the proclamation had drawn a crowd—farmers from villages outside Dradela and traders who had packed up their caravans but not yet departed. Tatsu wove through the gathering people, trying to disappear into the shadows of his hood. For once, he didn't worry about bystanders noticing his Runonian features. What he worried about was any one of them focusing on the bow strapped tightly to his back.

He made his way to the Iah district.

The smell of incense and spices dissipated as he left the market streets to turn into the alleys, the mud beneath his boots reeking of urine and rotted food as he got further into the winding pathways. The houses, if they could be called that, were small and built far too close together, with decaying boards and uneven roofs, and Tatsu tried not to focus on their terrible condition. Even with the moans coming from inside one of the shanties, he forced himself to keep going. He'd been to Iah only twice before, and he needed to keep his senses sharp to find what he was looking for.

Unfortunately, he found himself quickly turned around in the sea of tiny houses that were all in the same state of disrepair. Tatsu stopped at the next corner and paused. Making a complete circle, he noted the spires of the palace over the tops of the crumbling buildings, but all that did was orient him within the city itself. Frustration swelled in his throat. He didn't have time to lose, but he remained rooted to the spot without a clue of where to go next.

He waited for a second, and then another, growling to himself when the correct direction didn't appear. Turning one more time, trying to find a hint, he saw Ral standing in the middle of the grime, the hemline of her brown skirt muddied darker with the muck.

"Hello," she called with a smile. "Tatsu, come!"

"Ral?" he called. "How did you find me?"

She didn't answer. Tatsu made his way to her side, and she grabbed for his hand. The warmth of her skin and her heartbeat in their joined palms helped soothe some of the agitation in his blood.

"Come," she repeated and led him down the dirty street.

Houses flashed by them, all identical, and Tatsu was still disoriented within the slums. Ral didn't look back at him, walking with purpose, her gait strong, until they reached a shanty that looked like all the rest. Large gaps opened between the wooden panels of the ill-fitting door and the siding, and the handle jutted out from the splintered board that housed it.

A second later and the door opened.

"Ral!" Alesh said, emerging from the structure. "Where have you—"

Her voice cut off as soon as she noticed Tatsu.

"What are you doing here?" Her gaze shifted quickly to the street. Her cheeks looked pink even in the shadows, and Tatsu felt a pang of sympathy for showing up at her door. She'd always tried to keep the realities of Iah and her life there from him.

"I need your help," Tatsu said in a rush, and before she could respond, added, "All you have to do is tell me where to go. I won't put you or Ral in danger. I just need you to give me the best place in the city to do what I need to do."

Alesh's eyebrows furrowed. "And what, exactly, are you going to do?"

"I'm getting Yudai out."

"Goodbye, Tatsu," Alesh said as she started to close the door, but Tatsu threw his hand up to stop it from closing completely.

"I'm sorry. I'm sorry for the way I treated you."

Her eyes were cloudy with distrust, but she didn't push the door any further closed.

Breath quickening, Tatsu continued, "It was wrong of me to cut you out like that. I know you do everything for Ral. I know all you want is to make sure you can take care of her. And I'm sorry I couldn't see that."

"You cut me out as soon as I did something you didn't agree with." Alesh's fingers tightened around the doorframe. "You didn't even let me explain. You just threw away everything we had."

"I know," Tatsu whispered. "I know. I'm sorry."

Alesh's gaze shifted over his shoulder a bit. "And now you're begging me to help you do the same thing, when we finally just got out of the mess."

She turned to meet Tatsu's gaze, full of defiance. "I know it was my fault you were in the situation at all, and I'm sorry for that, but it's over. It's done. And we got our freedom back and you want me to throw it all away? This could be my chance, Tatsu. This could be how I get free of this whole dirty business. Isn't that what you wanted me to do all along?"

"Alesh—"

"Do you know how it felt? The job had gone horribly wrong, and Hesch was dead, and I was *terrified*, Tatsu. Everything was my fault. I was barely holding it together when I went to you, and you didn't even listen. You turned me away and cut me out. You broke one of the few good things I'd ever had without hearing my side at all."

Shame washed over him in a wave of dizziness.

"I loved you," she said, voice very low and thick with emotion.

"I know," Tatsu murmured. He wanted to close his eyes and block everything out, but he ground his teeth together and kept his gaze on her. He owed her that much.

"So, what do you have to say now?" Alesh asked.

"I had a brother," Tatsu blurted out and then wrenched his eyes away from her expression of surprise. "A half-brother. And he's dead."

Her eyes were wide. "Tatsu—"

"He was terrible," Tatsu said and laughed mirthlessly. "He was a terrible person. He was one of the mages who tortured Yudai for years. And I know that, but he was still my brother. He was still blood."

He shook his head, glancing at Ral. She gave him a small smile and a nod. *Keep going*, he imagined her saying.

"I never could understand why you made all those decisions," he said. "But I know you did because you had no other choice. You did the best you could to take care of Ral, and I judged you for it. I'll never really understand it, because I don't know what it's like to have a sibling like that. But I do know what it's like to want to protect someone else."

Alesh sucked in a deep breath, and although she didn't respond, the bare hint of tears shimmered in her eyes.

"Please," he said. "Yudai doesn't deserve this. He doesn't deserve to lose his whole life to being used like some kind of living weapon. And Chayd can't control it. They don't have the power to control him like the mages in Runon did. It's going to destroy everything."

When Alesh finally did look at him, her chin trembled.

"I need to get him out," Tatsu said.

The air grew heavy around his shoulders. Alesh's chest rose and fell with several hitching breaths. Then she looked at Tatsu and bit her lip, slowly bringing her teeth down on the soft flesh.

"Okay," she replied.

HE HAD TO keep his steps quick to keep up with Alesh. She was grumbling under her breath, and Tatsu couldn't quite make out the words. She darted through the city streets with a practiced ease Tatsu was unable to mimic, always a few steps behind her and clumsy along the same zigzag path. Whatever shortcuts she'd taken had gotten them out of Iah and back through the market district, where the cloying smell of too many bodies shoved together in the ever-growing crowd greeted them. At the edge of the noble estates and the line of sandstone stores stood the long, pillared entryway of the palace.

Alesh ducked behind one of the spice shops, and Tatsu followed. He found himself standing in the middle of old dye pots still full of dark liquid. The sharp, pungent smell of the concoctions nearly brought stinging tears to his eyes.

"Here," Alesh said quietly. "You can climb up the barrels and onto the roof. From there, it's an easy jump over to the tavern roof. The upper windows of the tavern give you a small section to hide behind to avoid being seen, and you can see the entire road to the palace from the east end."

"Thank you," Tatsu told her.

"How do you think you're going to pull this off? It's just you."

Tatsu shook his head. "I don't know. Maybe I won't be able to. But I have to do something. I have to at least try."

"Yeah. I get that," Alesh said, and her voice warbled a little. She ran her hands across her face, scrubbing at something invisible on her cheeks. "Well…good luck, then."

She started toward the main streets and then seemed to change her mind. She paused, turning to face him.

"This man...this Yudai," she began slowly. "He's a good person?"

Tatsu's breath caught in his throat.

"He's a brat," Tatsu barked out as a half laugh. "He's spoiled and haughty, and his pride will completely crush him one day. He spits out insults but can't quite handle when they're aimed at him. He—"

Tatsu stopped himself because Alesh's face had started to soften in a way he wasn't sure he understood. A shiver ran down his spine as he swallowed, feeling strangely vulnerable.

"Yes," he finally answered, a whisper. "He's a good person."

"Okay," Alesh said again.

Staring at her, Tatsu wondered if it would be the last time he ever saw her. Surely, if he failed, he wouldn't just go back to Aughwor. The queen would have him executed, publicly, to make an example of him. And Alesh had been right to point out the odds against him. He was just one person. What he was doing was impossible. What he was doing was suicide.

Something flickered in Alesh's features, and Tatsu guessed she was thinking about the same thing.

"Gods watch over you," she told him, and then she was gone, disappearing around the corner of the spice shop and leaving him alone.

Tatsu let his gaze stay on the empty space where she'd just been for several breaths before starting up the side of the building. The barrels were easy enough to step up, but he had to order his hands to stop shaking before he could pull his weight onto the roof.

The vantage point from the eaves of the tavern did indeed let him see the entire road. Midday lingered an hour away, before the start to the queen's announcement, and his position put him close to the palace entryway itself. The guards were keeping bystanders away from the marbled steps; Tatsu assumed this would be where the queen would make her announcement.

Soldiers patrolled everywhere in the crowd below, but the angle of the sun kept the roof behind the high windows covered in shadow. Tatsu crouched there with his head in his hands and waited, mind racing, until the bells signaled the beginning of the procession.

He suddenly had no idea why he'd thought he would be able to do anything.

Knees aching, he remained in position as the shadows slowly shifted around him with the movement of the sun overhead. Whether it was the shade's cooler temperature or his own apprehension that caused the chills on his arms, he couldn't tell.

As the crowd began to cheer and swell, Tatsu peeked out from behind his hiding spot. The palace doors had opened, and the court advisors were arriving first. A quick glance across the road and Tatsu could make out the armor of two guards watching from opposite rooftops, the glint of gold-plated metal giving them away. He would have to be quick and careful to avoid being seen.

As the cheering of the crowds increased, he assumed the queen's arrival was imminent, and he was right. Accompanied by the dark-robed mages, she arrived only a few minutes later in the most elaborate array of colored sashes Tatsu had ever seen. Draped over her arms and shoulders and billowing out behind her as she walked, they glittered in every color dye Dradela used. The effect was a ripple of jewel tones bordering on ethereal. The joyous, feral garb left nothing to doubt: she proudly wore a victor's attire. Tatsu was witnessing a pre-emptive triumph.

The queen's hair was coiled up in an elaborate mass of braids and ribbons, and gemstones hung on her forehead from a golden chain that roped up into the plaits themselves. Her features alight with joy—and success— she looked like the lore-inspired paintings of the palace entrance, and Tatsu suspected the effect had been deliberate.

She stopped just at the edge of the steps and the mages fanned out around her in a symbol of united power, but also a shield. Tatsu wondered if Leil was down there, tensed and waiting. He couldn't see anything in the shadows of the dark hoods.

"Citizens of Chayd," the queen began, and the crowd fell into silence to hear her, "I bring to you great news. We have spent decades at war. We have given our resources, our land, and the blood of our children. For too long, we have compromised, sacrificing the very core of our great kingdom. For too long, we have been made to bow at the feet of others.

"No longer will Runon bully us into submission. No longer will Joesar threaten to close down the exports to our doors. Today, we will turn the tide against them. Today, Chayd will reclaim its rightful respect."

Mutterings floated up from the crowd, but Tatsu didn't let himself focus on discerning them. He leaned closer to see the queen turn to the door. He stilled, breath catching, as a group of soldiers emerged from the palace entryway dragging a limp figure, suspended by his arms.

Yudai.

For a second, Tatsu couldn't breathe. The mage had been redressed in new clothes of brown, a symbol of the lowest status, a cruel taunt given his royal heritage. His arms were tied behind him, wrenched up in an impossible position as he was carried. A white cloth was looped around his head and pressed against his lips, slightly under his nose. It had to be soaked in the poisons they were using on him. The soldiers threw him unceremoniously to the ground, and the crowd gasped, but Tatsu barely noticed it because Yudai was moving. It was little more than an exhausted shudder, but it was there. He'd seen it.

They hadn't gotten the formula right.

"Runon was using this mage to drain the life from the surrounding lands," the queen said, with one regal hand outstretched as if to display the man in question, half collapsed and half kneeling in front of her. "They stole the life of the world for their own, leaving everything else desolate in the wake. And now, we have stolen their weapon. We will use it against them to reclaim the life they took. We will use it to show them that Chayd will rise above their foul, dirty greed!"

Tatsu focused on Yudai as the crowd began to cheer. He crept across the roof until he was at the southernmost edge of the inky shadows and then narrowed his eyes. Yudai was trembling enough that Tatsu could make out the movement of his brown clothes against the white marble backdrop. The poisons were keeping him nearly unconscious, but not quite. Maybe the queen didn't realize the extent of what the toxins needed to do. Maybe the mages simply hadn't put enough onto the cloth.

Another movement caught Tatsu's attention—Yudai's finger was moving.

His *index* finger.

Tatsu's breath caught in his throat. It took a split second to remember the other man's story from the cave with the blizzard raging outside. Tatsu had been racked with grief, but he recalled the sympathetic stirring he'd felt in his heart at the tale.

I wanted him to know I was aware of him being there.

Tatsu had to grab onto the roof to keep from falling. It could have been a fluke, or a trick in the light. He stared at Yudai's hand, willing his finger to move again. There was a second of nothing, and then it did: once, then twice, in deliberate, unhurried motions. Yudai knew Tatsu was there.

"Yudai," Tatsu whispered.

One hand reached for his bow. He didn't know if his plan would work. When they were in the mountains and Zakio had found them, Yudai hadn't been able to use his magic until he was threatened. His magic sensed the danger and rallied to protect itself. Zakio had commented on it—the effect had to be real. Tatsu pulled an arrow out of his quiver with unsteady hands.

After years of sedation, Yudai had rallied back into consciousness within a day. Tatsu could only hope that a few days of the same would result in a fraction of the delay.

He was counting on Yudai's magic to recognize the threat and return, and he only had one chance. As soon as the soldiers traced the arrow's origin, they would find him. It would be easy for them to follow the trajectory of it from their rooftop positions. The queen would execute him on those same marbled steps, and the same crowd of people would cheer. They would celebrate as his blood ran red down the road and the soldiers mounted his head on the palace walls.

Tatsu ran his tongue over his lips to wet them and pulled the bowstring toward his face.

"Please let this work," he breathed, as close to praying as he'd ever been.

He aimed the arrow at the knot of white fabric at the nape of Yudai's neck. If he sliced through it cleanly enough, the cloth would fall free from the mage's face, freeing him from the poison keeping him half-sedated. Any closer to his head and Tatsu would kill him. A sliver to the other side and he would miss completely.

It was all Tatsu could do to keep his arms from shaking.

"Don't move," he whispered to Yudai, to himself, to the arrow.

His whole body seized when he let the arrow fly. Part of him was desperate to look away, but he didn't dare to. The arrow whistled through the air and cut through the knot at the center of the white cloth, sending scraps of fabric flying to either side. The linen tumbled down from its place against Yudai's face.

Little enough time passed to draw a reaction from the queen, the guards, and the crowd before Yudai's eyes snapped open and his magic exploded into a windstorm around him.

Chapter Twenty

THE SHEER FORCE of it nearly knocked Tatsu off the roof. He grabbed hold of the eaves to avoid the killing fall, lowering his head in hopes the howling winds would glide over his body more easily. He tried to yell, but it was lost, ripped away on the wind. Several bits of the roof tore free, almost smacking into Tatsu's face.

When he looked up again, Yudai was the only thing visible at the center of it all, struggling up on his feet while the dirt and sand created a vortex with his body at the crux. Tatsu found his footing on the roof and crossed the jump back to the spice shop as quickly as he could, shimmying down the eaves and landing on the stacked barrels. He nearly tripped in his haste to get to the main street leading to the palace and *did* trip when he turned the corner too quickly, running headfirst into a noble woman. She was hunched over near the ground, her hands on her head in a desperate attempt in the furious gusts to keep hold of the gemstones hanging from her ears.

The road to the palace steps was engulfed in chaos. Splinters of crates flew wildly through the crowd; several barrels of liquid dye split and broke open, spilling their contents onto the street. There was a terrible crashing noise before an entire overhang on one of the stores broke free. As the wreckage built up on the wind, moving faster and faster, it swerved dangerously near the bystanders.

Most of the cries and wails were stolen by the wind, but a few made their way in a horrifying echo.

Tatsu picked himself up off the ground, holding his arm in front of his face to block the debris, and took slow, purposeful steps toward the palace entry stairs.

"Yudai!" he tried to yell, but he was still too far away.

Time slowed thanks to the resistance fighting against his movement. He pushed forward bit by bit, getting closer to the marbled steps. The nobles and advisors crouched over on the ground, some reaching out to one another, and even more losing the expensive baubles and jewels they wore, ripped away by the force of the wind. The brunt of the wind roared over the stairs, and a few paces from the start of it, Tatsu could push through no farther. A wall of stone might as well have been blocking his path.

"Yudai!" he tried again, and this time, he was close enough for the mage to hear him. Yudai's eyes met his from his position on the stairs, hands still bound. His face was creased with exertion and effort. Everything seemed to pause before a broken fragment of a pushcart smacked into Tatsu's right side, almost knocking him over. He stumbled and managed to keep his balance, but his entire shoulder began to throb.

"Yudai, listen to me!" he yelled and hoped that whatever gods there might be were on his side. "I'm here to get you out!"

Yudai raised his linked hands and there was a break in the wind, a tunnel that shot straight to where Tatsu was standing. The sudden absence of the howl against his head caused Tatsu's ears to ring. The force that had kept him from moving dissipated, and he fell forward, taking the steps two at a time to reach Yudai on the marbled dais.

Even as Tatsu approached, a shadowy distrust showed in Yudai's face.

"I can't hold it much longer," he shouted, the perspiration beading up on his forehead beneath the white strands of hair.

"How long?" Tatsu asked.

Yudai's response was to shake his head, so Tatsu reached forward to grab his arm.

"Then we need to go," he yelled. "Now!"

As Tatsu turned to take Yudai with him through the path created in the cyclone of wind and dirt, he saw the queen to the side of the podium. Her braids were whirling about her head, her elaborately embroidered sashes fanning out from her body. Something had struck her; one of the bits of wreckage had made solid enough contact to draw blood, and several of her brightly colored sashes had darkened with it. Bent over on all fours with her fingers digging deep into the dirt, her face was upturned toward them.

Her features contorted in fury as she opened her mouth and yelled something, but Tatsu couldn't make out the words. She tried to reach for them, wincing in pain from the injury, but was unable to get up.

Retribution hung heavy around their shoulders, and Tatsu had to look away.

They could not stay in Chayd.

"Tatsu," Yudai started, and Tatsu cut him off with a curt shake of his head. There wasn't time.

They continued to run through the wind. Two mages stood near the sides of the opening that Yudai created in the vortex, and even though their hands were raised, they didn't seem able to touch the screaming power circling them all. Tatsu avoided eye contact with them, keeping his gaze on the road in front of him. Then he did a double take and stopped so suddenly Yudai nearly crashed into his back.

The mage on the right was Leil.

In a split second, their gazes met and held, and Tatsu's heart lodged itself somewhere in his throat. She'd returned safely, it seemed, and if her attendance at the procession meant anything, she'd slipped effortlessly into her old position at the queen's side. Her face was streaked with tears, though whether from shock, pain, or fear, Tatsu didn't know. Her eyes darted to take in Yudai next to him, and then she threw her hands over her face and knelt forward, curling into a trembling ball.

Leil didn't move again. If she was letting them go, the gesture was useless. She couldn't possibly hope to control Yudai's magic windstorm. Her stillness rang more of guilt than anything else, which Tatsu had to push aside in order to keep moving forward. He couldn't afford to dwell on it, even though part of him, pulsing in time with each breath, was glad to see her still alive.

With each step they took toward the edge of the city, Yudai opened up a bit more of the pathway until they were off the main road completely and into the market district. The crowds were nothing more than mottled swatches of color lying flat against the road, shrieking in fear. The sandstone of the noble estates had protected the majority of the buildings from damage, but in the market, little had held the cart awnings in place. Most of them were gone, ripped free and hurled away, though several of them had wrapped around the remains of spice carts, and one lay in cinders in the molten forge of the smithy.

Tatsu was glad he couldn't hear any of the anguished screams above the furious howl of the wind.

His lungs were burning from the pace, but he pushed through it. Yudai stumbled twice, and it was only through Tatsu's vise-grip on his arm that he kept his footing. Tatsu wasn't sure if he had control over their direction, or if they were at the mercy of the gusts behind them. He had to jump over a young girl dressed in apprentice orange who had somehow stumbled out into the pathway Yudai was opening up.

"I can't," Yudai gasped from behind him, and his fingers nearly pulled from Tatsu's grasp.

But they were near the edge of the market, and Dradela itself. Beyond the gates, the caravans stretched out, and past them, the farmland filled with rows of date trees. They had to get out of reach of the queen and her soldiers. Even if many of the guards had been injured, Tatsu and Yudai were in no state to contend with a company of them.

There were several horses tethered outside the walls, near the brightly colored awnings of the trader stands.

"Yudai." Tatsu pointed at them with his other hand, hoping Yudai would be able to help, to stop before the horses were injured in the cyclone. But that was the moment the wind abruptly died around them. Yudai pitched forward, and Tatsu only just caught him. The mage's entire body shook.

"I can't," he rasped. "It's gone. I lost it again."

From the city behind them came the shouting and screaming of the crowd. Without the wind to hold them back, the soldiers would be after them. They had minutes, if that, to get far enough away to lose the guards.

Seeing no other option, Tatsu pulled his hunting knife from his sheath and raced to the caravan where the horses were tied. A boy, no older than twelve, stood near the post, and he jumped in fright when Tatsu approached.

"Go into the city," Tatsu demanded, holding the weapon out in front of him and hoping he looked threatening—or deranged—enough. It seemed to work; the boy scampered and fell over one of the hitching posts, and then disappeared through the city gates, leaving a cloud of dust in his wake.

With his knife, Tatsu cut through the leather holding two of the horses in place—a bay mare and a mottled gray stallion.

"I'm sorry," Yudai said as Tatsu handed him the frayed ends of the mare's rein. "I couldn't hold the magic. I can't help anymore."

"Can you ride?"

Yudai's red-rimmed eyes flickered up to the mare's muzzle. "Yes."

"Then get on. We have to outrun them."

Tatsu used the wagon posts to hop up onto the stallion's bare back, body clenching—without proper tack, he would be sore and protesting within the hour. The horses' bridles would suffice, and there wasn't time for anything else. Yudai followed suit and threw his leg over the mare's haunches, though Tatsu could plainly see his exhaustion.

Tatsu didn't dare to return west to the Shyreld again, and they couldn't go north into Runon either. The only choice was to head northeast to the edge of his woods and then into the Turend Mountain range. The peaks might be their only chance to hide their trail and slip away unnoticed.

"Tatsu," Yudai tried, voice angry despite his fatigue.

"Ride," Tatsu told him and kicked his mount into motion. "Follow me."

Horseback offered a much faster escape. With the breeze at his face, Tatsu could almost ignore the pounding of his heart against his ribs. The fire in his blood had faded away into a dull sense of nervousness. He checked over his shoulder as often as he dared, but not once did he see anyone following them. Yudai's destruction in Dradela's city center had delayed the soldiers long enough.

The sun followed its arc toward the rocky horizon behind them, until the sky was flushed with the reds of dusk. Tatsu pushed his borrowed horse to the edge of the trees, where the plains rose up to meet the bright, summer-green woods, and then he stopped. The stallion's neck was slick with a sheen of white sweat, and they couldn't push the animals any further.

He dismounted, landing badly, and had to shake out the pain in his ankle.

"We'll walk from here," he told Yudai, who managed to get off his mare with a bit more grace. Every muscle in Tatsu's body screamed in pain, but they had no time to rest. They'd bought themselves a day, perhaps two, but the soldiers would find their tracks eventually and come after them. Outside of Chayd's jurisdiction, they would have more freedom to hide. The mountain range was their best hope of slipping out of the queen's grasp completely.

Tatsu patted the horse's neck with one hand. "Thank you," he said quietly.

"You came," Yudai said, behind him.

Tatsu turned to face the other man. Yudai looked beyond exhausted, his hair matted to his face with sweat and dust and his chest heaving. But there was a brightness to his eyes that bordered on manic, and the emotion didn't fade from his gaze, locked on Tatsu as he closed the space between them.

"You came for me," Yudai elaborated. It was very close to a gasp. "You rescued me. *Again.*"

"I don't think the first time really counts," Tatsu replied, uncomfortable. "But I...I'm sorry."

Yudai's expression was guarded, but he didn't turn away. "For what?"

"I didn't mean to..." Tatsu began and then stopped, struggling to find the right words. "I didn't mean to give you to the queen like that. I didn't know she was going to use you. I didn't know that was her plan from the start."

Yudai stared wordlessly at him.

"Other than that, I've never given you a reason not to trust me," Tatsu continued, a bit desperate.

"No," Yudai agreed. "You haven't."

"And I know...I'm probably not the person you really want to trust," Tatsu attempted, distinctly unhappy as he ran a hand through his sweat-slicked hair. "I'm related to the two people who tried to destroy your whole life. But I didn't know that either. As it turns out, there's a lot I never knew. That's really no excuse for it, but...well, there it is."

Something in Yudai's face finally relaxed. "Blood doesn't dictate who you are."

"I hope not," Tatsu said.

Then, Yudai laughed. He threw his head back and the setting sun illuminated his hair, giving the mottled strands a faint pink glow. He spread his arms wide to either side, breathing deeply. Finally, he straightened and met Tatsu's eyes once more. His gaze held something fierce that Tatsu couldn't quite describe.

"What do we do now?" Yudai asked. "Where do we go?"

"The mountains. At least we can hope to disappear there. We can't stay."

"I know." Yudai's smile was neither sad nor angry, but something in between. He took another step toward Tatsu, fingers twitching at his sides. "Tatsu..."

A lump of emotion caught in Tatsu's throat. He tried to swallow it, and when that didn't work, he could only breathe around it. Yudai's gaze seemed to know too much as it roved over his body once, up and down, and finally settled on his face. Tatsu's lungs constricted, and then the mare whinnied softly, tossing her mane. Whatever spell had fallen over them was broken.

Trying to clear his head, Tatsu pulled his pack over his shoulder and took out his father's boots.

"Here," he said, handing them to Yudai and hoping he would ignore the thick, smudged dust on the tops. "Put these on; you'll need them."

While Yudai stooped to lace up the leather, Tatsu gazed out at the horizon and setting sun behind him. He could no longer see Dradela in the distance, hidden behind the wave of the land. The queen would come after them and send her guards to scout which direction they had taken, and, eventually, they would track them into the mountains. He could only hope his skills were better.

"I'm ready," Yudai announced as he straightened. His movements contained an air of finality.

Tatsu gave one last lingering look to the sloping plains, trying to memorize the feel of them.

Then he nodded. "All right."

"Tatsu," Yudai said quietly. "Thank you."

Tatsu didn't answer, but he did reach out and grasp Yudai's elbow to lend him support. He was too weak to make it far into the mountains without help. They would have to stop and rest soon and pick it up again the following morning. But at least they were together, and they were free.

With the setting sun at their back, they started off into the bit of trees that slowly ebbed upward toward the rocky mountain peaks.

Acknowledgements

This project began as a spontaneous novel-planning circle in the summer of 2016, when I was desperate to get back into writing again. Over the course of those six weeks, a group of like-minded friends and I worked through some of the main stages of planning a novel: outline writing, world-building, and the first sentence. Without that group and those friends, including Lindy Kelm and Lily Xavier, nothing in this story ever would have taken off the ground.

A huge thanks goes to Caroline Ziegler, my initial first draft beta reader, who saw everything as it left my fingers and offered comments and suggestions on it. She was perhaps the person who shaped the final product the most and pushed me to make it better. Her input and insights were incredibly valuable in the expansion of the story.

Of course, to all my friends and family who listened to me talk about this as I was writing it and gamely offered to read it pre-publication—you are all fantastic! And, last but not least, thanks to my husband who, despite not having the English language skill to read it himself, always encouraged me to spend time working on this.

About the Author

Kathryn Sommerlot is a coffee addict and craft beer enthusiast with a detailed zombie apocalypse plan. Originally from the cornfields of the American Midwest, she got her master's degree and moved across the ocean to become a high school teacher in Japan. When she isn't wrangling teenage brains into critical thinking, she spends her time writing, crocheting, and hiking with her husband. She enjoys LGBTQ fiction, but she is particularly interested in genre fiction that just happens to have LGBTQ protagonists.

Email: ksommerl@kent.edu

Website: www.kathrynsommerlot.com

Twitter: @KSommerlot

Other books by this author

Ibuki

Coming Soon from Kathryn Sommerlot

The Mage Heir

The Life Siphon, Book Two

From his vantage point atop an outcropping of stone on the east side of the mountain, Tatsu stared out over the horizon. The withered trees of the siphon's original devastation stood blearily out against the turning colors of the hill's opposite side. Twisted toward the ground, the old trees remained far enough away that they didn't pose a threat. Still, Tatsu stayed for a few minutes, enjoying the last bits of warmth on his skin from the setting sun as he gazed over the brown swath of long-drained land. With the season slowly cooling into autumn, they wouldn't be able to stay in the higher altitudes. Already, the sun's descent summoned a fierce chill that whipped against his cheeks, and the thought of remaining in the peaks, with relatively few provisions, didn't help the tightness in his gut.

As the sun dipped low behind the dark shapes of the mountain range, Tatsu sighed and made his way back down the rocky slope. The path, long abandoned and overgrown with weeds, snaked through the higher cliffs and coniferous trees, high enough on an old trade route that Tatsu didn't see any movement in the trees below. While escape had been the goal, the lull gnawed at Tatsu's subconscious. If anyone *had* followed them, he'd seen no signs of it.

Hunting sorely lacked in the clusters of dark-needled trees. The abandoned paths only went so far, and, after a while, they'd have to start looping over their own footsteps, which would impact any potential food supply.

As Tatsu wound his way along the path toward the small cavern they'd set up in, no noises, animal or otherwise, disturbed the peace. The mountain insects had already migrated down the slopes, and the birds and rodents would soon follow.

Yudai was sitting near the fire when Tatsu entered the cave.

"Anything?" Yudai asked. He didn't seem relieved when Tatsu shook his head. The white-drained ends of his hair hung ragged in front of his eyes, but the roots were growing in their natural black, and the transition between the colors formed a dark halo around the crown of his head.

"We have at most a few weeks of summer left," Tatsu said, taking a seat across the fire. He leaned forward to twirl the hare roasting over the flames, split by a makeshift spit. "Anyone on our trail will probably give up once the cold front comes down."

"And we'll freeze if we try to stay here," Yudai replied.

Tatsu kept his eyes steadfastly glued to the fire when he answered, "You're not wrong."

"You've been worrying about it for a week. I can see it on your face every time you come back from hunting."

When Tatsu didn't answer, Yudai shifted on the ground, stretching out his legs and wiggling his toes near the warmth. "How long were you going to stew over this on your own?"

"That's not what I was doing," Tatsu said, but the argument was weak.

"Well, you certainly weren't being truthful."

"What have I been lying about?"'

"We can't stay here much longer, and a lie by omission is still a lie," Yudai said, sounding a bit put out. "We have to find somewhere else to go."

Tatsu peered across the fire at Yudai, who raised both eyebrows and said nothing. As the silence grew too imposing, Tatsu sighed.

"I've been going over our options," he said, taking his time with the words. "I just can't come up with an end point. We can't go to Runon—"

"No, we can't." Yudai's eyes flashed dark and angry.

"—and we can't return to Chayd," Tatsu finished. "The queen's response at this point will be much worse than simply using you for revenge."

"I'd rather die," Yudai said, low and more of a growl. His gaze dropped to his fingers splayed wide in his lap, curling and uncurling in tandem. "I'd rather die than be used as a slave again."

After another tense moment, Tatsu said, "I know. I won't take you back there; you know that. Right?"

Yudai raised his head, teeth chewing on his lower lip. "Where will we go?"

"Far. Rad-em, maybe, or Joesar. Or we'll take a ship across the Oldal Sea to Dusset and hope luck is on our side."

"Wonderful," Yudai said with a mirthless laugh. "That's worked out well so far. And what are we going to do when I start draining the world around me while we sleep every night? You know it's getting worse."

"I don't have an answer for you."

Yudai laughed again. "We're leaving a bright trail for anyone hoping to catch us, without any plan where to disappear to, crushed under the hourglass hanging over our heads."

"Are you yelling at me or the world?"

"Myself," was Yudai's frustrated response before he pressed his hands against his face and stilled, lost in his own thoughts.

The hare was beginning to char on the bottom, so Tatsu spun the spit and sat again. Even while staring at the sizzling meat, his appetite had started to fade away. Apprehension returned, throbbing in time with his heartbeat.

"They must have done something to you in Dradela," Tatsu said quietly as the cavern closed in around them, threatening in its inactivity. "There's a reason the drain started up again. It can't be a coincidence the change came only after the queen tried to use your magic for herself."

"Knowing that doesn't get us any closer to shutting it off."

Tatsu couldn't come up with anything to say in response, at least not anything inspiring. Instead, he crossed his arms over his knees and tried to push the thoughts from his mind.

"You think this is a result of being a prisoner in Chayd?" Yudai asked.

"It makes sense, but I doubt you were in any state to remember what the Chaydese mages gave you."

Yudai's mouth formed a hard line when he shook his head. "There was only a vague awareness of people around me and nothing else. It's not very helpful."

"Then we're stumbling in the dark," Tatsu said and sighed. After a few seconds of observing Yudai, dejectedly hunched over on himself, he added, "I wish I could find you something else to wear. The brown is insulting."

"Is it?" Yudai appeared genuinely surprised. "I had no idea."

"That's the color the lowest citizens wear. For royalty, it's... something akin to a slap in the face, I suppose."

Yudai seemed to consider the information. "It doesn't bother me. Brown isn't an insult in Runon."

"When we found you, you were wearing white."

"Nota has a twisted sense of humor," Yudai agreed. "In Runon, white is the color of funerals."

"Fitting." A tightness banded Tatsu's chest. Across the fire, Yudai pushed up to his feet, his face still lined with bitterness there didn't appear to be a remedy for.

"Less talk of dying," he demanded, "and cut up that hare. I'm *starving*."

Also Available from NineStar Press

Connect with NineStar Press

www.ninestarpress.com

www.facebook.com/ninestarpress

www.facebook.com/groups/NineStarNiche

www.twitter.com/ninestarpress

www.tumblr.com/blog/ninestarpress

www.ingramcontent.com/pod-product-compliance
Lightning Source LLC
Chambersburg PA
CBHW032058180726
48284CB00002B/341